Esther

the Queen

OTHER BOOKS AND AUDIO BOOKS

BY H.B. MOORE

Out of Jerusalem: Of Goodly Parents

Out of Jerusalem: A Light in the Wilderness

Out of Jerusalem: Towards the Promised Land

Out of Jerusalem: Land of Inheritance

Abinadi

Alma

Alma the Younger

Ammon

Daughters of Jared

OTHER BOOKS BY

HEATHER B. MOORE

Women of the Book of Mormon: Insights & Inspirations

Christ's Gifts to Women

Athena

a novel

Esther
the Queen

H.B. Moore

Covenant Communications, Inc.

Published by Covenant Communications, Inc.
American Fork, Utah

Printed in the United States of America
First Printing: April 2013

19 18 17 16 15 14 13   10 9 8 7 6 5 4 3 2 1

ISBN-13: 978-1-62108-417-4

For my daughter Rose.
You remind me of Esther,
who makes the best of any situation in life.

Preface

FOR THE PURPOSES OF PACING this novel, I've condensed some of the time periods. King Xerxes I and Queen Esther were married about five years before Haman proposed his famous plan to exterminate the Jewish population in the Persian kingdom (Esther 2:16). In this novel, that time is greatly reduced. Also, the decree that Ahasuerus (King Xerxes) sent out to exterminate the Jews had an eleven-month lead time. I have shortened that to only a month.

It was about 480 B.C. when King Xerxes went back to war against Greece to avenge his father's (King Darius) loss in the first invasion of 492 B.C. This might explain why there were four years from the time King Xerxes put away his first wife, Queen Vashti (Esther 1:19), to the time he married Esther.

Acknowledgments

Writing a novel about Queen Esther was a bit daunting. Most of my historical novels have been about people who lived in Book of Mormon lands, but this novel takes place on another continent and in another time period. So I was back to square one on the research. Therefore, many thanks to my alpha readers, who went through the manuscript with a keen eye, including my parents, S. Kent Brown and Gayle Brown; fellow writers Debra Erfert, Susan Aylworth, and Taffy Lovell; and my critique group, Lu Ann Staheli, Annette Lyon, Michele Holmes, Sarah M. Eden, Robison Wells, and J. Scott Savage.

The support from my publisher has been amazing, and I'd like to thank managing editor Kathy Gordon for her support and editor Samantha Millburn for her careful editing. It's great to have so many people behind a single book to make the product really shine.

I'd also like to thank my daughter Dana, whose favorite Biblical heroine is Esther, because Dana prodded me to choose Esther when I was considering a number of heroines. Maybe she'll finally read one of my books.

Many thanks to my children and husband, as well as to my parents and my father-in-law, Les Moore, all of whom have been extremely supportive in all areas of my writing and publishing life.

Characters

* Ahasuerus, King Xerxes of Persia

* Esther, queen of Persia

* Vashti, former queen

* Mordecai, Jewish relative of Esther

Leah, Mordecai's wife

Children of Mordecai and Leah: Abigail, Ben, and Samuel

* Haman, prime minister

* Zeresh, Haman's wife

* Hegai, keeper of the harem

* Hatach, king's chamberlain, attends to Esther

* Biztha, king's chamberlain

* Meres, prince of Media

* Shaashgaz, keeper of the concubines

Gad, captain of the guards

Tarsena, former prime minister

Sons of Pharez: Aaron (married to Johanna), Dan, and Ethan

*denotes historical names

482 B.C.
Kingdom of Persia

And the king loved Esther above all the women, and she obtained grace and favour in his sight more than all the virgins; so that he set the royal crown upon her head, and made her queen instead of Vashti.

—Esther 2:17

Chapter 1

"*YOU* WILL BE THE BRIDE today," Abigail said, tugging on Esther's hand.

Esther smiled at her young cousin, whose face was bright with eagerness. It was hard to resist a request from the cherubic, round-faced girl. "All right, but who will be my groom?"

"Ben."

The children surrounding Esther shrieked with laughter. Ben, who was only seven, folded his skinny arms across his puffed-up chest. Esther fought back a smile and went over to her little cousin. His dark, curly hair stuck in all directions this morning as his face pushed into a pout.

"What is it, Ben? You do not want to marry me?" she asked.

Instead of smiling at the comment, Ben blinked his brown eyes. "I want to be the king."

The group of children went silent, and Esther thought quickly so Ben wouldn't crumple into tears. It would be a terrible start to an already early morning. The relatives she lived with—her cousin, Mordecai, and his wife, Leah—had gone to the holy place of gathering for Leah's purification. Their new baby, Samuel, was sleeping inside. As long as Esther could keep the other children playing outside, the infant wouldn't wake and want to be fed.

"Which king would you like to be?" Esther said, throwing a warning glance toward the other children. Abigail's laughter died, and she elbowed her two friends. At nine, she was a bright girl, but she loved to tease her brother.

"Xerxes," Ben said, his pout softening.

Esther's heart sank. She knew that if Mordecai or Leah heard their young son requesting to playact Xerxes, they'd be horrified. Xerxes might be their king, but he was not a Jew. He was a warrior first, had many concubines, and worshipped various gods, including the twin brothers Ahura-Mazda and Ahriman. And even worse, he had put away his queen, Vashti, for refusing his command to visit a war council and remove her veil in front of a room full of men, like a common maidservant in public. Esther couldn't even imagine going to the market without wearing a veil.

"But King Xerxes is not a Jew," Esther said in a quiet voice so the other tittering children couldn't hear. "Surely you want your cousin Esther to marry a good Jewish man?"

Ben shook his head, his eyes filling with tears.

"All right, let's pretend that Xerxes is a Jew." She looked at the other cousins and pronounced, "Prepare me for my marriage to the new Jewish king, Xerxes."

Abigail and the other girls rushed forward, their eyes bright with excitement. "Sit down, sit down," Abigail ordered Esther.

Esther perched on the stool next to the weaving loom. The girls combed her long, dark hair, which fell to her waist, and then they scrambled about the courtyard, plucking rosebuds to place in it.

"Don't pick too many," Esther cautioned, imagining Mordecai and Leah arriving home to a flowerless courtyard.

She smiled as Ben stood at the other end of the courtyard under the arched gate that led to the cooking room. It was as if he were waiting for his bride under a makeshift chuppah.

"All finished," Abigail said.

"Where's my veil?" Esther asked in a playful tone. "A good queen always wears her veil."

Abigail's dark eyes widened. "I'll fetch it."

"Don't wake baby Samuel."

Abigail returned in a moment, and thankfully, no crying followed her. She had brought one of her mother's nicer veils. It was a beautiful piece of fine silk. The pale-blue cloth was edged with Leah's fine embroidery, a skill Esther was still trying to perfect.

"Be very careful with that; we don't want to get it dirty," Esther said.

The girls arranged it on her head and then clapped their hands together.

"Your king is waiting for you," Abigail said.

Esther stood and walked slowly toward Ben, deliberately, as if every step was important. Ben smiled, despite the fact that his bride-to-be was about three heads taller than he was.

"Here is the cup of wine to drink," Abigail said, holding out a saucer of water.

Ah, so it is to be a Jewish wedding, Esther thought. At sixteen, she knew her own betrothal might be considered overdue by some. Mordecai and

Leah had started discussing the matter about a year ago, but when Leah became pregnant and fell so ill, it was apparent that Esther was needed more than ever in the home. Esther had been happy to help. She'd always felt an obligation toward her family members who'd cared for her since the age of four, when her parents had died.

Mordecai and Leah had been newly married at the time, and with Mordecai inheriting Esther's father's home, they had naturally agreed to care for Esther as well. Sometimes, Esther thought about what it would have been like to grow up in this home with her parents, but she also couldn't imagine her life without her dear cousins. Mordecai and Leah had become pillars in the community, with Mordecai the leader of the community affairs council and also a noted scholar, teaching mornings at the local school.

Ben took the cup first and pretended to drink. Then Esther took the cup and pretended the same.

"Now you must circle him seven times," Abigail pronounced.

The children giggled as Esther walked around Ben seven times, the number of perfection, and came to a stop.

"Give her the ring and lift her veil!" one of the children shouted.

Ben pretended to put a ring on Esther's finger, his expression solemn. Esther took off the veil, careful to hold it so it wouldn't wrinkle.

The children skipped over the blessings and cried out, "Throw the cup down and step on it."

"We'll pretend to throw it down," Esther said, looking at Ben.

He grinned and put the cup on the ground then acted like he was stomping on it.

"I missed the wedding?" a woman's voice spoke behind them.

"Mother!" Abigail said, running to Leah.

Esther felt chagrined to be caught holding one of Leah's best veils while surrounded by energetic children. But Leah just smiled in her usual way, her round face bright with pleasure at seeing her children.

Esther wouldn't be surprised if Leah had a dozen children. She always seemed so full of love for each of them and was endlessly patient, so it had been extremely difficult when she'd been ill with little Samuel and had to remain in bed most of the time.

"He still sleeps?" Leah asked over the head of her exuberant daughter.

Knowing Leah spoke about Samuel, Esther nodded.

Leah's gaze went from Esther to Ben. "Ah, my son has chosen such a beautiful bride."

His face pinked, which Esther found adorable. He lifted his shoulders and announced proudly, "I'm the king."

"Oh." Leah's voice went small.

"He's King Xerxes," Abigail informed her mother. "But he's Jewish now."

Leah's smile was indulgent. "Very well, then. I'm sure Ben made a wonderful king."

He beamed at his mother's compliment and followed her inside the house, chattering.

Esther looked over to see Mordecai, who'd hovered in the background during the interchange. His mouth was pulled into a grim line. A thin man, he wasn't much taller than his wife, but where Leah was jovial most of the time, Mordecai was serious.

Abigail saw him too and ran into his arms. His expression always softened around his daughter, and Esther's heart pinged. She'd been shown plenty of compassion and love by her relatives, but there was something different about the relationship between a father and his daughter.

Esther turned away from the tender scene and told the neighbor children they could come back later to play. The family would attend to their morning meal and prayers, with a long list of chores to follow.

The children passed by Mordecai, and before Abigail ran into the house, she fervently promised her friends they would be reunited soon.

Esther turned to follow her but was stopped by Mordecai's voice. "Can we speak a moment, Esther?"

She hesitated, not knowing if she should be pleased or worried. As of late, their conversations had been restricted to his wife's health. Leah had looked well enough, but there were definite tired lines about her eyes. Or perhaps Mordecai did not look so kindly upon Ben's playacting as king.

He led the way to the low wall that separated the courtyard from the vegetable garden. Sitting on it, he dipped his head, and Esther sat next to him.

"With all that has gone on with bringing Samuel into the world, I have neglected an important aspect of your life," Mordecai began.

Esther's heart hammered. This was not about Ben's playacting or about Leah's health.

"I was soundly reminded of it on the way back from the synagogue. We met Pharez on the path." He paused, and Esther felt his gaze on her.

Pharez had three sons. The eldest, Aaron, had married a couple of years before to one of her friends, Johanna. He was set to inherit his father's lands, and Johanna had been pleased with such a promising marriage.

The second son was Dan, and the third, Ethan.

"Pharez asked if you were betrothed yet."

Esther exhaled. Dan walked with a bit of a stoop, no doubt earned in his years as a scribe at the palace—a position of honor. Ethan had a wild look in his eyes, and some said he wasn't quite right in the head. She almost didn't dare breathe, wondering what Mordecai had said to Pharez.

Mordecai's hand patted her tightly clenched ones. She hadn't even realized she was gripping them together.

"Don't worry, Esther. You are not meant to be the wife of a second-born son. Dan may hold a royal position, but he will never look up from his clay tablets long enough to appreciate your beauty."

Esther stared at Mordecai. He'd just called her beautiful. She had never thought herself as such, although her friend Johanna had often said she wished she was as fair, which was nonsense since Johanna's flashing dark eyes could charm a rock.

Her chest tightened. So was it to be wild-eyed Ethan, then?

Before she could question, Mordecai said, "I told Pharez that we have plans for you, which we do, but they are not completed yet." He smiled one of his rare smiles. "Tonight is the opening night of the Rosh Hashanah festival. Keep your eyes open, and I will too. There will be many eligible men in attendance. Leah and I agree that it is time you were betrothed."

Mordecai left her then, and Esther took a steadying breath. She hadn't planned on going to the festival. She hadn't been anywhere, besides running errands for Leah, for months. By the time evening had approached each day, she'd been too exhausted from caring for her cousins and the household to think beyond a single night's rest.

She knew Mordecai was being more than generous. He was practically giving her a say in which man she would marry. Her mother hadn't even known her father when they were betrothed. Esther wondered if it was better to know the man beforehand or not. It wasn't as if she knew any men anyway. She'd worn her veil in public since the age of twelve, of course, so the men would only remember her as a twelve-year-old girl.

Esther heard the cry of a babe coming from inside the house and knew her help was needed. She left the stone wall, realizing she had a day of chores ahead of her but also holding close the seed of hope that now grew in her breast.

Chapter 2

"YOU ARE TRULY BEAUTIFUL, ESTHER," Leah said, startling Esther for the second time that day.

Leah had loaned Esther a soft, rose-colored, linen tunic imported from Egypt. The Egyptians were famous for making the highest quality of linen, and it was nearly as supple as silk. The tunic had been a wedding gift to Leah, and when Esther had pulled it over her head, she'd felt the transformation just from a simple change of clothes.

She studied herself in the polished brass circle Leah kept in her bed chamber. The rose color set off Esther's olive complexion and made her deep brown eyes look black, matching her hair. She looked older somehow, more like a woman, and the tunic followed curves that her everyday shifts didn't reveal.

Leah stood behind her, smiling, and put her hands on Esther's shoulders. "I have been praying that you'll see your future husband tonight. That you'll know it is he so you may be at peace."

Had Leah sensed her troubled thoughts stemming from her conversation with Mordecai? "How was it with you and Mordecai?" Esther asked, suddenly wondering if the question was too private.

"Oh," Leah said with a smile. "I knew Mordecai when I was a young girl. In fact, we were playmates. His family moved into another neighborhood when I was about eleven. But when our parents made the arrangements, I only had fond memories, so it was a happy union for us both."

Esther let out a small sigh. She knew all marriages weren't like Leah's, not even Jewish marriages sanctioned by the Lord. Yet, she hoped for the same measure of happiness she'd seen among her relatives. She knew part of their joy was that they were both devout in their faith and commitment to family, but another part of it was natural attraction.

Esther had experienced a little of that herself when she'd noticed a handsome man at the market. Nothing intense, or what she could call *love*, but a growing awareness. She supposed it was part of the Lord's plan to bring a woman and man together to create a serene family.

"I hope to have a happy marriage," Esther said in a quiet voice, mostly to herself.

"You are full of life and love." Leah squeezed Esther's shoulder. "I've no doubt that any man will consider himself very blessed to call you his own. Your temperament matches your fair countenance."

Esther gazed at her reflection and thought about where she might be this time next year. Would she be married, in her own home, and expecting a child? Her stomach fluttered as if in answer, and she wondered if she would indeed see her future husband tonight.

"Wear this veil tonight. It will complement the tunic." Leah held out the blue silk that Abigail had used in the "marriage" that morning.

"Oh, I couldn't," Esther said. "It's much too fine."

"And it's doing nothing but collecting dust." Leah pulled it over Esther's head and adjusted it so only her eyes showed. "Perfect. Your eyes alone will draw in all the men."

Esther flushed at the compliment.

As Leah moved away, a sense of loss flooded through Esther. "I wish you could go to the first night of Rosh Hashanah with us."

Leah crossed the room and picked up Samuel from his cradle. "It's too soon to take him into public. The children will stay home with me as well. You'll have other things to concentrate on, and Mordecai promised he'd escort you to sit with Johanna."

Seeing Johanna was something Esther looked forward to. It had been a few weeks since their last visit, and Esther loved hearing all Johanna had to say. It seemed her friend knew all the comings and goings of their community as well as those concerning Shushan.

Before leaving the house, Esther knelt by her mat and said a quick prayer. She hoped to know whom she should marry and possibly even see that man tonight. As she finished her prayer, excitement coursed through her. Maybe tonight she really would find her future husband—if it was the Lord's will.

On her way out of the house with Mordecai, Esther grabbed the basket she'd loaded with spiced crescent rolls. Everyone was expected to bring something to the festival, and the food would be shared. Esther had experimented with spices today, and she thought the crescent rolls had turned out better than usual. Maybe she could offer one to some handsome man and capture his interest that way. She smiled at her thought; she would never dare be so bold.

Once they left the neighborhood of Mordecai's modest estate, they reached the more crowded area of their community, with narrow roads and small houses. More than one family dwelt in some of these homes, and it amazed Esther how they all seemed to live together in harmony. She knew she was fortunate to have a bedchamber to herself. As they walked to the marketplace, it seemed everyone greeted Mordecai on the way. His hours spent in the service of his people made it easy for everyone to recognize him, and Esther considered him a great example.

She heard the music coming from the marketplace before they reached it. She marveled at the transformation. Flowers and leaves had been woven into garlands that draped the doorways. Beautiful cloth and ribbons decorated the food tables. Everyone looked scrubbed clean, wearing their best clothing, and the air was charged with excitement and resounded with greetings.

The tables of food were lined up end to end, already filled with the most delicious cakes of every variety and platters of fruits and vegetables. Esther made her way there first, stopping each time someone greeted Mordecai. She set the basket of rolls on the end of a table next to another basket of challah and wondered how many minutes would pass before it was consumed.

"There you are!" a woman shrieked behind her.

Esther turned and was enveloped in Johanna's arms. She laughed and pulled her close. "How's my married friend?"

"Tired and nervous," Johanna said as she released Esther.

Esther laughed again. It was a typical answer from her wise-mouthed friend. "And how are you *feeling*?" she asked, drawing out the last word.

"I'm not with child, if that's what you're asking." Johanna's eyes glittered above her veil piece.

Esther arched a hidden eyebrow. "Oh, I was definitely not asking *that*."

"You expect me to believe you?"

The two women laughed together.

Esther felt a tap on her arm and heard Mordecai clear his throat. Suddenly, she felt embarrassed. Had he overheard Johanna talk about being with child?

"I'll be making greetings throughout the crowd. If you stay on this side, I'll be able to find you quickly." He looked pointedly from Esther to Johanna.

Johanna linked arms with Esther. "We'll stay together near the food tables." Her eyes smiled at Mordecai. "After all, this is where all the single men will come to fill their bowls." She winked at Esther then looked back at Mordecai.

Heat raced through Esther at her friend's boldness, but Mordecai just bowed his head and turned to leave.

When he was out of earshot, Esther said, "You can't guess what task Mordecai has given me tonight."

Johanna gripped her hand. "Let's go sit down. I must hear every word."

The two women found seats in one of the many alcoves that typically served as a backdrop to a market stall. There, they could observe the crowd without being jostled.

"Are you to meet your betrothed here?" Johanna asked as soon as they were seated.

"You know I am not betrothed," Esther protested.

"I heard that Pharez questioned Mordecai this morning."

Esther stared at her friend. "How could you know that?"

"Rebecca was passing by, and she . . . Oh, never mind. Tell me which brother Mordecai has settled on. Is it Dan?"

"You are impossible. And amazing," Esther said. "How can you know so much—?"

Johanna laughed then delivered a sharp pinch to Esther's arm. "Tell me what your cousin said!"

"Ow! All right, all right." Esther rubbed the sting on her arm. "Mordecai told me that I would not be married to any second-born son. That Dan was too caught up in his tablets and would not appreciate my . . . beauty." She whispered the last word.

"Mordecai said *that*?" Johanna's eyes went wide, and she leaned close to Esther. "Mordecai knows everyone in the community, and he's greatly revered. It seems he wants only the best for you. If you married Dan, we would be sisters-in-law. I couldn't think of anything better—although I can't really imagine Dan being able to keep you content." She sat back with a sigh. "There is no limit to the man your husband could be. Why, he might be the richest man in the land."

Esther's face warmed at the attention, and she couldn't stop the laughter that bubbled up inside of her. "Perhaps he owns a wine press that will produce the best wine in all of Persia, so good the king himself buys vast barrels from him."

"Or he will be so handsome that every girl will fall in love at one glance," Johanna said with a wink.

"And he will be so kind and generous that even the children do his bidding at a single word."

Johanna grasped her arm. "He might be all of those things and more."

"Yes, I'm sure there are plenty of men walking around just like that," Esther said, scanning the crowd. "Perhaps he will approach the table at any moment."

A young man passed by them then, his hair prematurely thinned, muttering to himself. He stopped at the food table and picked up one of Esther's spiced rolls. After sniffing it, he set it down and wandered back into the crowd. He'd rejected her crescent roll based on the smell. Perhaps she'd overdone the spices after all.

Johanna burst out laughing then covered her mouth with her hand so as not to draw attention.

Esther stared after the man in disbelief. "I suppose that wasn't the man."

"Well, he might have been rich," Johanna said with laughter in her voice. "But definitely not handsome."

"Nor kind," Esther said with a smile.

Johanna brought a finger to her eye to capture the moisture. "Not kind in the least, or he certainly would have eaten your delicious roll and gone for second helpings."

Esther leaned against the stone wall. The evening air had finally cooled off enough that she was glad for her veil. It did provide some warmth.

A group of musicians struck up a tune on the other side of the marketplace, and some of the children were already forming a dance.

"Have you heard the latest news about the king's bride?" Johanna said.

"I've heard no news. I didn't realize he'd chosen already," Esther said. The king and his armies had returned only a few weeks before from a failed invasion of Greece.

"He hasn't. But he's no longer considering only royal candidates now that he's back from the Greek invasion."

Esther arched a brow. "Who else could a king marry? Surely he won't marry a foreign woman?" Yet she realized it was entirely possible for King Xerxes to choose a foreign princess, especially if it furthered his political cause. Maybe he'd met women he favored in the recent Athenian battles.

"It's said that he's looking for the most beautiful and fair virgin, no matter her descent. She might be royal; she might be a peasant."

Esther was quiet, trying to comprehend. "It's such a debacle to begin with. He put away his first wife for living the laws that society is governed by."

"She disobeyed the king," Johanna said.

"She didn't have a choice."

"Her choice cost her dearly."

"Yes," Esther said, wondering what the former queen thought of her husband's antics. "And now he's searching for another wife."

Johanna nodded. "Not only that, but the king sends out officers to find fair virgins and has them 'purify' themselves for an entire year before granting an interview."

Esther felt herself growing hot with indignation. "Purify? You mean 'preen.' A full year of preening, yet none has pleased him? It's unbelievable."

"It's not like he can go out into the city and court a woman at will." Johanna leaned back with Esther, their shoulders touching.

Esther's temperature continued to rise. "He chose his first wife without all of this parading."

"His father chose his first wife."

Esther paused, thinking of the arranged marriages among her people. A king's marriage must be politically sound as well as produce an heir to the throne. The king had put away Vashti three years before, and it was said that she lived in her own palace somewhere in the east mountains. She retained dozens of servants, yet her status of queen was gone forever. If the king hadn't decided to invade Greece to try to avenge his father's loss, he'd probably already have a new queen. Now it all seemed to be a cruel sport for him.

"What happens to those women he rejects?" Esther asked.

"I suppose a few elect will be elevated to concubines, but the others will be sent back with a handsome dowry to tempt a suitor," Johanna said.

"Of course," Esther said, bitterness creeping into her voice. "All very convenient for the king, but life-changing for the women." She smoothed out the delicate fabric on her lap. "Our lives may be dull and predictable in our community, but at least we don't have to be concubines to a negligent man."

"Esther," Johanna said, her loud whisper sounding like a reprimand. "You shouldn't call the king negligent in such a public place."

Esther pursed her lips together and nodded. Johanna was a good friend, a faithful friend. And even though she was an eager gossiper, Esther also knew Johanna wouldn't betray the most important details.

"Some women might feel that being a concubine to the king is a great honor," Johanna said in a gentle voice.

"I suppose it is in its own way. They have their own quarters and aren't turned away from the palace when they become with child by the king. The concubine children of King Darius hold plenty of titles in the land. But what about the harem? Those women are practically slaves to whichever royal man happens to visit."

Johanna shuddered. "I couldn't imagine anything more awful. Yet, it is better than starving."

Esther knew that not all of the people in Persia had a wonderful place to live like she. There were beggars and slaves mixed in with the royal and elite. Melancholy settled over her as she thought of the fate of some women, women she didn't even know but somehow felt pity for anyway.

She and Johanna watched the children clapping and dancing together. Later, the adults would join in.

Dan and another man walked toward the food table. Dan's head was lowered as usual, his dark locks shadowing his features. He seemed to be listening intently to what his friend had to say. Unlike Dan, the second man was wide, with a round belly.

They stopped at the food table, and Johanna elbowed Esther. "There's Dan and . . . is that Reuben?"

Dan walked along the table, not paying attention to the food. But Reuben moved more slowly, eying the platters. He paused in front of her basket of rolls and picked one up.

"Oh, it looks like Reuben is interested," Johanna said.

He took a bite and smiled.

"He's a bit short," Esther said with a soft laugh.

Johanna nudged her. "But has very nice taste."

"Merchant? Farmer?" Esther said.

"Merchant, definitely. He's as pale as alabaster."

Esther couldn't stop her laughter. "Maybe it's better to *not* see the groom before the wedding."

She fell silent as Dan backtracked and picked up one of her rolls as well.

Johanna squeezed her hand. "Be patient. You'll see someone who captures your interest soon enough. And I'm sure he'll be devastatingly handsome and rich and—"

"Kind and wise . . ." Esther smiled. "But will he love me?"

"He would be foolish not to," Johanna pronounced.

Esther wished she had that kind of confidence. She hadn't spied any young man tonight who had piqued her interest. Maybe marrying Dan wouldn't be so bad after all.

Chapter 3

"WATCH THE LINE," AHASUERUS SAID, scanning the terrain below, where two ibex grazed.

Meres slackened his hold on the bow and realigned the arrow. "Like this, Your Majesty?"

"Perfect. But keep it steady, and just before your hand starts to shake, release." Ahasuerus had been hunting with the prince of Media all afternoon and had finally come across this golden spot as twilight descended.

One slain ibex had already been carted away to their tents to add to the largest prize captured the first day of the hunt—a massive lion. This second ibex would be a gift to Meres . . . if his aim was true. The small-boned prince might appear delicate, but there was a wiry strength in him.

The bow pinged, and the arrow shot through the air, hitting the ibex just below its shoulder.

Both men stood up and watched the beast run a few dozen paces then stagger and fall. Meres looked over at Ahasuerus, a smile on his flushed face.

"Well done, my friend," Ahasuerus said, grinning back. "You'll be joining me in hunting lions very soon."

A rush of feet sounded behind them, and several chamberlains and servants came running up and stopped at the ridge to see Meres and Ahasuerus's handiwork.

Cheers erupted when the group spotted the fallen ibex. The chamberlain named Biztha, who stood closest to the king, seemed to remember to curb his enthusiasm and acknowledge the king first. He prostrated himself right there in the dirt.

Ahasuerus's mouth twitched into a smile as the others prostrated. They'd all have dirt and bits of grass on their tunics now.

"You may rise, all of you," Ahasuerus said. He'd enjoyed the last three days devoid of the usual palace conventions back in Shushan. The prostrating chamberlains brought it all rushing back. In the morning, the tents would be packed, the dozens of servants rerouted, and the entourage started on its homeward journey.

They would all be back to the palace formalities, the only way to keep a kingdom the size of Persia organized. Now in his sixth year of reign, Ahasuerus had thought he'd be more comfortable in his role as king, but truthfully, he loved the wilderness more than anything. And it was refreshing to get away from all of the councils on war—the chamberlains and some of the princes were already pressuring him to launch another invasion against Greece. But the king knew Persia needed to recover from the last failure. First, his father had lost against the Athenians, and now he had as well.

Out here, Ahasuerus could forget the war debates, if only for a few days. The fresh air, vast sky, scent of grass and wild plants, and thrill of hunting dangerous beasts spoke to him like nothing else.

Inside the palace, he wore elaborate robes and delicate jewelry and had to sit in council from dawn until well after dusk. The women brought some delight in the evenings, but with the banishment of his wife, Vashti, he'd grown tired of the tittering girls who swooned when he so much as looked in their direction. Despite all of Vashti's vanity and self-centeredness, being married to her had at least kept the other women from vying for his attention so openly.

In fact, Meres had been there that fateful night of Vashti's fall from grace. The war council that month had dragged on as arguments had made their circular rounds of how best to quell the Greeks once and for all. Wine and dancing were introduced each night to pacify the seven princes of Persia and Media, and the men vied for the most beautiful of dancers.

Even three years later, Ahasuerus still questioned what had made him send the chamberlains to his wife and demand that she display herself in front of the men. Was it the wine or the knowledge that his wife would never look at him the way these dancers eyed the assembled princes? Whatever the reason, he had ordered Vashti sent for so he might boast of her beauty. The command proved to be the dissolution of their marriage.

He had been foolish, yes, but she had put him in a position to hold her up as an example to all men and women in the kingdom. If the incident had occurred in front of a few court members, the outcome might have been different. But in front of his chamberlains and seven visiting princes, it did no good to have Vashti blatantly refuse his command.

They hadn't even produced an heir, and Ahasuerus wondered if there had been a child to consider, perhaps the chamberlains would have been more forgiving.

"Your Highness, supper is ready," Biztha pronounced with an eager smile pulled across his two very crooked front teeth. He started to move into the prostrate position again.

Ahasuerus raised his hand to stay him. "You've enough dirt on your clothing already."

A few chuckles surrounded them. Laughter and good humor were plentiful out here on the hunting ground. Back at the palace, the stiff formality would return.

With a nod, Biztha turned and called out, quite unnecessarily, "Make way for King Xerxes," as if no one else had heard the man's announcement of supper.

It had taken months to get used to the Xerxes title, but now Ahasuerus liked the sound of it. It was abrupt and powerful, much like he viewed himself. Only those closest to him ever called him by his given name.

They made their way across the rocky ground to the large billowing tent, its sides vibrating in the wind. Out here, the wind seemed never to stop; it just altered its level of strength. But Ahasuerus didn't mind. It reminded him that time was always moving forward and a king had only a small portion of it to make an impact, improve his land and people, and avenge previous wrongs.

Three Magi were already positioned inside the tent, waving their clay lamps of incense. The pungent smell greeted the king like a slap. After the fresh air, the inside of the tent felt stifling. But he had to admit, he was ravenous.

The center rug was piled with gold platters of roasted fowl topped with pistachios, ripe peaches, and boiled wheat sweetened with figs. He sat down, and the Magi chanted a short prayer of thanksgiving to Ahura-Mazda, the god of truth and light. The king mouthed the familiar words in earnest. When the prayer ended, the chamberlains took their place at the other end of the rugs.

Ahasuerus enjoyed the companionable silence as they ate. In the palace, there would have been music, entertainment, and required conversation. Here there were no petitions to hear, no concubines to choose between, and no worry about selecting the next queen.

Well, almost no worry. This excursion had been precipitated by the outcry when he dismissed all of the royal virgins who had been waiting in the harem for his final decision. He'd honestly tried to choose one of the women—there was no lack of beauty and attraction among them—but he wanted a true companion.

Vashti had created a strong political alliance with her connections to the outer provinces, including the ever-restive Medes and Bactrians. But

like most of what had been established in his life, Vashti had been chosen
by his father, King Darius. Ahasuerus didn't fear an arranged marriage,
but now that he was king, he found the suggestion from his officers to
interview the fairest virgins to be very interesting. He just hadn't expected
it to take three years. And there was the matter of the Greek invasion that
had taken him away from other concerns in the kingdom.

Ahasuerus was not getting any younger, and he needed an heir. He was
already in the sixth year of his reign. This hunting trip was meant to clear his
head and give him more resolve when he returned. The gossip would have
certainly died down by now, and he could set to the critical task of selecting
a queen.

The more he dwelled on it, the more he was determined to delay no
longer. He recognized that it wasn't fair to the kingdom and his people to
keep them unbalanced for so long. He needed to ensure the succession.
Persia needed a queen to revere and a palace full of legitimate children.

A servant came to refill his wine goblet, but Ahasuerus placed a hand
over it. Only one cup was desirable. He needed his wits about him at all
times. He'd learned his lesson well enough with Vashti, and regret still burned
deep inside. Because of that, he was determined to choose a wife who was
more than just beautiful. Vashti had been the epitome of royalty, but that had
also come between them. It seemed that in her mind, she was so superior to
everyone else that she was never pleased.

She was also never happy. Ahasuerus had rarely seen his former wife smile.
He thought of her in her palace in the mountains, spending her inherited
wealth and never being satisfied with anything less than perfection. Of course,
Ahasuerus's actions in divorcing her probably hadn't lent to Vashti's happiness—
if it were even possible for her to find any fulfillment.

He blew out a breath. He had to get that woman and his mistakes out
of his mind.

"Meres," he called across the length of the tent. "How would you like
to ride back with me to the palace tonight?"

The prince's thick brows arched. "Tonight?"

"There's nothing like a ride in the fullness of the moon, and I'll be able to
show you the more quiet side of Persia. We'll ride through some communities
and perhaps surprise a few people."

Meres chuckled, his eyes gleaming. "That we shall no doubt do."

"Wear a cloak," the king said, rising to his feet. Everyone else rose as
well, going into their deep bows. "And select four guards to come with us.
We'll leave at once."

Chamberlains and servants scrambled into action. Ahasuerus strode to the private section of his tent, and Biztha scurried after him, locating the king's cloak in a moment.

"Your Highness might consider more guards," he said with his head bowed.

"Perhaps if the people knew we were coming back early, but four will do tonight." He let Biztha position the indigo cloak about his shoulders. In the light of day, the fine weave would give it away as a royal garment, but in the dark, it would look like a commoner's.

Meres was waiting when the king exited the tent. The prince stood next to a Nisean stallion, its dark coat gleaming in the late afternoon sun. Another gift from Ahasuerus to the prince. One of the guards held the reigns of another stallion, and the king smiled. His horse was one of the finest in the land; it hadn't let him down yet. He'd even tried the horse out at races, which, predictably, he'd won.

"Ready for an evening run, boy?" Ahasuerus stroked the horse's muscular jaw. It closed its long-lashed eyes as if it enjoyed the attention from its master.

The king mounted, and the four assembled guards mounted their own steeds. They wore military tunics with the royal insignia, consisting of a silver embroidered circle with wings in the center. The clothing of the guards would make it obvious whom they escorted. Before they set out, the king turned to the guards. "Stay a good distance behind us. I don't want my identity to be known."

"Your Highness—" Meres began.

Ahasuerus laughed. "I like to see what's really going on in the kingdom from time to time." He gripped the reigns and shouted, "Aiyah!"

The cooling wind pushed his robe behind him as he rode, Meres hard on his heels. Ahasuerus had no doubt the guards could keep up, but they were following his command and allowed a fair gap. The king rode hard for about an hour then slowed as the first farms came into view. He was home, yet he felt as if he were leaving a true part of him behind in the hunting grounds.

Meres's horse slowed to a trot next to the king's, and Ahasuerus grinned at him. "How was that?"

"I'll be sore enough tomorrow," Meres said, matching the king's grin.

They laughed together.

"It's beautiful this time of day," Meres said, looking out over the vast valley.

Ahasuerus couldn't agree more. The harvest was just coming to a close, and overturned fields of rich dirt spread almost as far as he could see. The setting sun warmed the earth and turned it a dazzling orange. The wind was quieter now, only a soft breeze that cooled the perspiring men. The king glanced behind him. The royal guards were a good distance away, just how he liked it. He knew that one raise of his hand would close the space with a fierce gallop.

The two men watched the glow of the sun fade as twilight descended. Shadows lengthened until they matched the night sky. Tiny specks of light flickered across the capital city as people lit lamps and stoked cooking fires. The twilight had brought a peaceful feeling, and for a moment, the king felt free of all burdens. Words weren't needed to describe the feeling to Meres, who seemed lost in his own thoughts.

A lazy fly landed on Ahasuerus's arm, breaking him from his revelry. He urged his horse forward and rode at a canter toward the first buildings. He and Meres stayed along the outer perimeter, seeing the people enjoying the cool of the evening without being noticed themselves. Though it was dark, the moon was bright enough to guide the horses.

When they were about to the middle line of the city, the king's thirst got the better of him. In his haste, he hadn't taken time to bring a wineskin. At the next gravely road, he turned toward the dwellings. "There is usually at least one well along these larger roads," he said to Meres.

A couple of young boys skirted out of the way of the approaching horses. They pressed against an outer wall of a home and stared at the animals. As Ahasuerus passed them with a nod, he heard them chatter in excited voices. It wouldn't be long before the guards would turn down the same road and the boys might figure out who had just ridden past them.

He smiled to himself. Light from oil lamps spilled onto the road, making the path easy to follow. The dark form of a well stood out ahead, unmistakable, even at night. "Here we are," he said.

Prince Meres brought his horse to a stop. "I'll fetch the water for you," he said, dismounting.

"We can wait for the guards." Ahasuerus turned to see them just entering the road behind.

"I'm already down," Meres said with a laugh. He strode the few steps to the well and felt around the stone opening. "Where's a cup?"

Ahasuerus was enjoying watching the prince of Media grappling around. "Perhaps you're supposed to bring your own."

"Most likely." Meres moved to the other side of the well. "Ah. Here's the rope to fetch the water but still no cup."

The king shook his head. "Bring the water up; I'll drink straight from the goatskin."

Meres started to tug on the rope then stumbled forward. "What's attached to this thing?" A distant splash sounded. "Oh, I think I just knocked something into the well."

"The cup, perhaps?" Ahasuerus said.

Meres looked up and glared at the king.

"It appears you need help after all," Ahasuerus said, climbing down from his horse.

A woman's laughter came from around the corner, and voices carried, echoing off the stone. One female voice rose above the other. "You used to be more adventurous. Trust me, we will not be caught. No one is in the streets now."

The speakers came into view. Two young women walked, carrying oil lamps that illuminated their faces. The shorter one had tightly curled hair and a pleasant, round face. The second woman, who'd obviously been trying to talk her friend into something, wore her hair long. It rippled over her shoulders, framing a delicate face and large, luminous eyes.

Ahasuerus stared at the second woman as her gaze met his. Her expression went from surprise to what he could term only as complete astonishment. The color faded from her glowing face and was quickly replaced by a deep rose, perfectly matching the tunic she wore.

The king was amazed at the collection of expressions this woman showed in just mere moments. If only all of his court members could be read like her, he'd never have to second-guess a person's intentions.

She gripped her friend's arm and gave a little shriek.

Ahasuerus wanted to laugh but thought it might frighten her further. He was about to explain his presence when the women turned toward each other, frantically grabbing at something between their hands. Then the king understood. They were trying to put on their veils. He chuckled to himself and watched as the shorter woman was immediately successful. But the woman in the rose tunic pulled hers on backward. She twisted it furiously until her friend forced her hands still and adjusted the veil so that only her eyes showed.

He could imagine how red her face was now.

"We apologize for startling you," Ahasuerus said. "We're just about to fetch some water, but it appears that my . . . companion . . . is having trouble with the goatskin. It seems to be weighted down."

"Oh," the taller woman said, her eyes burning through her veil at him. Strangely enough, his heart rate quickened.

"It gets stuck frequently," the woman continued. "I avoid this well when I can." She hurried over to Meres, who stepped aside. Giving a hard tug, she seemed to dislodge it. "It's freed now. But let me fetch the water for you both."

Ahasuerus couldn't stop staring. Even though the woman was now veiled, her voice was sweet and mellow, and her quick actions had impressed him. Although her tunic was fine enough, he sensed she was not aristocracy. She moved with the ease of a woman used to working, including fetching water from a well. Yet, she was elegant and graceful at the same time. An interesting mixture.

He had the sudden desire to question her about her name, her family, her interests. Then he noticed the other woman had prostrated herself on the ground. That could mean only one thing. His guards had arrived.

A gasp from the taller woman drew his attention. "Ahasuerus?" she said as their eyes locked, and then she too was on the ground paying her obeisance.

Now she knew who he was, yet he had no idea who she was. And she'd called him *Ahasuerus*.

Meres didn't comment on the familiarity of the woman but moved to the place she had abandoned and proceeded to pull up the now-detached goatskin. "I'm afraid I caused something to fall in the well—perhaps a cup?"

"Most likely a rock," the tall woman said from her place on the ground.

"That's a relief," Meres said. "No one will miss a rock."

The king chuckled then realized the women were still on the ground. "Please rise," he said.

As the taller woman rose to her knees, he crossed to her and held out his hand.

She hesitated.

"I promise I'm not angry," he said, keeping his hand extended, waiting.

He thought he heard a sigh as she took it and stood. For some reason, he was reluctant to let go of her warmth. Hers wasn't like the hands of the women of his court. It was sturdy and somehow comforting, with strong fingers. She released his hand and stepped back, her head bowed.

He was already missing those vibrant eyes. The shorter woman, who had scrambled to her feet on her own, had pressed herself against the wall of a house. Perhaps he should send out a decree that he was not to be feared, especially in the neighborhood streets with only four guards. But he could very well imagine the tales they might have heard filtering from the palace.

The guards dismounted and took over Meres's task. "We should have brought wine," one of the guards said.

"I can fetch wine. It won't take but a moment," the tall woman said. She wasn't huddled against the wall like her friend. Her head was still bowed, but her voice was clear and strong.

The king's curiosity burned, but he didn't want to pester her with too many personal questions in front of Meres. Who knew how far the tale would spread. "Do you live nearby?"

Her eyes darted up to meet his. "Not exactly, but I can certainly fetch wine from the nearest home. I'm sure they would be only too happy to oblige."

An absurd image popped into his head of this woman bursting into the home of a family just sitting down for supper and demanding that they give her wine for the king. His mouth curved into a smile. "Well water will be refreshing enough. Our travels are nearly finished."

She nodded slightly. "Please forgive me, Your Majesty, for calling you by your given name. I was startled, and my wits fled."

Ahasuerus studied her bent head as the silence stretched around them. He couldn't get the image of her glowing face and unbound hair out of his thoughts. "No need to ask forgiveness. I'm quite fond of my name and rarely hear it spoken. But you are right—you should call me King Xerxes the next time we meet."

That got her attention, and she raised her head. Looking into her eyes, the king was again struck by their expressiveness. They crinkled at the corners, and he realized she was smiling at him. He smiled back but was interrupted when Meres said behind him, "Your water, Your Majesty."

Along the road, several people had come out of their homes, staring at the scene. One by one, each individual dropped to the ground.

Meres thanked the women for their service, and before the king could ask anything else, the women were hurrying away, clutching each other's hands.

Ahasuerus turned to the closest guard and lowered his voice. "Find out that woman's name." The guard set off after the women, and the king drained the water skin then handed it back to Meres.

Too many people were congregating for the king to wait for the guard's return, so he mounted his horse and turned back the way they'd come. He'd stick to the perimeter until they reached the main palace road. He had plenty to ponder tonight without anyone else gawking at him.

Chapter 4

ESTHER'S FACE BURNED AS SHE tried to keep herself from running down the road and screaming at the sky. The king had seen her with her veil off. The king had held her hand. The king hadn't minded that she'd called him by his given name.

King Xerxes. The king of all of Persia. The man who commanded armies of thousands, conquered women by the dozens, and displayed his wealth in palaces of marble and gold.

And she'd called him "Ahasuerus," like she was his intimate. Her mind couldn't comprehend it, and the only reason she believed it herself was that Johanna was next to her, fleeing as well. They turned a corner then another. Finally, when she thought she'd burst, Esther tugged Johanna to a stop, her breathing labored.

"I should be hanged from the highest scaffolding ever built," she whispered in a fierce voice. "Did we just meet the Great King? And did I just tell him I would fetch him wine from the closest stranger's house?"

"You did," Johanna said, her breathing coming in short gasps.

"And did we just appear before him without our veils, laughing like crazy birds?"

"We did." Johanna leaned against the alley wall, her hand over her heart. "And he didn't seem to mind one bit." Her head snapped up. "Did you see how he looked at you?"

The thought of his piercing gaze sent a jolt into Esther's stomach. His eyes had been warm yet deep, as if there was no end to their depths. He wore a rather plain cloak, and his dark wavy hair touched the back of his neck. For some reason, she'd noticed a scar above his left eyebrow, no doubt from a fierce battle. And his hands . . . that had touched her. His fingers had been strong, warm. "He stared at me like he was trying to decide if he wanted to order our execution or laugh himself sick."

"No," Johanna said, her voice steadying. "I don't think that's how he was looking at you. He looked at you like you were the most beautiful woman he'd ever seen."

Esther snorted then started to laugh. She didn't know whether to blame her nerves, her complete embarrassment, or her fear, but she couldn't stop laughing and shaking. She sat down on the road, leaning against the wall, and covered her mouth. The king had smiled at her, a genuine smile, and his eyes had searched hers as if to question her, as if he were interested in speaking with her further.

Johanna sat next to her and patted her shoulder. "Are you all right?"

Tears spilled out of Esther's eyes, and her nose started to run. "No, I'm not all right. The king wouldn't genuinely notice someone like me. He's interviewed princesses and the most beautiful virgins of the city. He has a harem full of concubines. Women faint when he so much as looks at them, let alone helps them to their feet and jests with them."

Esther's laughter faded, and Johanna moved closer until their shoulders and arms were touching. She placed a hand on Esther's knee. "I speak the truth when I say that King Xerxes certainly *noticed* you. The way he looked at you made *my* face heat up," Johanna said in a quiet voice.

"Johanna!"

"On my life, I've never spoken anything truer," she said.

The sound of horse hooves reached them, and Esther stood, her entire body trembling at the thought of the King of Persia noticing her. A man on a horse came around the corner, and even in the deepening darkness, it only took a second for Esther to realize he was a royal guard.

He stopped when he saw them. "Are you the women who helped King Xerxes at the well?"

"Yes," Johanna said because Esther couldn't form a coherent word.

"He wishes to thank both of you for your services," the guard said. "And," his eyes focused directly on Esther, "he wants to know your name."

Still, she was speechless, so Johanna did the practical thing. "Her name is Esther."

The guard bowed his head. *Bowed to them!* "Thank you." Then he reined his horse around and was gone as suddenly as he'd arrived.

"We must get you back home," Johanna said, her voice sounding far away to Esther. "Mordecai will wonder what became of you."

Johanna grasped Esther's hand and tugged her along the alley then out onto a small road. It intersected with the one the king had been on, but when they reached the crossroad, there was no sign of him in either direction. Esther gripped Johanna's arm. Her mind whirled at all that had happened, but she knew one thing for sure. "You can't tell Mordecai of this. He would certainly disapprove."

"Of meeting the king?"

"Of not wearing our veils," Esther said. "Surely if he hears the story of young women meeting the king and he knows that we did as well, he'll connect that we didn't have our veils on." Her stomach knotted. Mordecai was a leader in the community, and he wouldn't stand for his cousin acting so foolishly. Besides, she'd be ashamed to hurt him in any way. He and his wife had been nothing but generous toward her.

After the excitement of the night, the streets seemed painfully dull and quiet. Esther still hadn't caught her breath when she reached the courtyard of her home. Johanna embraced her, saying, "Don't worry, I'm sure the story will never reach your family. My lips are silent."

"Thank you," Esther said, clinging to her friend. Her heart still thudded as she thought about everything the king had said to her.

She hurried through the gate and into the house. She wanted to step out of the rose-colored tunic as quickly as possible so as to not damage it with more perspiration. Once in her room, she breathed a sigh of relief as she slid on her sleeping robe. She finally felt like herself again. If the king saw her now, surely he wouldn't give her a second glance.

"Esther? Are you home?" Leah's voice came through the hall.

Esther tied her sash into a knot and walked out of her chamber.

"Who did you come home with?" Leah asked. "Mordecai is still not here."

"Johanna walked me." She took a deep breath, hoping Leah wouldn't notice what were sure to be flushed cheeks.

"You're glowing, Esther," Leah said with a smile.

She noticed. "It was a nice festival. But spending time with Johanna was the most enjoyable part." *Not to mention when we met the king.*

"Come into the cooking room, and I'll get you a refreshing drink. You can tell me all about it."

Esther followed Leah to the cooking room; it still retained heat from the fire that had cooked their evening meal. Esther opened the outside door, letting in the night breeze. "I'm quite warm from the walk," she said.

Leah produced a cup of cool pomegranate juice, and both women sat on stools at the table. Esther had to force herself to drink it slowly. The cold sweetness was delicious.

"Did you see anyone who interested you?" Leah asked.

Esther was grateful there was only one oil lamp lit, hanging from the rafter of the house. It certainly hid the flame that again touched her cheeks. "I think Johanna and I discussed every eligible man in attendance." She laughed nervously, her thoughts going to the Persian man she'd met that night. "Johanna probably gave me too much information about each one."

Leah reached across the table and patted Esther's hand. "All women have to put up with some flaws, just as the men accept us with our quirks as well."

"Yes." Esther took another sip. The king certainly had flaws—all those women available to him; he was someone used to indulgence.

"Surely, besides Johanna's insights, you saw someone who caught your eye?" Leah's eyes twinkled with anticipation.

For an instant, Esther considered telling Leah everything, but something held her back. It was ridiculous to think that she'd ever see the king again. Maybe someday she could tell Leah, years from now when it was but a faded memory.

"Dan was there," Esther said instead. "He actually ate one of my rolls."

"Oh?" Leah said. "He has a nice future. He'll certainly move up in King Xerxes's service and provide any woman a good home."

At the mention of King Xerxes, Esther's heart flipped. *Stop that*, she commanded herself. "Dan is definitely nice."

"But you don't want to settle for nice?" Leah asked, her eyes probing.

Esther lifted a shoulder in a shrug. Maybe she just needed more time. Dan would grow on her, or there would be someone else interested.

"Well, I did hope that my prayers for you to see your future husband tonight would be answered." Leah smiled. "Perhaps they were, and you saw him but didn't realize it."

Esther's heart raced. "Perhaps." She finished the fruit drink, suddenly wanting to be alone with her tumbling thoughts. Leah seemed to be lost in her own thoughts when Esther excused herself and went to her bedchamber.

She said prayers then moved onto her mat, pulling the soft woven rug up to her chin. Closing her eyes, she willed sleep to come quickly. But her mind only wanted to recall the king's image—his dark wavy hair, the scar above his left eyebrow, his long fingers that were strong yet elegant, the way he smiled at her, and the intensity of his deep brown eyes.

* * *

Esther awakened well before dawn, gave up trying to get back to sleep, and slipped out into the courtyard. She climbed the north wall and perched on what had become her regular spot. From there she had an excellent view of the sky and, with the close of the harvest season, the bright constellations.

Mordecai had pointed them out to her one night when she couldn't sleep as a young girl. Since then, she'd learned so much more about the maps in the heavens—for that was what they were to her. Intricate paths intersecting in fascinating maps. Mordecai even had a clay tablet collection with stories from the Greeks that told of ancient legends of their gods. She couldn't read it, but he'd indulged her from time to time and read to her.

Yes, she was adamant about keeping the true faith and worshiping the supreme God, but it was interesting to learn about other people's beliefs. Persia was a divided country when it came to religion. The majority of the population followed after Ahura-Mazda, whom the king, and his father before him, worshiped. But as a people who had been exiled from Babylonia, the Jews were at a disadvantage. Even after many years, they were, for the most part, considered foreigners. They served in a few mundane positions at the palace but nothing that was politically influential. All of the king's closest advisors were connected to King Darius—they had served with Darius or were the sons of Darius's commanders.

Glimmers of the rising sun made themselves known in the softening gray of the sky. The bright constellations started to fade, and Esther yawned. She could not go to sleep now; there was a full day of chores ahead.

As she climbed down the wall, Mordecai exited the house. "You shouldn't be out here alone," he said when he saw Esther.

He had no idea how much time she spent outside alone.

"I couldn't sleep and wanted to see if I still recognized any constellations."

A rare smile came to his face. "Did you find the seven marks?"

She nodded, smiling back. He studied her for a moment until a flock of sparrows descended in a nearby pistachio tree.

"What did you think of the festival?" Mordecai asked, and Esther sensed what he was really asking.

"It was a nice event," she said in a careful voice.

Understanding showed in his eyes. "Very well. I have a full day and won't be back until sometime after the supper hour. Can you let Leah know?"

"Of course," Esther said, wishing she could tell him that she had found someone at the festival whom she was interested in. But the truth was, the king was still on her mind. She might be able to make better sense of things when he faded from her memory and she had a few nights of good sleep behind her.

Esther bade farewell to her cousin and went inside to begin the morning meal of wheat cakes and to check on the progress of the yogurt she'd made from goat's milk.

The rest of her day included scrubbing the baby's clothing, setting it out to dry, and keeping Ben from underfoot so Leah and the baby could take an afternoon rest while Abigail went to her friend's home for a few hours. By the time supper came, Esther was exhausted.

Leah was setting bowls on the table when she said, "Why don't you have a nap? It will be cool enough for the children to play in the courtyard after supper, and their noise won't disturb you."

Esther was more than grateful, so after supper, she curled up on her mat and fell asleep almost immediately.

It seemed like only a few moments later when she was awakened by Mordecai tapping her shoulder. The glowing lamp in her room told her that it was fully dark outside. She blinked up at her cousin's face and wasn't sure how to read it. His expression displayed concern.

"Is everything all right?" she asked. "Where's Leah?"

"They're all fine and settled in for the night. You must have overdone it today."

She sat up on her mat and smoothed her hair. "I didn't mean to sleep so long—"

Mordecai held up a hand. "Don't worry about that. I've come to talk to you about news that's all over the city." He hesitated, studying her carefully. "I didn't know what to make of it at first, but the more information I gathered, the more things became clear."

Esther was fully awake now. Her stomach tightened. What could her cousin be talking about?

"It was you, wasn't it? You and Johanna are the two who met King Xerxes last night at the well."

She opened her mouth to explain but realized the less she said, the better. Mordecai had obviously heard the rumors. The question now was, what did he really know?

"Yes," she whispered. Instead of anger crossing his face, Mordecai smiled, surprising Esther. Maybe he didn't know about the veils.

Relief drummed through her as warmth returned to her limbs. "We were very surprised to see the king, of all people, near the well. We were taking a bit of a walk so we could visit before returning to our homes."

Mordecai didn't say anything, just watched her as she spoke.

"He was with another man and four guards. I was surprised that he'd travel with such little protection." She'd seen his great processions and marches, although from a distance. No one was allowed close to the militia that surrounded him at those events.

"At first I didn't recognize who he was, and then I saw Johanna prostrate herself, and I realized . . ." Her voice trailed off. Mordecai's expression was one of wonder, even awe. Perhaps he'd heard a greatly inflated tale. The way rumors and gossip could compound was amazing, but Mordecai wasn't one for sensational stories.

Finally, he spoke. "Is it true he sent a guard to inquire after your name?"

Her mouth dropped open. "Yes. I was . . . very surprised. It was, in fact, Johanna who spoke to the guard."

"And she told him *Esther* and nothing else? Not your father's name or my name or your mother's name?"

"No, just Esther."

Mordecai gave a short nod.

"What is it? What has been said?" She dreaded Mordecai bringing up that he'd heard she'd worn no veil when she first saw the king.

"There's been a private edict sent to all community elders," Mordecai said, his voice a bit unsteady. "The king has requested that a woman by the name of Esther, whom he met at the well last night, be presented at his harem. He says he's renewing his search for a queen."

Chapter 5

AHASUERUS STARED STRAIGHT THROUGH THE assembled vocalists. The women were all fair and reasonably talented, as were most who performed in his court, but his mind was far removed from the night's entertainment.

Had only one day passed since he'd met the young woman he now knew as Esther?

The name tumbled in his mind, only to bring up fresh images of her. Those eyes had mesmerized him in a way he thought he'd never experience in his lifetime. He had a harem of dozens whom he could promote to concubine at any moment or make one his wife and elevate to queen. Many of them were more cultivated and beautiful than Esther.

It wasn't just her face though, nor her graceful movements, but her boldness that mixed with her humility at the same time. An astonishing blend.

Next to Ahasuerus, the prime minister, Tarsena, lounged on a pile of cushions. He was in his fiftieth year, excessively heavy, and one of the most indulgent members of the court. A leftover from King Darius's reign. Ahasuerus had been careful to retain some members of his father's court in order to appease the people and make the transition smoother from king to king.

To replace the prime minister was nearly impossible, especially when Ahasuerus could find no fault with him, at least politically. There were plenty of personal faults in the man.

Tarsena clapped as the vocalists finished their song. He leaned forward over his great belly and called out to them, "Well done." He turned toward the king. "Where are the dancers?"

Ahasuerus looked into the man's greedy eyes. "They have been delayed."

The expression on Tarsena's face tightened. Then he looked back to the vocalists with a sigh and made a motion with his hand for them to continue. As they began the next lilting tune, the prime minister leaned over and said in a too-loud voice to be private, "Why don't you just order the girl to your bed instead of going through all of this foolishness?"

Ahasuerus stared at the man. It seemed Tarsena had forgotten to whom he was speaking.

But the prime minister wasn't cowed. "Your obsession will be gone by morning, and we can move on with finding the next queen." He tapped the king's arm. "She must be from a royal lineage; the people expect it. They're already restless. They want security, and that means a queen in the palace and heirs running in the halls."

Ahasuerus agreed, although he wouldn't force Esther to his bed in order to get her out of his mind. His father might have embraced such a suggestion, but not he. The people expected him to marry a royal princess, and he'd done it his father's way once. There had been no heirs from the union with Vashti, and it had ended badly anyway. This time finding a queen would be done with more consideration and through Persian tradition.

If Ahasuerus bypassed the customary twelve-month purification process, his people would never accept Esther as queen.

"It was a mistake, you know," Tarsena continued. "Sending back all of those beautiful royal virgins." He shook his meaty head. "Such a waste."

Ahasuerus rose to his feet, and the singing abruptly stopped. All eyes of the assembled guests looked at him. "I will retire for the evening," he said.

The chamberlains scrambled up from their trays of sweets and assembled to escort him back to his private rooms.

"Do you need my services?" Tarsena asked, lumbering to his feet and bowing.

"Enjoy the dancers," the king said with a sardonic smile.

The man nearly salivated.

Ahasuerus stepped off the platform where his golden throne sat. He walked past the silent singers and the finely clothed courtiers. Was it so bad for a king to want to spend an evening alone, in a quiet room, with no prying eyes or elaborate entertainment?

He walked swiftly along the marble corridors until he met with one set of guards who stood outside the main door to his chambers. They moved aside, and he walked down a second hall that served as the corridor for the family rooms. Only he lived in them alone.

It was quiet, and the quiet seemed to mock him. In the banquet room, he'd craved the silence, but now that he had it, he wanted to fill his head with things other than his failures with Vashti and his uncertainty of finding a queen who could enrich his life.

Another set of guards stood before his private quarters. He turned to the chamberlain, Biztha, who quickly prostrated himself.

"I will be left alone now. If I need anything, I'll send for you."

The man scrambled to his feet and made another deep bow. "Yes, Your Majesty."

Once alone, Ahasuerus crossed the thick rugs to the balcony window and opened the doors. The view overlooked the whole of Shushan and was spectacular in the sunset. But it was well past sunset now, and few lights twinkled against the darkness below. The majority of the people were asleep.

The king leaned against the balcony wall. Below him, guards were stationed, even though it would be a rare feat for an arrow to reach him at this angle. The stars were plentiful tonight, brightening the sky against the dark valley below. The breeze tugged at his robe and ruffled his hair. It was a fine night. And he had no one to share it with. Or no one he wanted to share it with.

Was Esther looking at the same stars from her home? No, he decided. She was asleep like any reasonable person. It was only the king's court that seemed to stay up all hours of the night, doing who knows what, as if they were afraid if they closed their eyes, the very palace would disappear by morning.

The edict had been sent out this morning, and there had been no report from Hegai, the keeper of the women, that she had arrived today. Maybe he should have made it a command instead of a request. Again, that was something his father would have done.

He left the balcony, keeping the doors open, and drew off his robe. It was after midnight but still early for him to retire. He was sure that under the direction of Tarsena, the court would feast and entertain into the early morning hours. Ahasuerus sat at his writing desk and withdrew a square of parchment from a silver-embossed box. What if he wrote her a personal letter?

She won't be able to read it.

He set the parchment back in its place and closed the silver lid. Then he stood and crossed the doors of his inner chamber. Cracking the door open, he said to the guard, "Bring Hegai to my chambers."

The guard nodded and hurried from his post. The king shut the door and waited for the knock.

* * *

It was after midnight when Esther slipped out of the house into the courtyard. She climbed to her favorite perch on the north wall. The stars were brilliant tonight, but that wasn't why she'd come outside to sit beneath the sky.

She was hoping the Lord would tell her what to do about the harem.

Mordecai wanted her to go. No Jewish man or woman held any position of political influence in all of Persia. Her cousin had explained that having Esther positioned with an ear to the king would benefit the Jewish people.

"He doesn't know I'm a Jew," Esther had told Mordecai.

"You'll tell him when the time is right," was Mordecai's response. As if there would be another time.

Even if Esther did as the king requested and reported to the harem, she couldn't believe she'd be chosen as his queen. There was a vast difference between her and the women who'd been raised to marry royalty. Esther knew nothing about proper court conventions, and the news of scandals that had come from the palace had made her stomach churn.

And what would happen to her when she was rejected? Would she become a permanent part of the king's harem, sent for at will or used to entertain a prince? No proper Jewish woman could return from a palace unscathed in reputation. The king might be able to secure a dowry for an aristocratic Persian woman, and she could recover, but Esther couldn't imagine someone like Dan taking a bride who had been part of a harem.

And the life of a concubine wouldn't be much better.

And the life of a queen? . . . Esther squeezed her eyes shut. He had sent out an official edict . . . *for her.*

What did he want with her? It was impossible that he was serious about interviewing her for the role of queen. If Johanna was right and the king *was* interested in her, was it just to add her to a harem of women to be under his control? To be at his mercy? His fancy?

Esther's face burned. She had not been brought up to be in a harem or live as a concubine. So if she went and she was not chosen as queen, she would spend the remainder of her days without a husband.

But how could she tell the king no? How could she tell Mordecai no?

She pulled her knees up and wrapped her arms about her legs. She'd never been more surprised than when Mordecai had told her she should accept the king's request. That was not the Mordecai she knew—the day before he'd been talking about suitors like Dan, not King Xerxes.

Her people had always lived separately in their worship, their holidays, their prayer rituals, and their dietary laws. The Jews had been fortunate when the king of Persia had allowed exiles from Babylonia to return to their lands. But not every Persian was happy about it. There was plenty of disagreement among merchants and disputes over land, not to mention those who served in positions of power. A Jew might be a scribe at the palace or a member of the royal treasury but never a military leader or personal chamberlain.

Whether or not the king wanted Esther as part of his harem, or even as a queen, the people would never accept a Jewish queen. And once King Xerxes knew her true religion, he wouldn't accept her either. Perhaps Johanna should have told the king's guard Esther's Hebrew name, Hadassah. That would have told the king plain and clear who she really was.

O Lord, she whispered, bowing her head. *Unto thee I pray. Hearken to my cry and consider my plight. Favor me with Thy will, and guide me along the right path.*

When she ended her prayer, she kept her eyes closed, listening and feeling as the night surrounded her with stillness. She waited for her stomach to tighten, for breathlessness as she worried over what would happen at the harem, for perspiration to break out on her skin, but none of these things happened.

Instead, warmth tingled through her, spreading until even the cold stones beneath her no longer felt cold. The fear had left. Just like that. She hugged her knees as tears pricked her eyes then fell onto her cheeks.

She touched her wet face, her hands trembling. Even though the fear was gone, she now sensed the weight of what the Lord was asking her to do. How was it possible that He wanted her to report to the harem of the Persian king?

"Can I really do this?" she whispered.

Her mind rushed through the possible consequences of ignoring the peace she'd just felt—and ignoring the king's request. She knew that if she refused, she was at risk of incurring the king's wrath. He'd put away his first queen for disobeying his command. Was Esther willing to incur the same punishment?

It wouldn't be hard for the king to track her down and eventually link her to Mordecai. What if Mordecai and his family were somehow blamed for not delivering Esther? They were her guardians and would surely be held accountable.

How can I be responsible for bringing vengeance upon Mordecai?

The weight of a dozen stones seemed to press down on Esther's shoulders. By giving herself up at the harem and letting go of any future chance at a husband, a home, and children growing up in the Jewish faith, she'd protect Mordecai and Leah and their three children. The thoughts of the sweet faces of Abigail, Ben, and Samuel tugged at her heart. But the sacrifice was so great!

The weight of knowing what she must do increased into exhaustion, and Esther at last climbed down from the wall and made her way to her bedchamber, where she collapsed onto her mat.

Chapter 6

It was in the early mornings that Haman, the son of Hammedatha the Agagite, had the best chance to watch the woman he loved. The sun had yet to crest the eastern hillside while he waited in the copse of trees a short distance from the small hut.

He still couldn't believe Rebekah had chosen this hut—and the man who now emerged through the door—over *him*.

Haman's lip curled as he watched the stout man walk across the yard to a goat pen. Rebekah had married a goat herder. A man who wore leather straps about his arms and a tunic of what looked to be a tent panel. It probably was.

No, Haman couldn't have offered her a traditional marriage—he already had a wife and three concubines—but even as his concubine, Rebekah would have been well taken care of. Much better than the squalor she now lived in with that Jewish man.

Out of curiosity, Haman had been inside the hut, sneaking in when the couple was gone. It consisted of only three rooms: a cooking area, an adjoining gathering room, and a back room that barely had enough space for a double sleeping mat.

He clenched his hands into fists, feeling his jeweled rings dig into his skin. Compared to this *Jewish* man, Haman was two heads taller, and he had been complimented on his distinguished looks his entire adult life. The Jewish man's beard was unkempt, his hair was cropped too short, and he had more fat than muscle. And apparently, he made very little income herding goats.

Haman was wealthy, having been appointed a judge in King Darius's court and been elevated to the status of chief judge in King Xerxes's court. A laugh burst out from the Jewish man, and Haman narrowed his eyes. The man was actually inside the pen, laughing and playing with his goats.

Goats!

Haman knew the goat-man's name, but the man wasn't worth thinking of by name. And Haman had forbidden Rebekah to ever speak it in his presence. Anticipating Rebekah's appearance, his heart sped up. If he knew her habits well enough, she'd be coming out of the hut at any moment. He could hardly wait to see her, even at a distance.

"Joshua!" a woman's voice called before Haman could see her face.

And then she was there—standing at the hut's door, framed by the dawn's soft yellows and blues. Haman inhaled sharply and clenched his hands tighter. Her dark hair was loose, curling around her shoulders and bordering her delicate face. She wore no veil, not when she thought her husband alone could see her.

Haman's fingers remembered touching that face, and his mouth remembered kissing hers. Even from here, her eyes were the most arresting of all—a light brown mixed with gold. He used to call her his lioness. She would laugh at that and kiss him then laugh again.

But now, there was no more laughter, no more kissing. Not for months. Rebekah had married in the spring, and she'd said she needed to be faithful to her husband. Haman knew it was only a matter of time before Rebekah would become disenchanted with her marriage and her sense of what a "good" Jewish wife would do.

And he would be waiting for her when it happened.

She was walking toward the goat-man now, her alabaster-colored tunic sliding off one shoulder—a shoulder Haman used to caress. Longing pulsed through him, and as he watched Rebekah's walk, he realized he wouldn't be able to leave as soon as he had planned.

He held his breath, trying to hear what Rebekah was saying. He cringed when she smiled at her husband and leaned forward to kiss his cheek. At least it was just the man's cheek. Haman didn't know if he could handle watching any other type of kissing.

He forcibly unclenched his hands, trying to remain calm. If he acted on his instincts, the goat-man wouldn't live to see the sunset. For a wild moment, Haman wanted to laugh at himself. He was like a lovesick boy, hiding to spy on a girl, when in truth, he was one of the most well-respected members of the court of Persia.

His wife, Zeresh, was a cousin to Prince Admatha. Zeresh had born Haman six children, four sons and two daughters, and his concubines had delivered him six more sons. In his household, his word was law. So that was why today Haman hid behind trees, feeling disgusted with himself.

How was it possible that this nothing-of-a-man Jew could come between one of the most powerful men in the land and his true love? Haman took a deep breath. He had yet to tell his wife about Rebekah, but when he did, she would not complain. She dared not complain about any of his activities.

Yet there was no use telling his wife and disturbing his household until Rebekah agreed to become fully his. And that would take either Rebekah's complete cooperation or the death of her husband.

Of course, Haman had visualized the goat-man's death many times. Some of the enactments involved only Haman, such as well-placed poison or an accurately shot arrow. Other ideas were centered on recruiting help: anything from blockading the hut door and setting it on fire—after rescuing Rebekah—to a horse stampede in the market.

Haman's heart leapt as the goat-man waved to Rebekah and set off toward the hills, followed by his scraggly goats. A few of the smaller ones remained in the pen, bleating pitifully at the departing adults. The man headed straight for Haman, but Haman was well hidden and knew he wouldn't be discovered. He'd seen Rebekah's husband take the same route many a morning.

Haman waited several minutes after the Jew's departure and Rebekah's return inside the hut before standing. His legs ached from being in a cramped position for so long, but the wait would be worth it. Seeing Rebekah unveiled and kissing another man had stirred the desire in his chest to a frenzy. The sun hadn't even spilled onto the land yet as Haman left his hiding place, so he knew there was plenty of time for his unscheduled visit before returning to the palace for another day of court hearings.

A small goat bleated as Haman passed the animal pen and entered the dirt courtyard, if anyone could consider it a courtyard. There was no proper stone wall, nor any flowers in sight. He knew Rebekah kept a modest garden behind the hut—he watched her tend to it on the afternoons that court was not in session.

He stopped before the door, his heart thudding. Was he really going to do this? They hadn't spoken in months. *Yes, I am.* The door was partway open; Rebekah hadn't even bothered to shut it, let alone latch it. It was a sign from the god Ahura-Mazda, Haman decided. This was meant to happen, here, now.

Rebekah was humming, and for a brief moment, Haman closed his eyes. She used to hum around him. The melody seemed to caress his body, spreading fiery warmth straight to his soul until he could not wait one more moment before seeing his beloved.

A half smile framed his face as he pushed the door open all the way. Rebekah was bent over a basket of grain, but she turned when he entered.

"Josh—" She let out a gasp and straightened. Her hand went to her heart. "What are you doing here, Haman?"

He just stared at her for a moment, not answering. Truthfully, he didn't know what to say. He'd been prepared to say something, but now . . . standing in the same room with her, it was like every memory they'd ever shared came tumbling at him with full force. He could hardly breathe for the power of it.

She took a step back, her hand still on her chest as if she was having trouble breathing as well.

"I thought I told you to not come here. Ever." Her voice trembled, and it only endeared her more. "You shouldn't be here. My husband . . ." Her voice trailed off, and her eyes burned into his, first in surprise then in desire so tangible that it seemed to touch him from across the room.

He still couldn't speak. There were no words that could express what he wanted to say. So, instead, he strode toward her and pulled her to him. She tried to push him away at first, but the effort was weak, even for a woman. She stopped struggling as he pressed his mouth against hers. He didn't know at first if it was because she realized he wasn't going to let her go or because she had missed him as much as he had missed her.

She remained frozen in his arms as he kissed her over and over. When he pulled away, she wouldn't look at him. Haman slid his hands up her arms and behind her head then slowly kissed her again. Only then did she relax against him, and her hands moved tentatively up his chest.

That was all he needed to lead her into the back room.

Chapter 7

"ESTHER," A VOICE SAID. "YOU must wake up."

She opened her eyes, startled to see Johanna peering down at her. Then everything came flooding back. Meeting the king, the edict Mordecai had told her about, her prayer to the Lord. She sat up, brushing back her tangled hair that had become sweaty about her neck and shoulders. A glance toward the window told her that dawn had just arrived.

"What are you doing here?"

"The news is all over, and people are whispering your name on every road," Johanna said, her eyes wide as if she couldn't quite believe it herself. "It's astonishing, Esther. I thought he showed interest in you, but I never imagined . . ."

Esther drew her knees up to her chest, disbelief lodged in her mind. "I don't understand it either. He has dozens of women to choose from. He has several concubines, and he's already put away one queen."

"I know," Johanna said. "But there's no one like you, Esther. You are so kind and generous and clever . . . and beautiful." She reached out and touched Esther's cheek.

Her friend's touch made Esther dissolve. A sob escaped her throat, and she threw herself into Johanna's arms.

Johanna held Esther tight and let her cry.

"How can this be happening?" Esther said. "The other night, we were comparing the virtues of Dan and Rueben."

Johanna drew back and offered a gentle smile. "And now we are speaking of a chance for you to become the queen of Persia."

Esther sniffled. "I know, isn't it horrible?"

Johanna burst out laughing.

"There's nothing funny about this," Esther said, but a smile tugged at her face. "Have you spoken to Mordecai and Leah?"

Johanna sobered. "Yes, they are waiting in the other room for us. I told them I'd talk to you." She paused, watching Esther carefully.

Esther felt slightly faint. "So you agree with Mordecai?"

Her friend reached for her hand and squeezed. "It's an amazing set of coincidences. Leah told me she'd been praying you'd meet your husband the night of the festival. And for a king to take such notice of you—"

"Just because I go to the harem doesn't mean he'll choose me."

"I know." Johanna let out a sigh. "We all realize that, but perhaps the Lord is giving you this opportunity for a reason, no matter the outcome."

Esther's eyes filled with tears as the warmth filled her soul just as it had out on the wall a few hours before. It was undeniable now. She knew what she had to do. Using the back of her hand, she wiped away her tears.

"Oh, Esther. I'm so sorry," Johanna said, pulling Esther into her arms.

But Esther drew away. "You don't understand. I'm crying because the Lord has told me I need to obey the king's edict."

Johanna stared at her, her own eyes glistening with tears now. "I will pray for you every day."

Esther nodded, feeling numb, overwhelmed, but strangely courageous. "I'll be praying for myself as well."

Her friend cracked a smile.

"And for all of you." Esther rose up from the mat and grasped Johanna's hand to help her to her feet. "We'd better not keep them waiting any longer."

* * *

"I won't wake Abigail or Ben, but I want to kiss them good-bye," Esther said, meeting Leah's gaze.

Leah nodded and walked back into Mordecai's arms, where he held on to her tightly. After Johanna had left, they discussed what Esther should do once she reached the harem and how she should explain her family when asked.

"Do not reveal your religion yet," Mordecai had cautioned her. "Not until you are given a fair chance at a successful interview with the king. And even then, we'll have to decide when the time is right to let him know."

The deception weighed heavily on her heart, but with the Lord's confirmation that she should at least take this first step, she had to trust in Him. Walking into the bedchamber Abigail and Ben shared, her throat hitched. She'd miss these children so much. She bent over their sleeping forms and gently kissed their foreheads. She wondered how Leah would explain to her children Esther's absence.

The time a woman spent in the harem before being presented to the king was twelve months. Since the Persians thought the king was also deity, they believed it took twelve months to reach full purification before a woman was truly free of contamination and could be presented to the king. Abigail and Ben would change greatly in that amount of time. Esther hurried out of the room and gathered the satchel she'd packed. She wore the rose-colored robe again, the finest clothing in the house. Inside the satchel was her mother's marriage ring and two of Mordecai's tablets on the constellations. She couldn't read them, but looking at the diagrams would make her feel closer to home.

She took a final look around her room. She'd been lucky to have a chamber of her own. The rug was folded on her mat, and her collection of colored stones she'd put together as a young girl sat on a wood shelf, as did a collection of dolls that Leah had made for each birth date celebration. She'd have to tell Leah that Abigail could have the dolls now. When, and if, she returned, she wouldn't need such things.

Leah stood in the doorway, and Esther turned to embrace her.

"If there is anything you need, send a message to Mordecai," Leah said in a quiet voice. "He'll be outside the palace gates every morning waiting for any word. And he'll be applying for a position in the palace today."

Esther drew away. "What about his duties in the community?"

"Esther," Leah said. "Your chance at becoming queen *is* his new duty. Do you understand what it would mean for our people?"

A lump grew in Esther's throat. "Yes."

Leah kissed her on both cheeks. "May the Lord preserve and keep you."

They walked arm in arm into the gathering room, where Mordecai waited. His expression was somber, but his eyes were alive with anticipation. "I'm sorry there isn't more time for farewells," he said. "But I dare not delay your arrival any longer. Surely the king will not forget his edict."

Esther embraced Leah one more time, and then she was out in the courtyard, following Mordecai through the gate. It was still early and well before the vendors traveled to the market square, but Mordecai insisted on taking the side roads. He didn't want to encounter any delays or raise any curiosity.

Esther had forgotten how far the palace really was until she realized that each step toward it was a step away from the only home she'd known. She had to hurry to keep up with her cousin. When the palace came into view, Esther's heart plummeted and soared at the same moment. The huge columns seemed to reach to the sky, and the intricate sculptures were breathtaking when she considered that she'd be living inside the massive structure.

She and Mordecai bypassed the portico that stood in front of the main gates, surrounded by statues of the Persian god Ahura-Mazda. Mordecai led her onto another side road that met with a smaller entrance not generally used by the public. Although she'd never noticed this entrance during the handful of times she'd been near the palace, she was sure Johanna knew all about it. The thought brought a bittersweet smile to her face.

Mordecai approached the guards who manned the entrance and did not hesitate or apologize. "I've come at the king's request. I've brought the woman Esther to meet with Hegai, the keeper of women."

Esther tried not to stare at the guards and wonder if one of them had been the one who'd asked her name the other night. Their uniforms of rich-indigo tunics all looked the same, so it was difficult to tell.

None of the guards moved but simply stared at Mordecai.

"I've brought the edict." He held up a clay tablet, and one of the guards took it.

The guard looked down at the writing, and Esther had the sudden urge to look at it too before she realized it was probably written by a scribe and not the king himself.

She also realized the guard couldn't read. He just stared at the message then handed it over. A third guard picked up a small trumpet and blew into it. Then all three guards went back to their impassive, stoic expressions.

"Now what?" Esther whispered.

"Now we wait." Mordecai folded his arms and smiled at the guards.

None of them responded.

It seemed as if an hour passed, but it could have been only a handful of minutes when Esther heard a woman's throaty voice say, "Why must I be summoned at all hours of the day? Is there no other task you can attend to? Perhaps the stones need another scrubbing."

She came into view on the other side of the arched entrance, and Esther's eyes widened. It was a man. She blinked then lowered her gaze, trying not to stare. Something inside her mind knew that the keeper of women must be a eunuch, but she had never thought about it applying to someone she might actually meet.

The man wore a luxurious robe, brilliant blue with gold embroidery on the sleeves and hem. His head was shaved, and he had the kindest and largest eyes Esther had ever seen.

"Who is this?" the eunuch demanded, his voice no longer sounding exactly like a woman's but still decidedly feminine. His eyes were on Esther as if they could see every plane of her face through her veil.

Mordecai stepped a bit closer to her. "May I present Esther, who has—"

The eunuch clapped his hands together. "It is she!" He held out his hands to Esther. "Come here. Let me see you."

Mordecai nudged her, and Esther took a step closer then another one.

The eunuch grabbed her shoulders, nearly causing her to stumble back in surprise. "Turn your heads!" The guards' faces flushed, and they turned away. In one swift movement, the eunuch lifted Esther's veil. She didn't have time to react before the man let it fall back around her face.

"Come with me," he said, grasping her arm in a firm grip. He looked over at Mordecai. "You may come once a month for a report. But your daughter will not be seen in public until twelve months have passed and she has completed her interview with King Xerxes."

"I am not her father," Mordecai said quickly. "I was commissioned—"

"Thank you for bringing her," the eunuch said. "Her baggage will be searched by the guards before it is allowed inside. You may leave it and return to your home." He paused, looking around. "Where is it?"

Esther lifted the satchel she carried. "This is all I brought."

The eunuch's face drew into a tight frown. "Leave it with the guards."

She handed it over then felt a tug on her arm as the eunuch pulled her through the entrance. Her last glance at Mordecai showed his forlorn face. They had not said a proper farewell, and she wondered if he was having any second thoughts.

A heavy door shut behind them, and Esther realized they had passed through a long arched entryway and were now turning to the right. The door shut out the entrance, and before her was a large courtyard. Vines climbed the outside walls, and flowers grew in colorful arrangements. Clusters of trees grew all around, and it was as if the harsh sun never touched this garden.

The scent alone was heady, but the eunuch was already guiding her through the labyrinth of blooming plants.

"Excuse me, sir," Esther said, disengaging her arm from his hand.

He paused, his face crossed with annoyance. "There's no time to waste. It's too late for farewells."

"I've said all my farewells," Esther said in a quiet voice. "I'd like to know your name."

A thin eyebrow arched as he studied her.

Esther found herself holding her breath. Had she been too direct? Did Persian women not ask eunuchs their names?

He smiled, and Esther was amazed at the transformation. If he'd had hair and had retained his masculinity, he would have appealed greatly to the ladies.

"My name is Hegai, and I'm the keeper of the women, in case you wanted to know that too."

Esther couldn't help but laugh. It was certainly the last thing she'd intended to do in the palace harem—laugh. It was then she realized they weren't alone. A woman sat on a stone bench not far from them. She sat as still as a miniature statue. Her hair hung in deep curls, framing her delicate face, and the paleness of her skin surprised Esther. She wore a cherry-blossom robe with such sheen it had to be silk.

When the woman blinked and looked away, Esther realized she'd been staring.

"Who is that? She's beautiful," Esther said in a quiet voice.

Hegai took her hand and patted it. "She's your competition."

Esther tugged her gaze away from the woman on the bench. "I only came because of the edict."

The eunuch looked at her, and Esther was grateful for her veil. His stare was so probing it made her skin flush.

"Come with me. The women in the harem are not too fond of being disturbed in their hour of garden peace."

"The women take turns in the garden?" Esther blurted.

Hegai didn't respond, and Esther followed him to the other side of the garden, where they reached another archway. This one led into a sort of gathering room. Cushions were piled at one end, and at the other was a low table.

"You will stand on the table for the inspection," Hegai said as two women entered, carrying folded clothing or robes. These two were certainly not women preparing to interview with the king. One was old enough to be Esther's mother, the other perhaps a few years older than Esther. Their robes were plain, with only the royal symbol embroidered below the shoulder, and their hair was pulled into severe knots.

"Esther is here," Hegai said, his tone lifting. "Send Shaashgaz to deliver the message to the king."

One of the ladies bowed, handed her pile of clothing to the other woman, and left the way she'd entered the room.

The second woman was already surveying Esther, her painted brows pulled together into a point. She had hair the color of a deep brassy sunset, and she was perhaps the shortest woman Esther had ever seen. Her voice was scratchy when she spoke. "Remove your veil and your robe."

Esther removed her veil then glanced over at Hegai.

"We need to begin the inspection," he said. "If you are salvageable, then we'll admit you into the harem for purification."

The words jarred together in Esther's mind. *Harem* and *purification* didn't coincide. Esther reluctantly removed her outer robe so she stood in only her undertunic, a linen shift that made her feel as exposed as she was.

Hegai still stood there, and Esther looked at the woman, who was folding the tunic and laying it on one end of the table. Their eyes met, but there was no yielding on the woman's part. So Esther was surprised when the woman said, "Hegai, leave us. I'll give you a full report."

Chapter 8

HEGAI GLANCED FROM THE WOMAN to Esther, but Esther couldn't read his expression. Had the woman done something that might cause trouble for her? But then he turned and left the room, his green robe billowing behind him.

Relief washed through Esther at Hegai's departure, but she still felt uncomfortable removing all of her clothes.

"He won't stay away long, so if you want privacy, you must hurry."

Esther pulled the tunic over her head, her skin burning with embarrassment. The woman walked around the table, looking for who knew what, while Esther closed her eyes and counted to ten over and over.

The woman muttered several things, some indistinguishable, others sounding like, "Cracked feet will take months to heal. Dry skin will never do. Legs need a double waxing. Calves too wide. Hands are . . . deplorable."

Esther opened her eyes and looked down at the bowed head inspecting her hands and fingernails. "I have a poultice I use when they get very dry, but I haven't had much time lately."

The woman held up her hand. "Anything you used outside the palace is not acceptable in here. When the twelve months are up, you will not remember any of your coarse ways."

Esther felt as if she'd been slapped. The woman's tone had been even enough, but the words bit into her heart.

"Put this on please," the woman said, holding out a pure white linen tunic, not much different from the one Esther had just taken off. "You will have to go through inspection in two weeks. There is so much work to be done that it will take me all morning to find everything. The girls will get the worst fixed."

Esther took the garment and pulled it over her head. She instantly felt the difference of weave and quality of fabric compared to her old tunic. The fine cotton of the new one was nearly as supple as silk. She almost smiled as she looked at the woman busily folding the veil and old tunic. "What's your name?" Esther asked.

The woman's hands paused, but she didn't look up. "Sarah." She placed the veil on the folded stack of Esther's clothing.

"Can I ask you a question, Sarah?"

Sarah didn't answer but lifted a robe from the pile of things she'd brought in. When she held it up by the shoulders, it fell to the ground in a soft wave of luxurious cloth. The deep blue color bordered on violet.

"How beautiful," Esther said, awed by the fabric.

Sarah's brows pinched together again.

"Have you served in the palace long?"

This captured Sarah's attention. "Step off the table." She traded Esther places so that Sarah was nearly as tall as Esther as she stood on the table. "Now turn around."

Sarah draped the robe over Esther's shoulders and smoothed out the creases. "This way again."

Esther faced the woman. The fine cloth felt like water enveloping her, and the weight of the garment only added to its luxurious feel.

"I was sold into King Darius's harem in my thirteenth year," Sarah said in a quiet voice that rattled with emotion, her eyes lowered. "You might say that I've been here a lifetime." Her hands shook as she adjusted the front of the robe.

Thirteen was so young, and to be *sold?* Esther had heard of such practices done by extremely poor families, but she'd never known any of them. It was below the pride of a Jew to do that to a child. This woman had spent years here. Was this Esther's fate as well?

"My family lived in a small town in the mountains," Sarah continued in her throaty whisper. "They were poor goat herders, and my days were spent out on the range, watching over the animals because my two older brothers had died."

Sarah looked up at Esther, her eyes moist. "I have not thought about those goats in years." A sad smile crossed her face. "I must assume both of my parents are now gone. There was never a way to get any news about them."

The sound of footsteps echoing against marble grew closer. Sarah's expression changed back to a steady calm.

Hegai was back. He strode in carrying her satchel, his sandaled feet slapping against the floor. Esther was glad to see her possessions. In his other hand, he held a cup of steaming tea. "Ah, good. You are presentable. Here is a special tea we brew only in the harem."

Esther took the cup and sipped the steaming liquid. It was sweet yet bitter but strangely appealing.

Hegai looked at Sarah. "And what is the verdict?"

"She needs a full moon's worth of work before I can complete my evaluation."

Hegai barked out a sudden laugh. "Very well. We must begin right away." He handed the satchel to Sarah. "Deliver this to her chamber."

Esther watched the satchel change hands, and Sarah collected her clothes.

"You will not need your veil in the harem," Hegai told Esther.

Following him out of a side door, Esther stepped into a long, open corridor that looked like it was a garden in itself. She drew in a breath. If the rest of the harem was like this, it was beautiful. She walked slowly, savoring both the tea and the scenery.

The floor sloped until they reached a wide staircase. The change in the air and temperature was palpable, and moist heat rose up from below the stairs. They left the morning sunshine behind as they descended.

As her eyes adjusted to the new dimness, Esther realized they were entering an underground bathing room. A soft melody floated around her, but she couldn't tell from which direction the flute was being played.

At the bottom of the steps, Esther paused, looking over the large square pool of water. Tiny mosaic tiles made up the intricate floor, and plants stood in painted pots scattered along the edge of the pool.

Two women were soaking in the pool, wearing wet tunics. At least she wouldn't have to completely undress, she thought.

Another eunuch sat on a stool in the corner of the room, his hands clasped together, his eyes closed. He looked much younger than Hegai, closer to Esther's age.

Despite the savory tea, she swallowed against the lump in her throat as she thought of a perfectly healthy male being made into a eunuch—all in the name of serving in the king's harem.

A woman hurried forward, the same one who had arrived with Sarah. "I will hold your cup and take your robe," she said with a bow of her head.

Esther handed her the cup, which the woman set on a low table, then made a move to remove the robe herself.

But the woman shook her head. "You must let me do it. It's part of the process of preparing you to meet the king."

Helping me with clothing? Esther wondered. She allowed the woman to remove the robe, and once again, Esther stood in a thin tunic.

"I'll return in an hour for her," Hegai said then headed toward the stairs.

"Thank you," Esther said, and Hegai's foot paused on the step. Then he started climbing again.

The woman took Esther's hand and guided her toward the pool. "The steps into the pool can be slippery," she said.

Esther looked into the woman's narrow face. She was perhaps five or six years older than Esther and younger than Sarah. Her features might have been fair but for an obvious misalignment of her teeth. Her upper lip jutted over a receding chin. Yet her eyes were lively, and Esther sensed this woman missed little. When Esther asked her name, the woman was quick to smile.

"Nanacee, but you may call me Nan," she said, her smile growing broader. "You have impressed Hegai. Well done."

"I have?" Esther said. Together they stepped into the water. It was warm, soaking her up to her ankles. Three more steps and they were at the base of the pool. It only reached to Esther's midthighs. "I'm afraid I've only bothered him with questions."

Nan smiled again and released Esther's hand. "He can handle the questions. I have been serving for three years, and no one has ever told him *thank you*."

"No one?" Esther found it hard to believe.

Nan glanced in the direction of the other two women who soaked in the pool; they'd moved to the far end. The eunuch still hadn't opened his eyes. Nan lowered her voice, "The other women come from more . . . privileged homes." She raised an eyebrow as if waiting for Esther to explain her background.

Exhaling, Esther knew she could say very little without giving away her heritage. "My parents both died, and I live with a relative."

"Ah," Nan said. "My parents died as well." She reached over and squeezed Esther's hand. "We are sisters in our loneliness. Yours is only temporary though."

Esther was about to question her when a woman's voice rang out.

"Call for Hegai! The water is too hot today."

The eunuch on the other side of the pool snapped his eyes open. He rose to his feet and shuffled away with a pronounced limp. A glimpse below the hem of his robe showed a deformed foot.

"What happened to his foot?" Esther asked Nan.

Nan moved closer to Esther, and as the eunuch slowly walked up the stairs, she whispered, "He was born like that. Some say he is King Darius's illegitimate son, which, of course, would make him one of perhaps dozens."

Esther fell silent, watching the man struggle up the stairs. His hand moved along the stone wall, but it offered only minimal support. He needed something to hold on to.

"You will soak for an hour," Nan said. "Submerge yourself up to your chin, and then I'll come back, and we'll go to the washing room." She walked through the water and spoke briefly to the other two women, both of whom barely acknowledged Nan.

Esther sat back into the water, and the warm wetness flowed over her. She'd never been to a bathhouse like this before. There was a small one reserved for monthly purification in her community, but only one woman went in at a time. Public baths were for men only. Although this wasn't exactly public, it was strange to share it with others.

She looked over at the other women, but they had their eyes closed, seemingly content to keep to themselves. So Esther relaxed in the water and thought of how a few days ago, her concerns in life were so different.

She'd been worried about keeping the older children busy in the courtyard so they wouldn't wake up baby Samuel while Leah was gone. The memory of playacting the marriage ceremony with little Ben suddenly struck with great irony. He'd wanted to be king, so she had played the queen. And now she was in the pool beneath the king's harem.

Her breath went shallow. Did Ahasuerus know of her arrival? What had he thought? Would she be summoned soon or would she wait the customary twelve months of purification?

Esther moved to the side of the pool, where she could rest her head on the edge and relax more fully. She thought of Mordecai's forlorn face and Leah's tearful good-bye. Johanna had promised to send her messages through Mordecai, but Esther knew that it wouldn't be the same. She exhaled as tears burned her eyes. She hadn't been able to hug the children. It might have been better for the children not to have a tearful good-bye, but her arms ached to hold them one more time. They were like her siblings, and she'd miss them terribly.

The longer Esther stayed in the water, the more tired she grew. She hadn't slept well for the past couple of nights, and now that she was finally here at the palace, she realized how exhausted she was. And the warm water was making sleep feel very welcome.

Her head bobbed forward, her chin submerging into the water. She opened her eyes with a start. The two women were gone, and the eunuch with the lame foot was at his post again, eyes closed, hands clasped together.

Esther moved forward in the water, her legs and arms feeling strangely numb. She could barely keep her eyes open. She just wanted to let herself sink into the water and let it wash over her entire body. Something moved to the side of her, and Esther turned to see Nan. She hadn't even heard the woman come into the water.

"Are you all right?" Nan said, but it was hard for Esther to hear her. She seemed to be talking in a garbled voice.

"Hegai!" Nan called out.

Arms lifted Esther from the water, and she felt herself being lifted higher and higher before she remembered nothing else.

Chapter 9

"MOISTEN HER LIPS AGAIN," A voice said above Esther.

She tried to remember who it might be. Not Leah, not Johanna. Then she remembered. The harem.

With a groan, she opened her eyes a crack. The light was soft, and shadows moved back and forth in front of it. Then a face came into view. "Sarah," she croaked, her throat on fire.

"She's awake!" Sarah said, and another face appeared.

Esther recognized this one too. "Hegai . . ." Her voice faded as her thoughts tumbled together.

He placed something cool on her forehead. "Stay with us, Esther," Hegai said in a firm tone.

She tried to keep her eyes open, but it was as if she had no control over them. Then a breeze floated over her body, and Esther made another effort and forced her eyes open.

The face staring down at her now was not Hegai.

"Ahasuerus," she whispered.

He smiled, and Esther wanted to reach up and touch his face, but she couldn't move. Besides, something told her it wouldn't be proper to do such a thing . . . because he was King Xerxes.

She stared at him, her eyes burning from being open so long. "What are you doing here?"

He continued to smile, and she thought he spoke to her, but she wasn't sure. Had he heard her? Or was she just speaking inside her mind?

"I'm sorry for all of this trouble," she managed to whisper, and then he was holding her hand. She must really be ill if the king was here to see her die.

She wondered if any of the women in the harem had died before their time. Focusing on the warm grasp of the king, she tried to speak again. "I didn't mean to call you Ahasuerus again."

He bent toward her until she could feel his breath on her cheek. Then he pressed his lips against her skin, and she closed her eyes, deciding that maybe she was already in heaven. But why was the king there too?

Then his touch dissipated, and when she opened her eyes again, the room was dark. Nan sat next to her bed, humming. She watched Nan for a moment. Then Esther moved her toes and her fingers. Apparently, she was not in heaven.

She swallowed, wincing at the pain of her raw throat. "What's happened?" she whispered.

"Oh," Nan said, looking startled but pleased. She touched her arm. "How do you feel?"

How did she feel? Awake and . . . "Thirsty," Esther said.

Nan laughed. "Wonderful. It seems that you'll recover after all. The king will be pleased."

"The king?" Esther stared at Nan's smiling face. "He was here, wasn't he?" It came out as a whisper, but the words thundered in her heart.

Nan poured something from a jug into a cup. She helped Esther lift her head and drink.

The lukewarm liquid was like a balm to her throat. She laid her head back. "How long have I been in bed?"

"This is the third evening," Nan said.

Three days. Esther had never been ill for so long.

"We were all so worried about you. Only Hegai seemed to think you'd be fine, but he sent for the healer anyway. You probably don't remember his visit." Nan dabbed Esther's brow with a cold cloth that had a lemony scent. "We were all surprised when the king insisted on coming." She looked toward the door as if she expected someone to come in at any moment. "You should have heard the envy from the other women."

Esther turned the information over in her mind. She didn't know any of the other women preparing to meet the king, but she could imagine the stir this would have caused. They were probably upset at seeing any favoritism. Had the king truly been concerned for her? The thought made her chest swell. She wondered if Mordecai had been notified of her illness. But she didn't know how to ask Nan without raising too much interest.

"The others will want to know that you're awake and thirsty," Nan said then left the room.

Moments later, Hegai came in, followed by Sarah. They looked as if they'd both been awakened. They hurried to her side. Hegai put his hand on Esther's forehead, and Sarah clasped Esther's hand.

"Praise the Creator," Hegai said. "Sarah, send news to King Xerxes."

"It's the middle of the night," she said.

He withdrew his hand from Esther's skin. "The king leaves in the morning for the mountain borders. It would do well for him to know that Esther is recovering."

Sarah bobbed her head and left the room.

Was the king really so concerned about her health? Esther wondered.

"Is there anything you need?" Hegai asked her.

"No," Esther said, looking from him to Nan. "I am grateful to you for all your care."

Hegai nodded. "I must ask you about the tea you drank." A shadow crossed his face. "It's important that you describe the taste."

Esther tried to think back; she remembered taking a few swallows of the delicious tea. "It was sweeter than I'd ever tasted but had a hint of bitterness to it as well. I didn't drink very much of it by the time Nan took it."

Hegai's mouth drew into a line as he listened. "It's as I thought. We're giving you the best suite in the harem. We'll move you there as soon as you are well, and I'll bring women from the palace to attend to you. I pray that you'll be well and strong soon." He bowed, his eyes shimmering with emotion.

When he left the room, Nan turned to Esther, her eyes wide. "You have been elevated above the other women in the harem. Hegai has never done this for anyone. It's like he wants you to get used to acting like a queen, with ladies in waiting to do your bidding. And straight from the palace! They will be able to train you in all of the conventions."

Esther tried to smile at Nan's enthusiasm, but why had Hegai questioned her about the tea. "What did Hegai mean when he asked me to tell him about the taste of the tea?"

Nan's gaze faltered, and she leaned forward, lowering her voice. "We think someone poisoned the tea."

A jolt shot through Esther. "Someone wanted to poison me?"

Nan exhaled. "The competition is fierce in the harem. You'll realize that soon enough, although we never thought this might happen." She drew herself up. "You don't need to worry though. We are watching everything carefully now, and you'll be very protected in your new chamber."

I was poisoned, Esther thought with astonishment. How could someone want her dead? She hadn't done anything but obey the king's edict. So that was why the king had visited . . . She *had* been close to death. What would the other women think now if she took the upgraded chamber and had chambermaids? Would they hate her more?

She rose up on her elbows, and her breath immediately grew shallow. "I am perfectly fine in this room." She couldn't see much in the dim light of the oil lamps, but it seemed cozy and clean. Not unlike her room at home, but she hadn't had such a soft, luxurious bed as she did here.

"Hegai's word is law, at least in the harem," Nan said. "I'll be overseeing all food and drink preparation for you from now on. I prepared this drink myself." She poured another cup for Esther to drink. She let out a huge yawn, then she lay down on a mat on the floor. "I'll be right here if you need me."

Esther lay back. She had little strength now, but when she gained it back, she'd insist that she receive no special treatment. She closed her eyes, praising the Lord's mercy in silence. Why He had preserved her, she didn't know, but she was grateful to be recovering. Even if it meant she had to ignore the jealousy of others who saw her being favored.

* * *

The morning brought a new awareness to Esther. Everything in the room seemed rosy, and she realized the coverings over the windows were a light red. It was a beautiful room, a little larger than the one she had occupied at home, and the drapes reached to the floor and looked like silk. At the edges, indigo flowers had been embroidered by an expert hand. A table with a wash jug stood in one corner, and a divan with silk cushions sat in another. She wondered why Nan had chosen to sleep on a mat on the floor.

A thick rug spread across the floor had intricate designs of flowers and animals woven into it. Instead of bareness, the walls contained massive frescoes of intertwined lovers. Heat rushed to Esther's cheeks, and she looked away quickly. She might be glad to leave this room after all. Who would have chosen such pictorials?

Esther gingerly rose out of bed, testing her strength. She sat on the edge for a few moments until she felt ready to stand. Her body felt thin and wasted. With no food and little drink over the past three days, she was grateful to be alert again.

"Esther?" Nan said, startling her.

Esther plopped back down on the bed.

"You shouldn't be trying to walk by yourself." Nan was on her feet and by Esther's side in one fluid movement.

The strength seemed to drain straight out of her, and Esther nodded her agreement. "Is there a bit of bread I might have? I feel as if I haven't eaten for a year."

"I'll be right back," Nan said. "Don't try to walk by yourself again." She hurried out of the room and was back within moments with a platter of meat dishes and figs.

One of the dishes held meat that looked like pork with an orange glaze, which Esther couldn't eat because of the law of Moses. There was also a milk mixture with bits of meat—probably squirrel or rabbit. Esther bypassed that one too. She reached for the moist figs and scaled fish, both of which were permitted. Everything inside Esther seemed to have shrunk, and she could eat only a little. Fortunately, Nan didn't comment on her food choices.

Throughout the rest of the day, Nan stayed with her, and Esther continued to eat in small portions. She soon found out that Nan had no trouble regaling her with stories about the harem. In that way, Nan reminded her of Johanna.

"You are so different from the other women," Nan said, not for the first time. "None of them would ever just sit and listen to me tell stories. I'd be dismissed right after bringing in their meals."

Esther let her ramble on. It was nice to hear that she was "different." But she couldn't tell Nan that it was because she prayed to a different god and that her finicky eating habits were due to the Jewish dietary law. She also knew part of it was that she didn't fit the same mold as the other women since she'd been raised to work hard—much like the servants in the palace. Compared to the other women, she was more servant than mistress.

* * *

Two days later, when Esther was able to walk without assistance and felt nearly back to normal, Sarah came into her room. "Your new chambers are ready." She bowed her head.

Esther's first instinct was to tell her that it wasn't necessary to bow her head, but it was the way things were done in the harem and, presumably, throughout the palace. An inferior would always show respect to someone of a higher status, although Esther knew that in the Lord's eyes, they were all equal. But how could she explain that to anyone in the harem without giving away her true identity?

She followed Sarah along the corridor then through the exquisite main garden. Breathing in the scent of flowers and trees again, Esther smiled. It was good to be outside in the fresh air. Another prayer bloomed in her heart as she silently thanked the Lord for her healing and the chance to be alive in such a beautiful place.

A group of women sat in the middle of the gardens, dressed in colorful robes. They wore their hair in elaborate plaits, with blossoms and ribbons intertwined. Dark kohl lined their eyelids, and berries stained their lips. Each woman was beautiful in her own way. Esther smiled a greeting, but they all turned away and continued to talk as if they hadn't seen her.

"What are their names?" Esther asked Sarah.

"In the yellow is Anne; she came just a few weeks before you arrived. The other two, Tamar and Elisheba, will have their interviews with the king within a few moons."

Perhaps it was better not to get to know the other women. It wasn't likely they'd see each other after being dismissed. As she walked with Sarah into another corridor, laughter from the women followed her. Had it been about her? Her heart beat a little faster. Esther didn't have much experience with female friends. Johanna had been her closest one.

Suddenly, Esther missed her friend so much that breathing became painful. She slowed her step and tried to catch her breath. Just then, Sarah came to a stop at a set of double doors. The knobs and hinges were a lustrous brass.

Sarah opened the doors, and Esther joined her. She stared into the most beautiful room she'd ever seen.

The room was awash in white and gold. White marble inlaid with gold made up the floor. A massive bed was bedecked with white and yellow silk, and sheer drapes hung from the gold bed posts. Rows of windows lined two sides of the room, giving it an open-air feel. Small flowering trees set in gold jars were amassed in each corner.

"Is this the queen's room?"

Sarah closed the doors and turned to answer. "Queen Vashti stayed in here the month leading up to her wedding to King Xerxes. After the marriage, she moved into the private family rooms in the center of the palace."

Esther walked into the room, marveling at the beauty and opulence. If this was a room in the harem, what did the rest of the palace look like? She moved around the bed and froze. A lion skin spread across the floor, its mouth open and teeth bared in silence.

A hand on her heart, Esther pointed with her other hand. "Was the queen also fond of this?"

Sarah smiled. "That was not her favorite, but it was a gift from the king."

Esther looked around the room then back at the fearsome lion skin. A wave of melancholy passed over her. She was here only because the other woman who occupied this room had been banished and her title stripped. Did Vashti have any idea how her life would turn out when she was staying in this room, awaiting her marriage?

And even though the lion skin was something that did not belong in a woman's private chamber, the fact that it was a gift from Ahasuerus to his future wife was endearing nonetheless. She sat on the edge of the raised-platform bed, its softness drawing her in. Did people really live like this? It would have been impossible to imagine if she hadn't seen this room.

A knock sounded on the massive doors, and Sarah went to open them.

Hegai breezed in, several women following him. They wore elegant white robes with the royal insignia. Hegai waved his hand with a flourish. "These are your seven maidens. They will assist you in all things and prepare you for life in the palace."

Esther's mouth went dry; Hegai spoke as if she'd already been selected as queen. It was all too much, too fast. Her head felt dizzy as he introduced each woman and they stepped forward to bow to her.

She didn't remember a single name, only the curious dark eyes on her.

The next days were a blur, filled with daily soaking in the baths, although not the full hour, oils worked into her hair and massaged into her skin, and the shaping of her nails and brows. By the time two weeks had passed, one of Esther's maidens escorted her to again meet with Sarah in the inspection room.

Esther knew to remove her robe and stand on the low table, and Sarah knew to dismiss any eunuchs. Esther's sense of modesty had already spread throughout the harem, which created tittering and giggling from the other women behind her back.

"Your skin is responding well to the oils and bathing," Sarah said, her voice more hoarse than usual. She picked up the ends of Esther's hair and inspected them closely. "We will have to cut some off after all. The lower ends cannot be salvaged. At least I will be able to give a positive report to Hegai this time. He will be pleased."

Esther felt different, pampered, although she thought there was so much more she could do rather than indulge in skin treatments and hair oils. There must be something she could do in the harem to serve others.

When Esther had dressed again, Sarah said, "Family visits are tomorrow. You'll wear your veil, and your family will be escorted into the garden for a short time."

Esther wondered if Mordecai would come. Perhaps he'd bring Leah and the children, but she knew immediately that that would be too risky. One of the children might say something that would give away her true identity.

"Instruction on palace decorum will be this afternoon. Hegai will conduct."
Sarah started to cough low and deep.

"Let me make a tea for you that I used to make for . . . my family," Esther
said, putting a hand on Sarah's arm.

The woman shook her head. When she had breath to speak again,
she said, "I've tried all the teas in Persia, and other drinks I can't identify."

"You haven't tried mine," Esther said with a smile.

Sarah's mouth twitched. "Very well. It couldn't make it worse."

Once Esther had returned to her opulent rooms, she called one of the
maidens, named Karan. "Fetch fresh lemon and orange leaves for me. We
will steep them in a tea overnight for mistress Sarah."

The maiden, an eighteen-year-old who was ready to please Esther, hurried
out the door to fulfill her errand. It was nearly an hour later when Karan
returned, the requested leaves tied into a bundle of linen cloth.

"Gather around," Esther said, and the other maidens came from their
various duties to watch. She poured water into a jug then added a few measures
of wine. She put in several lemon and orange leaves and covered the mouth of
the jug. "It will sit overnight, and in the morning, we will transfer the tea into
a bowl. Then I'll show you how to create a special drink for Sarah's throat."

The maidens smiled, remaining silent as Hegai had commanded them
to do. They would respond only when given permission. Esther wasn't used
to all of the silence that surrounded her. The other women in the harem
hadn't been responsive to her friendliness, but the smiles from Nan and
Sarah and her maidens helped ease the loneliness somewhat. At times, she
missed Leah and the children with a fierceness; other times, they seemed an
entire lifetime away.

That afternoon, two of the maidens accompanied her to the lesson from
Hegai. He nodded when she entered the arched chamber that served for
palace instruction. The other women were already seated on their cushions.

Esther wasn't late, but it seemed to be a contest among the women of
who could arrive first. Anne perched on a large cushion, Tamar and Elisheba
on either side of her. There was always a bit of a triumphant look in Anne's
eyes, as if she expected to be treated like she was already queen of the palace.

Esther sat on a cushion and folded her hands in her lap so they rested
on the soft silk. She still hadn't quite grown used to her silk robes. Today,
she wore a deep yellow robe trimmed in gold embroidery.

Hegai began the instructions with a brief prayer chant to Ahura-Mazda,
something he did at the beginning of any formal gathering. Esther bowed

her head in respect and moved her lips, but she did not repeat the words aloud after him. She said a silent prayer to the Lord God, praying that He would understand the position she was in, that she had to maintain this disguise in order to fulfill her promise to Mordecai.

"We will review the customs of eating with the king," Hegai said, looking at each woman in turn. Esther met his steady gaze with one of her own. "Form a circle. I will represent the king."

When the women were settled into their circle, a line of chambermaids came into the room, carrying platters of food. Hegai stepped to the edge of the circle, and Esther immediately prostrated herself, as did the other women. It seemed they all knew that obligation well.

"Rise," Hegai said.

And the women rose.

He then sat down on his own cushion. "The king waits until the Magi have cast their blessing over the food. Sometimes he sits beforehand, other times he sits after the blessing. But only after the king is seated, the blessing said, and he has taken the first bite, can everyone else turn to their own meals."

A chambermaid placed a platter of melons, grapes, and oranges in front of Hegai. He took a bite of the fruit then gave a little nod.

Esther wasn't particularly hungry—her appetite had been very slight since her illness. She took a few bites of her fruit anyway. She marveled how every type of fruit seemed to be in season at the palace. She didn't touch the meats, even though some of it was clean according to the law, but she assumed it had not been prepared according to the law. Outside her own community, few butchers followed the Mosaic practices.

Hegai explained the different courses and the protocol behind how each was served. Then he said, "The king dines privately in his chambers for the morning meal. The midday meal is usually shared with those on his council or those he might be hosting that week. Evening meals are lavish events with entertainment."

He paused, and the women all had their eyes on him. "The wife of the king does not concern herself with the entertainment. Unless she is specifically requested to stay, she will leave with her maidens and return to her rooms before the entertainment begins."

Esther straightened her back, wondering why the queen would be excused. Then the giggling from a couple of the women told her what she needed to know. Esther very well knew that some entertainment would be considered unholy and definitely ungodly but appropriate for a worldly king.

She swallowed against her dry throat and took another sip from the gold goblet. *O Lord,* she prayed silently, *if I am chosen as queen, how will I support such evening activities in the place that will be my home?*

And how could she also accept the idea of the harem and concubines?

Chapter 10

FROM HER BENCH IN THE garden, Esther watched the families enter. Her veiled gaze searched for anyone she recognized. An elegant couple greeted Anne enthusiastically, and they withdrew to a canopied bench to continue their animated conversation. It seemed that Anne had much to report.

Finally, Esther saw Mordecai.

She almost cried out a greeting, but instead, she remained still, only her rapid heartbeat an indication of her excitement. She didn't want anyone to know he was more than a visiting acquaintance.

Waiting patiently, she watched as Mordecai glanced about at the other women with various family members. Finally, his gaze landed on her, moved away, then came back. His brows lifted slightly, and Esther knew he hadn't quite recognized her. Even veiled, she'd changed a lot in the few weeks since she'd arrived.

He was by her side in a moment, and she reached for his hands. She wanted to embrace him and cry on his shoulder, but she kept her back rigid. If the others saw her embracing Mordecai and discovered he was a Jew, they might suspect she was one too. She'd have to settle for the coarse warmth of his hands, which made her feel even more emotional.

"How are you, my dear?" he whispered.

"I have been preened and primed, and it's only the beginning," she said in a low voice, trying to keep the emotion concealed.

Hegai and the other eunuchs stood on the edges of the courtyard, keeping watch over their charges. It wouldn't do for her to break down; it would be most unroyal.

Mordecai was looking at her soft hands, their nails stained a deep mauve.

"They are molding you into what a queen should be," Mordecai said.

Esther looked down at her hands, which seemed like baby's skin next to Mordecai's. "The queen is only a symbol representing the kingdom. She is not allowed to have real feelings or any sort of life outside her duty."

Mordecai's eyes darkened for a brief moment. "A queen who is beloved by her husband will have his ear."

Exhaling, Esther wondered if Mordecai was right. Marriages like Mordecai and Leah's was nothing close to the marriage between the king and queen. If Queen Vashti had had her husband's ear, would he have sent her away? Would he have listened more to his chamberlains than to his own wife?

And how could there truly be love and respect between a man and a woman when the man housed concubines and employed a full harem? Not to mention unseemly entertainment not fit for his wife's viewing.

Esther's chin trembled, and she blinked rapidly. Now wasn't the time to confide her fears to Mordecai. There were too many people around them.

But Mordecai seemed to sense her distress. "You must look beyond your tender heart. The dreams you had last month need to be different dreams now. Grander dreams. Ones that do not include what other women yearn for but dreams of being the Lord's servant."

Esther lowered her head, fighting back the tears. Mordecai's words were true, and they brought added assurance, but the selfish part of Esther still reared up. "I have not been chosen yet," she whispered. "But the keeper of women has given me the queen's old quarters and seven maidens from the palace."

Mordecai did not seem the least bit surprised by the news. "It is as I have heard from within the palace, my dear Esther."

She lifted her head to look at Mordecai. The term of endearment startled her. In his gaze, she sensed true concern and even love.

"I have secured a position in the king's treasury." Mordecai shifted slightly closer to her and lowered his voice again. "I plan to serve well in this position of trust, and it will allow me to have contact with you—however indirectly."

"But our community relies on your counsel and guidance," Esther said. Mordecai had brought up that he'd try to gain employment in the palace, but she'd thought it was a slim chance.

"Esther. You must listen to me closely." His whisper was fast and urgent now. "What you are doing here is noble and good. It is also sanctioned by the Lord Himself. You may struggle with happiness in your marriage, but you will find happiness serving the Jews. That is the greater purpose, and the Lord will care for you."

Tears dripped onto Esther's cheek. Speaking to Mordecai had reminded her that she was but an instrument in the Lord's hands, and that should be her purpose no matter whom she married, no matter if her sons were farmers or princes.

She couldn't speak.

"There are men in power who despise the Jews. Dan has told me about some of the conversations he's overheard. Even the chief judge, Haman, is known as a persecutor. And he is a *judge* trusted by King Xerxes, making decisions for the land and the people. Not to mention prime minister Tarsena. He is a vile man who has mistreated Jewish women. Tarsena acts as if he has rights to all the women in the kingdom."

Esther's stomach tightened at the thought. She hadn't ever seen Tarsena, but she'd heard of the brutality of some of the royals against the Jewish people.

"We need someone on our side who has political influence," Mordecai continued. "Having this chance can only be the will of the Lord."

Esther felt the weight of Mordecai's words press against her breast. Why was it such a challenge for people to live in harmony? Didn't they all want the same thing? Peace and prosperity?

Mordecai's voice softened. "Everything that concerns the king is talked about in the palace—everything. I've heard your name spoken more than once." He touched her shoulder. "Leah and the children prayed for you during your illness. They pray for you night and day. Johanna stops by often to inquire of any news. Of course, I can tell her nothing specific, just that you are well now."

Esther let out a breath. What she wouldn't give to spend just a few moments with those she loved. "How does everyone fare?"

"Very well. We have been blessed, and I've no doubt that it's because of your service here. Samuel is sleeping through the night, and Ben is doing well with his letters. Abigail never stops talking about you."

Esther smiled, her heart swelling.

"It will grow easier with time," Mordecai said. "Know that I am close by, with my eyes and ears open." He patted her hand. "Until next moon. May the Lord preserve you."

Esther remained sitting as Mordecai weaved his way out of the garden. She'd seen the kindness in his eyes and, more importantly, the conviction. She looked at her clasped hands in her lap, tightening them together, knowing she had to be strong. Many were depending on her—for what, she wasn't exactly sure. But for some reason, the Lord had placed her here at this time for His purpose.

And now she had to trust in that.

* * *

The evening shadows had long since cooled the garden by the time Esther rose and walked back to her room to join the maidens. They must have certainly been wondering what she was doing sitting for so long by herself. Esther knew she was never truly alone, but it had been nice to sit for a while after all of the families had gone. She felt nothing like a queen, even after weeks of living in opulence, but she did feel comforted by Mordecai's words.

It was as if she and Mordecai were in this journey together—he working in the palace and she living in the harem. Would Mordecai have brought her to the harem if he thought she had no chance? She knew they both feared repercussions of not obeying the king's edict, but what if there was a greater purpose behind it?

Esther chastised herself for repeatedly questioning. She couldn't forget the peaceful reassurance she'd had while praying before coming here, but the doubts continued. It was quite fantastic to believe that she, a simple Jewish woman, would be chosen above the beautiful women who had trained their entire lives to manage a royal household. In that light, the fact that she was here could only be due to the Lord's hand.

Once she reached her chamber, she greeted the maidens. "Now we will check on our tea." She lifted the cloth from the jug and transferred it into a large bowl.

The maidens gathered around to watch, fascination in their eyes.

Esther cleaned her hands then reached into the bowl and ripped all of the leaves into tiny bits. It took a couple minutes, but the maidens patiently watched. When she finished ripping the leaves, Esther transferred the liquid back into the jug.

"We will pour a cup at a time and heat it for Sarah," Esther said. "If she takes it three times daily, she'll soon find relief." She looked around at the faces filled with anticipation. "Should we take her some now?"

The maidens giggled their agreement.

Esther and her maidens created a small entourage as they walked to the harem workers' quarters. Esther had never been to Sarah's room, but it wasn't hard to find with the direction of a young eunuch, who gave her a questioning look. Esther simply smiled and knocked on the door that was said to be Sarah's.

When Sarah opened the door, Esther said, "We've brought you a soothing tea. Before you say no, please give it a try for a few days."

Sarah looked from Esther to the maidens, all gathered in a tight group in the corridor, waiting for her reaction. "Very well," she croaked with a slight wince.

Esther's heart tugged, and she hoped the carefully prepared tea would aid this good woman. "Here is a jugful. Heat a cup three times a day and drink down the entire cup."

Sarah nodded and took the jug. "You will hear my report soon enough. Sooner if it's not to my liking."

Esther laughed, and Sarah allowed a smile to creep onto her face. Esther wanted to tell Sarah that she would keep her in her prayers, but she dared not. It would have to stay between Esther and the Lord.

The following morning, three of the harem women were ill. Hegai strode from room to room enquiring of the other women. When he reached Esther's, he said, "The family visits brought illness to the harem. How are you feeling?"

"I am well," Esther said.

"Stay inside your quarters today, and perhaps longer, until we know whether it will spread."

Esther nodded. "Can I send an inquiry for Sarah?"

Although Hegai looked a bit wary, he agreed.

"Ask her how her throat is this morning, and tell her not to fail in taking the tea."

Hegai nodded and left, leaving Esther to wonder how long it would be before she'd know about Sarah. The answer came at midday, after hours of idling in her room, wondering again if there were not better uses of her time.

The knock on the door was Nan, who came inside, smiling. "Sarah says to thank you. Her throat is soothed already. She wants to know the recipe."

Esther leapt up from the divan, where she'd been making a clumsy attempt at embroidering. "Wonderful."

The next time Esther saw Sarah, she told her how to make the tea. Esther marveled at the change in Sarah, who seemed to walk a little taller and smile more often. The pain had left, and her voice sounded remarkably better.

* * *

Esther spent the following weeks and months receiving more instruction from Hegai, continuing to bathe for purification, and gleaning plenty of information the harem workers delivered. Hegai had no idea how much Esther hung on every bit of news that came in from outside the palace. She longed to know how the tensions in the city were solved and how the various people managed to work out their differences. She soaked in every bit of news about how the king and his judges ruled the land.

"You are only months away," Nan said one bright morning. It was early spring, but the heat was already barely tolerable, so they spent their days in the cool of the marble chambers. The baths were no longer heated but were purposely left cool. "We must plan what you will wear for the king's interview."

"So soon?" Esther said.

"It can take many months for an order of silk cloth to be completed."

"Where is the silk coming from? China?"

"Yes," Nan said. "It's only the best for the prospective queen."

"Is this how the other women planned?"

Nan's brows drew together. "Hegai is regretting that he did not order the silk from China for Tamar. She was sent back this morning after her interview."

"The king turned her down?"

"Yes," Nan said in a quiet voice. "Even though it's clear you are Hegai's favored choice, it's still disappointing when one of the virgins is rejected." She let out a sigh. "We've been doing this for years, and with no queen selected yet."

"Perhaps the king doesn't want a queen?" Esther said, but Nan quickly shook her head.

"He's made it clear that he is intent."

"Where will Tamar go? Back to her home?" Although Esther hardly knew Tamar and only saw her as a shadow extension of Anne, she wondered what kind of life Tamar would now face.

"The king will return her to her family with a generous dowry," Nan said. "There will not be a shy suitor where she is concerned."

Esther considered what Tamar might be feeling right now. Would a sizable dowry make up for her rejection by the king? Would Esther receive one as well? Would her dowry be enough to restore her marriage prospects to a humble Jewish man?

Nan grasped Esther's hands. "Let's talk of more pleasant things. I have some silk cloth swatches to show you."

Chapter 11

HAMAN COULDN'T HELP BUT WHISTLE as he rode his horse beneath the pale-gray sky. It seemed the land might enjoy some rain today, and the change in weather quickened his heart. That, and the fact that he was riding to visit Rebekah.

She'd assured him the week before that her husband would be gone visiting a cousin in Media and that they would have an entire day to themselves. Haman had made sure he would not be expected at court. He also wore a simple robe of rough make and a plain turban wrapped about his head. No passerby would take him for a member of the royal court unless they inspected the fine horse he rode. But Haman wasn't worried about encountering anyone at this time of the morning. Dawn was still a good hour away.

A smile spread on his face as he thought of his beloved. Since the morning weeks ago that he'd been so bold as to walk into her hut and she'd accepted him into her arms, he had never felt so happy. He'd spent less and less time at home and more and more time watching Rebekah's hut for any glimpse of her. If her husband left for any reason, he hurried into the hut to be reunited with his love.

Now he had only to convince her to leave her husband. Each month Haman felt he was getting closer to persuading her. She could change her name and her entire identity. No one would have to know where she came from or that she was Jewish. He'd already selected a house for her to live in and was in the process of purchasing it.

He'd had to keep the creditor away from his home so his wife wouldn't find out anything until the transaction was completed.

When he reached the meager hut, he tied his horse out of sight. Rebekah's nearest neighbor was a good distance away, but there had been more than one close call. Once he was forced to wait in the back room while an elderly woman told Rebekah more than everything anyone would ever need to know about scrubbing stains out of linen.

He chuckled to think of it: the chief judge of Persia cowering in the back room of a hut because he didn't want an elderly Jewish woman to see him. At the time, he'd been upset, but he could see the humor in the situation now. Haman reached the door and decided not to knock since no oil lamp burned from within. Rebekah must still be asleep. He couldn't imagine anything more delicious than to see his beloved while she dreamt, although he thrilled at the chance to wake her.

Walking through the dirt-floor rooms, Haman felt his anger stirring. Rebekah deserved so much more. She was like a sparkling gemstone in this place of filth. He pushed aside the curtain that separated the gathering room from the bed chamber—if a couple of mats on the floor could be considered a bed.

Rebekah was lying on her side, sleeping with a rug pulled up to her waist. Her arms were bare, and Haman wanted nothing more than to have them around him. He crept into the room then knelt beside her. Leaning over her, he kissed her bare shoulder.

Her eyes blinked opened, and when she saw him, her mouth softened into a smile.

"Good morning," he whispered and slipped beneath the rug next to her. He started to kiss her, but when she stiffened and pushed against his chest, he drew back.

"What is it, my love?"

Her eyes were wide as she stared at him. His pulse quickened—whatever was wrong now?

"Haman, we must talk."

He didn't like the tone of her voice; he'd heard it before. *Please, Ahura-Mazda, don't let her start any foolishness again. I am so close to persuading her to become mine permanently.* "We'll talk later," he said, reaching for her and burrowing his face against her neck.

"No," Rebekah said, her tone firm.

Haman lifted his head, keeping his arms wrapped around her. "You can tell me anything, my love. I am here for you always."

She wriggled out of his grasp, and annoyance pulsed through Haman. He had missed her all month, waited to be with her, and now she was pushing him away? He'd even turned down a dancer from the harem in anticipation of being with Rebekah. Her husband was gone, and she was the one who told him to come. Now she wanted to start an argument?

He sat up and glowered at her. "Can't we just enjoy the day together? I don't have any court appointments, and I chose to come *here* to be with *you*." His tone conveyed that he easily could have gone elsewhere. Any other woman wouldn't reject his kisses in the early morning hours.

She moved away from him and pulled the rug around her as if she was suddenly concerned for her modesty. "Haman, I'm with child."

He stared at her. "Whose child?" he demanded.

"Your child." Her eyes filled with tears.

"How can you know?" He hadn't discussed it with her, but she must still be sleeping with her husband.

"I haven't . . . been intimate with Joshua in a while . . ." Her voice trembled. "It was one of the reasons he left without me. He believes that some distance between us will repair our relationship."

Haman wanted to shout for joy. This was better than he could have ever prayed for. Ahura-Mazda was smiling down from heaven on him. He hadn't known that Rebekah and her husband were at odds. That meant he was closer than he thought—but seeing the distress on her face told him he must take care in how he reacted.

"My dear," he whispered. "We'll find a way to make everything right." He moved toward her and stroked her cheek. Finally, she let him hold her.

"Haman," she said, clinging to him. "I need you to understand that I have been an evil woman in the eyes of the Lord. I have broken my marriage vows. I have broken the Lord's commandments, and now my husband will discover what I have done when I start increasing. He will know it cannot be his child."

"Hush, my love," he said. "What is between us is beautiful. If your god does not approve, you are worshipping the wrong god. For, you see, I have been praying to Ahura-Mazda, and he has answered my prayers."

Rebekah went still in his arms. "What do you mean?"

"I have been praying that we will be brought together at last. Not in these secret meetings, after which you return to your husband and I return to my wife and children, but that we will be united forever. You and I."

"You still want me to leave my husband and become your concubine, forsaking everything I've ever known." Her voice was flat, but at least she'd stopped crying. "I've already given you my answer for that."

He smiled, knowing she could not see him. "Don't you understand? Your pregnancy with my child is a sign that the gods want us together. It's our destiny."

"Your god cannot want a woman to leave her husband, just as my god cannot."

"You have already left, Rebekah. I have your heart." His fingers moved through her hair then down her back. "Do you really think your husband will want to keep you once he learns about us? Learns about what you have done in his absence? He will find out when he sees your growing belly."

Her sobs started, and Haman held her, waiting patiently. When her tears subsided, he kissed the top of her head, then her face, then her neck. When he lifted his head, her eyes were closed.

He stroked her cheek. "I have it planned already. I've been waiting to tell you—when you were ready." He kissed her mouth, but she didn't respond. "I've bought you a beautiful home. You'll have luxuries and servants and everything your heart desires."

She shook her head, and he moved closer, stealing another kiss. "In time, you can visit your family again, but for now, it's best you come in secret." His heart hammered with excitement. "We can leave now. You don't need to bring a thing—I'll provide all that you need."

"No," she whispered, opening her eyes. Then she spoke louder. "No, I cannot."

"You might be homesick at first, but I can help you with that." His hands captured her waist and pulled her against him possessively.

"My heart is breaking, Haman," she said, leaning back.

He pressed his lips against her throat. "My heart only breaks when we are not together."

"Haman, stop." She removed his hands from her waist and scooted away from him. "Becoming your concubine is not the Lord's will." She stood and moved to the curtained entrance. "I have rededicated myself to the Lord and His will." Her voice rose in pitch. "I won't come with you. I'll stay married to Joshua and pay whatever consequences that requires. What we have must end. Now."

He stared at her, hardly believing she'd dare speak those words, especially after what they'd shared. They'd been living in ecstasy. How could she not want that? And how could she believe her husband wouldn't put her away when he discovered she was carrying another man's child?

"You don't know what you're saying, Rebekah. I am giving you a way out of being disgraced. What will your husband say when he discovers your pregnancy?" He stood and moved toward her. "He will put you away. Or worse, he'll order you stoned."

She brushed at the tears on her face. "I have broken the Lord's commandments. If it is His will that I am punished, then so be it."

"Beautiful, stubborn woman." he said in a breath, reaching for her. "You cannot leave yourself at the mercy of your husband. Come with me, and I'll hide you and protect you."

He couldn't have been more surprised when she turned away from him.

"I made my decision already," she whispered. "I won't change my mind. I have always known what I should do. Now I must have the courage to do it."

He couldn't believe she truly intended to take such a risk. She was ignoring the plain sign from god—whether it was his god or hers, the sign was unmistakable. "Rebekah, you're confused. You don't understand what you should believe. What is between us is real—just as real as everything your god and my god created."

He stepped toward her, but she shrank from him. "I'm sorry, Haman. I cannot be with you anymore. I cannot see you again."

Haman grasped her wrists. "You invited me into your bed because you *wanted* me. Don't think you can sleep with me for months then turn me away whenever you want and use your god as an excuse." He squeezed her wrists harder, knowing he was hurting her, but he had to make her understand. She couldn't reject one of the most powerful men in Persia.

"You're hurting me." Her voice trembled as her tears came fast.

"You'll come with me now," he said through gritted teeth and pulled her through the curtain into the gathering room and across the pathetic dirt-floored room she insisted on living in.

"No!" she gasped.

"Keep quiet!"

She screamed and twisted from him.

Haman's anger burned through him. And before he could stop himself, he struck her, and she crumpled to the floor, sobbing. He stared down at her, horrified at what he'd done to his most beloved—at what she'd *made* him do. Kneeling, he scooped her into his arms, but she lashed out, scratching at his face.

"I would rather die than follow you to hell," she shouted, spitting at him.

He released her and staggered back, not wounded physically but feeling like he'd had a dagger driven straight into his heart. "You would rather *die?*" His head felt like it was on fire, and every part of him raged with anger. "Be careful of the words you speak, harlot."

"*Leave!*" she yelled, lashing out at him again.

He moved quickly to avoid her clawing fingers. A terrible urge came over him to grab her and make her pay for the horrible things she'd said to him.

They were lies, he knew it. Someone in her family had planted false ideas in her head. He knew he could overpower her in an instant if he wanted to. Make her yield to him. Humble her until she realized she could never defy him again. No one rejected the chief judge of Persia.

But deep down, beneath the anger that boiled inside him, he wanted her to come to him willingly, to love him truly and submit. His shoulders sagged at the realization. When he'd entered this hut, this was not at all what he'd envisioned happening. His temper still pulsing through him, he knew he had to leave before he did something worse—something that would be irreparable. He hurried out of the hut, leaving Rebekah a sobbing mess behind him.

As he untied his horse and mounted to ride away, he knew one thing for certain: Rebekah would be his, or she and the foolish Jews who advised her would pay a price greater than she could ever imagine.

* * *

The day promised to be perfect, Ahasuerus thought, smiling to himself. He was sure to win the horse races because Meres's horse had gone lame. The king had lost to that horse three times now, and he'd seemed unbeatable. Truly, it was Ahasuerus's own fault, since he'd been the one to give the horse to Meres during the previous harvest season. Now, finally, the stakes would be equal.

The king traveled with several dozen guards and various members of the nobility, including the prime minister, Tarsena. Ahasuerus wasn't sure how long Tarsena would last in the heat, and he never raced. Perhaps he'd stay beneath the tents with the women. The king's concubines had come along, all five of them with their children, riding in litters beside the traveling horses. It could be a long, hot day, with plenty of dust and smell. But spending the day outside just endeared Ahasuerus more to the upcoming race. For a moment, the king wondered what Esther would make of the horse races.

He was surprised at how much he thought of her—and at the oddest times. She'd been in the harem several months now, and there were many women waiting to be interviewed before she was, but still, thoughts of her pestered him, and he wondered what she might think of all the horses and the thrill of the race. For now, the king pushed Esther from his mind.

When the king arrived at the racing ground, Meres was already there with a new steed. The beast was huge and black, its dark eyes even blacker.

Ahasuerus laughed out loud as he neared his friend. "You couldn't stand to miss one race, could you?"

Meres grinned. "I think you'll find I'm still a good match, even with my other horse lame."

"We'll see about that."

Although Meres's new beast looked fine indeed, it wasn't a proven racing horse. And the king was quite confident in his own steed. He hadn't even ridden it to the track to save the animal's strength. He glanced over at the royal steed now and was rewarded with an eyeful of brown fur shivering over stone-hard muscles.

"I think my horse is ready to taste his winnings today," the king said.

Meres shook his head with a smile. "You may have superior hunting skills, but on a horse, I wouldn't have trouble even if I had to ride a filly against you."

Ahasuerus was close enough to Meres now to slap him on the shoulder. "Good luck, my friend."

Meres laughed and moved away, allowing the king to pass by. Ahasuerus rode into the arena, his entourage dividing into their separate duties. He slowed his horse as he reached the edge of the track. The field where spectators watched from was nearly empty. There were maybe a hundred people assembled instead of the usual five or six hundred.

Meres had ridden in behind the king, so Ahasuerus turned to the prince, puzzled. "Where are all the spectators?"

Meres looked over at the scant crowd then called to one of his men. "Did the notice go out that there is a royal race today?"

"I sent the notice myself, along with the others," a burly guard with spaced teeth said. "We were told there is a Jewish holiday today—for the next seven days, it seems—and the Jews cut their work days short and spend the evenings in their houses to observe it."

Meres glanced at Ahasuerus. "*Seven days?* What do they do on this holiday?"

"Uh," the guard began. "Whatever Jewish people do. Pray and eat strange food."

Ahasuerus heard Meres chuckle, joined in by Tarsena, but the king didn't find it very amusing. He'd heard his father, King Darius, threaten the Jews who worked in the palace not to miss any days of work, even for a religious holiday. And they hadn't.

Was not a decree from the king to attend a royal race a commandment? He looked from the guard to Meres then to the meager gathering. Racing would hardly be the same without the cheering crowds.

Ahasuerus knew what his father would do—send the guards into the Jewish neighborhoods and fine them, perhaps even whip a few. It didn't take long for the king to make his decision. "Bring me the leaders—whoever they are—of the neighborhoods where you delivered the decree."

The guard bowed and hurried away. By the time Ahasuerus had his horse warmed up and realized that, yes, Meres would most likely beat him again today, the guard had returned. He had three men with him.

Beneath one of the open tents that had been set up for the royals to keep out of the direct sun, Ahasuerus took a seat on the temporary throne adapted from one of the litters. The prime minister joined him, muttering under his breath, "We should just throw them in prison. Then they can spend their holiday there."

The Jewish men stepped forward, their heads bowed and their eyes lowered. Their robes were dark and plain, showing the dust from the road.

"Your father would never have tolerated this," Tarsena said, his voice not quite a whisper.

Ahasuerus should have been used to Tarsena's side comments about how King Darius had run things, but the comments bothered him. His father had been dead for more than seven years, and still, Tarsena referred to him constantly.

The king turned his attention to the Jewish men. "Did you know that an edict from your king is a command? Whether verbal or written or delivered by a judge or guard, it is to be obeyed."

"We work extra hard during the day so that we may be at home in the evenings with our families to celebrate our holidays," the man who seemed to be the leader said. "We believe we should not put the things of man before the Lord."

"Not even your king?" Tarsena burst out. "King Xerxes holds your lives in his hands. I'd advise you to obey *him*, not some invisible god."

The Jewish man paled, but the other two men next to him didn't look quite as cowed.

"Each of you will pay a fine of fifty silver talents, due by sundown," the king said. He knew the prime minister wanted more action, but Ahasuerus was determined to enjoy his race day and not have three executions shadowing him.

The Jewish men scurried away, and the king was reminded of a bunch of vermin, dark and dirty and always in the way.

"Your father wouldn't have been so generous," Tarsena said.

Annoyance pulsed through the king at the continued reminder. "My father is no longer king."

Tarsena chuckled then turned his attention to the neighboring women's tent.

The king glanced over at the women. His concubines had settled onto cushions, and little children ran around, on and off the carpets that had been brought in. The younger ones played in the dirt. It bothered Ahasuerus that Tarsena was ogling the concubines. The harem was at Tarsena's disposal; the king's concubines were not.

They were beautiful, yes, and Ahasuerus couldn't exactly say he was in love with any of them—the women served their purpose and brought him pleasure when he needed it—but that didn't mean the prime minister had a right to enjoy watching them.

"How's your family, Tarsena? Is your wife well?" the king asked.

Tarsena's head snapped back to the king, his eyes narrow. "Fine. They are all fine."

The king smiled. "Good to hear." He rose and left the tent, ready for the race to begin.

Chapter 12

HAMAN WAITED FOR REBEKAH'S NEIGHBOR to leave the hut. But the elderly Jewish woman was still inside and had been for two hours. What could they possibly be talking about? Rebekah's husband must still be gone since he didn't return at dusk. Was that why the elderly woman was still there? Surely she had to leave soon so she wouldn't lose her way in the dark night.

A faint light flickered from within. So Rebekah had lit her oil lamps. Would this give the neighbor woman cause to leave?

Haman could wait no longer. He had to do something to get time with Rebekah since he was giving her one more chance. He had a new plan, one that even she couldn't turn down. She would live with his female cousin, have the child in secret, and the cousin would claim the baby as her own. Rebekah could remain in the household under the pretense of being the child's caretaker. She wouldn't even have to give up her worship practices. She could be as Jewish as she wanted.

And then Haman would be able to visit without anyone questioning his relationship to a Jewish woman. That should make Rebekah happy—and her god happy as well.

He rose from his hiding place and, welcoming the growing darkness, walked around the back of the hut. He crept to the side of her bedchamber window. That was when he heard the moaning.

He moved closer and peered inside, risking being seen by the neighbor woman. Perhaps her eyesight wasn't good and she wouldn't notice him. What he saw shocked him. Rebekah was curled up on her sleeping mat, her face bathed in sweat while the elderly woman rocked above her, praying.

Rebekah was ill, seriously ill. Before he could think of the consequences, Haman hurried around the hut and burst through the door. In a few strides, he was in the back room, facing the startled neighbor. Rebekah didn't even look up from her curled position.

He knelt beside Rebekah, ignoring the other woman's sputtering. "What's wrong?" he asked, touching Rebekah's shoulder. "What has happened?"

Rebekah's eyes opened, and her mouth moved in a whisper. Leaning down, he heard her say, "I lost the child."

Haman sat back and scanned her trembling body. It wasn't uncommon for women to lose a child so early, but he didn't realize it could make them so sick.

He looked over at the woman, who was staring at him, wide-eyed. "Leave." His voice was barely controlled. "I'll take care of her. Do not speak of this to anyone, or else your entire family will be killed."

The woman's incredulous stare faltered, and she snapped out of her trance then hurried out of the room. Haman waited until he heard the door of the hut close before turning back to Rebekah.

"What happened, Rebekah?"

Her eyes opened again, and they seemed clearer now, more focused. Her voice was hoarse when she spoke. "The bleeding started this morning, and now the child is out of me. It is over." She exhaled. "It's the Lord's will, Haman. The Lord has given me a just punishment for loving you. We are not meant to be together."

His stomach twisted. How could this woman, who was so sweet and beautiful, believe that her god would do this? To herself? To their child? He wanted to scream, to rage. He wanted to sob.

Instead, he closed his eyes. He breathed in and out. He had many children, but a child with Rebekah had become his greatest desire since she'd told him the news. He thought he could come here tonight and convince her to come with him. He could give her a chance at a new life where no one in her religion would condemn her.

But now . . . if she truly believed her god had caused her to lose the child . . .

He opened his eyes and stared down at the woman he loved more than any woman he'd ever known. He'd been a fool and had allowed his obsession with her to control everything in his life, to master his emotions. But still . . . he wanted her to be his. And he'd do anything to have her.

He touched her forehead; it was as hot as a fire. "Rebekah, my sweet, you're very ill and don't know what you're saying. You need a healer, and then when you are recovered, we'll decide what to do. Many women have lost children too early. It's not a sign from your god."

Rebekah's eyes remained closed, and she didn't even respond. Her face was so pale, and her body seemed so fragile. It was physically painful to think of losing her. His hand moved along her face, to her neck, to her shoulders. He realized she was still in danger. How could he go on if something happened to her?

Time could not be wasted. She needed a healer immediately.

He rose and walked out of the hut to find the neighbor not yet far. Haman grabbed her. "Go fetch a healer. Rebekah's life depends on it."

The woman grappled for words. "She said that she wanted no one."

"She's not in her right mind. Find someone now! And bring them in the upmost secrecy."

The startled woman nodded. As she hurried away, Haman looked up at the sky. "Tonight I need your help, Ahura-Mazda, more than I've ever needed it."

He went back inside the hut and rummaged through the cooking room until he found a goatskin of wine. He took it to Rebekah and got her to drink a little. It seemed like hours passed before the neighbor returned with a healer.

The man hardly looked at Haman but immediately attended to Rebekah. He asked a couple of questions then set to work lighting incense he'd brought with him and chanting strange prayers.

At one point, he ordered everyone out of the room, and Haman could only listen helplessly to Rebekah's moans.

When the healer emerged, he looked pale and drawn. "She will live, but she has bled much." His gaze focused on Haman, although there was no surprise in his eyes, just a look of weariness as if he'd seen this situation many times.

"She needs several days of rest." He handed a wrapped package to the neighbor woman. "Use these herbs in a tea and give it to her every few hours."

"You will be well paid for your silence," Haman said. "No one will know that I was here."

The healer nodded then looked at the other woman. "See that she rests." One more glance at Haman, then he was out the door.

Haman stayed with Rebekah through the night. Sometime in the early morning, the heat left her body, and she slept peacefully, her forehead cool to the touch.

The neighbor spent the night in the gathering room, probably too afraid to leave Rebekah with Haman. The curious glances she sometimes gave him let him know she wondered what he was doing here with another man's wife.

When dawn graced the sky, he found the Jewish woman in the cooking room, mixing the herbs left by the healer. "You'll be rewarded for bringing Rebekah back to health and keeping me informed of her well-being. My involvement must be kept a secret, or I'll make good on my threats. Do you understand?"

The woman nodded. "Yes."

"Where do you live, that I might communicate through a messenger?" Haman asked.

The woman met his gaze then quickly looked away. "I live in the first house on the other side of the river. Next to me is my son, who is keeping Joshua's goats while he's away." Her voice faltered, and he heard the accusation in it. He wondered how much Rebekah might have told her or if she only guessed.

* * *

Duties at court prevented Haman from returning to check on Rebekah until the following evening. He rode his horse to the small hut but found that it was dark. He thought perhaps Rebekah was asleep, but why would the neighbor who was caring for her want to sit in the dark?

He tied up his horse to a nearby tree and crossed the barnyard. Without bothering to knock at the door, he opened it and stepped inside to total darkness. Something didn't feel right. Heart pounding, he walked through the rooms and entered the bedchamber.

In the moonlight coming through the window, he saw that the mats were gone. In fact, the room was empty of everything else too. He turned to scan the gathering room. The two stools and low table were gone, and the single wall hanging that had been there was missing.

She'd left. Rebekah had moved out of the hut. She'd left *him*.

For a desperate moment, he wondered if she had simply left her husband, but something in his churning stomach told him that wasn't the case.

Despite the darkness, Haman easily found the neighbor woman's hut on the other side of the river. Light spilled from the single window, lighting the courtyard paved with cut stone and bordered by flowers. He knocked on the door and heard the sound of voices.

He'd have his answer soon.

The door creaked open, and two dark eyes peered out at him. The woman opened the door wider and stepped back to allow him to enter as if she had been expecting him. Her gaze fell to the floor, and Haman folded his arms across his chest, waiting.

"She's moved away. Her husband came home this afternoon and saw that she was ill." The woman took a breath. "She told him everything." Her eyes slowly raised to Haman's then flickered away again.

"Did her husband show mercy for her condition and allow her to rest?"

"No," the woman whispered. "He was more afraid of your return than Rebekah's health, and she agreed to go with him." She twisted her hands together. "He gave her a choice, and she chose to leave with him."

The woman kept her eyes lowered, and for that, Haman was glad. Emotions rocked through him. The goat-man hadn't put away his wife, hadn't stoned her, but had taken her away.

"Where did they go?"

"I don't know," she said, still not looking at him.

Haman's hand grasped the woman's upper arm, and he leaned closer. "Your family's life depends on your choice of words."

"They didn't tell me, but I heard him mention his cousin's—in Media. That's my best guess. After Rebekah's pleadings for forgiveness, he consented to start anew." The woman raised her eyes. "She seemed stronger by the time they left, and she was walking fine."

Haman nodded, grateful to know Rebekah was stronger. But he was angry at himself. He should have never left her—to be found by her husband. What choice did she really have when faced by her husband? Of course she felt compelled to confess. Haman should have rescued her before the man returned. In her ill condition, Haman could have transported her to his cousin's and cared for her there. They could have grieved the loss of their child together. When she recovered fully, she would have seen his love for her.

By the time Haman returned to his horse, he had a new plan in mind, and it would start immediately. He would send someone to find her and watch her and report back to him. She would surely be miserable without him. She'd start to miss him, come back to him, and beg his forgiveness.

He rode into the night until he reached his home. He owned one of the larger estates in Shushan. Only the prime minister and the royal princes had places larger than his. His breast swelled with pride as he reached the immaculate courtyard with its fountains and exotic flowers.

This was a place fit for the beautiful Rebekah and her stubborn heart. He'd never understand the Jews' fanatic devotion to their religious beliefs. He should have known he was entering the fire pit when he first saw Rebekah over a year and a half ago out gathering wild flowers. Her veil had been discarded as she had walked along the riverbank barefooted. Haman didn't know what had attracted him more—her bare feet or her blush when she'd caught him staring at her.

His lips curved into a smile to think of it, but it was quickly extinguished as a servant hurried across the courtyard to take the horse's reins. Haman climbed off the horse as the servant bowed deeply.

"Judge, there has been a message from King Xerxes."

All thoughts of Rebekah fled. "What is it?"

"He's invited you to join his hunting party in the morning."

Haman hid a broad grin. The king invited only his most favored subjects to his hunting excursions. It was one thing to be considered loyal to the king; it was quite another to be considered a friend. And with this invitation, Haman's privileges and importance in the kingdom had just increased.

His plans for Rebekah would be delayed, but it would be worth it.

Chapter 13

THE DAY ANNE LEFT TO interview with the king had Esther's stomach clenched into knots. Anne was beautiful and graceful. She was also cunning and would no doubt be able to charm the king no matter how short the interview period.

Also, if Anne failed to be chosen, Esther would be the next woman to interview with King Xerxes.

O Lord, my God, give me strength, Esther prayed silently as she went about her usual activities in the harem. Her maidens followed her to the bathing pool, and Esther noted with satisfaction the wooden rail that had been installed on the staircase. When she'd mentioned the eunuch's difficulty to Hegai, he'd obtained permission to build the rail.

She ran her hand along it as she descended, marveling at the fine craftsmanship. Everything here was expertly built, and this rail was no exception.

After the pool, two of her maidens oiled and massaged her body, which should have relaxed her, but all she could do was imagine conversations between the beautiful Anne and the king. The harem was always quiet as the eunuchs waited inside the palace on the mornings there was an interview. When Esther returned to her rooms, she was surprised to see Hegai waiting for her, along with Sarah and Nan.

Hegai's expression was gravely somber, making Esther's heart jolt. Had something happened? To Anne? To the king? Then her stomach felt like it was ready to tumble. Mordecai?

Her gaze moved to Sarah and Nan, surprised to see they were barely concealing smiles. Surely the news wasn't awful then. Still, her heart hammered.

Hegai didn't bow as usual but said, "There has been a new development. Anne has been dismissed, and the king wants to see you today."

"Today?" Esther's hands flew to her cheeks. "Anne was supposed to . . . I thought . . . what happened?"

"She was in there for only a few moments," Sarah said in a quiet voice. "We aren't sure what was said, but she came out furious."

Hegai nodded. "The king followed moments later. Fortunately, Anne was out of sight and he didn't hear her angry mumbling." He paused as if he had to catch his breath. "King Xerxes asked me how many women waited in the harem."

Seven, Esther knew.

"He asked who was next to interview," Hegai continued, "and when I told him your name, he fell quiet."

Esther felt the tears threatening. Could this really be happening? She stared at Hegai and saw only seriousness in his eyes. Sarah smiled—a genuine smile—but she remained quiet.

"The king told me to send you in after the midday meal."

Only an hour away. And then I shall be face-to-face with the king. Esther's hands started to tremble, a quaking that spread through her entire body. She couldn't reply, for she didn't know what to say.

"We will fetch your clothing and begin right away," Sarah said.

Nan's head was bowed, but Esther practically felt her smiling. This was excellent and exciting news for the harem workers. They had all been waiting for this day, but for Esther . . . There was no turning back now. The king had sent for her.

While she waited for Sarah and Nan's return, Esther left her maidens to fret inside her chambers, and she walked into the garden. More than eleven months had passed since her arrival, and the garden had become her sanctuary, where she listened for further impressions from the Lord.

It was hard to believe so many months had passed and, in that time, how much she'd changed, both in appearance and thought. Her skin was smooth and sculpted and her hair thick and silky. Yet she was still fearful. It wasn't because she knew she'd have a lonely marriage should the king choose her. It was because she worried about being righteous enough to become what the Lord expected.

Besides fear, Esther also felt sadness. Many of the servants in the harem had become dear to her, but after today she would not belong here with them. She also knew the home she once had and the prospect of living in the palace would never come together and coexist after today. She'd either be sent home or become queen. To live in one world, she'd have to give up the other. And the harem wouldn't be part of either.

Unbidden, tears filled her eyes. Standing among the beauty and serenity of the garden made her heart swell as she realized she'd miss this lovely place. The garden made her feel that she was surrounded by the Lord's art, as if it were all created for her. Her former life seemed but a distant thing yet something that remained close in her heart. Still, from the many experiences she'd had listening to the whisperings of the Spirit, she knew she was in the right place, as unbelievable as it seemed.

Esther bowed her head and began her silent prayer . . . pleading with the Lord to preserve her people and to guide her in whatever ways she might aid in accomplishing the Lord's plan. *Thy will be done, O Lord, my God. Preserve my people and let peace reign in the land of Persia.*

In the quiet of the garden, she plainly heard footsteps approach. She turned to find Nan.

The woman bowed deeply. "Mistress, Sarah has the clothing ready. We cannot delay a moment longer."

* * *

The Chinese silk flowed from her shoulders to her ankles, its luminescent violet color changing hues as she walked out of the harem into the brilliant sunlight. Hegai led the way, and Esther followed, flanked by Sarah and Nan.

They crossed a courtyard of laid marble and passed a magnificent fountain that Esther might have stopped to admire if she had had any of her senses about her. Beyond the thick walls surrounding the courtyard, she thought she heard a man's laughter, but it was quickly gone.

She kept her gaze forward, neck erect, head steady, and steps sure and purposeful, just as she'd been trained. Esther wore no jewelry, save for her mother's marriage ring hanging from a chain around her neck, which she kept concealed beneath her robe. Her simple white veil was trimmed in violet and gold to match the beautiful robe Sarah had constructed.

Esther knew she was dressed no fancier than a lady at court—or a lady in the harem, for that matter—but the clothing made her feel royal nonetheless. To her, it was exquisite and more than enough.

Her heart thundered at double the pace of her footsteps, and she wondered how much the king remembered her. It had been nearly a full year since she'd met him that night at the well. The wait had seemed eons, yet it felt as if it had happened only days before. She remembered the king as a handsome man, large in stature, the size of a warrior.

She also remembered his smile and his eyes that seemed so interested in her. But perhaps she had imagined it all. Perhaps she wasn't now walking through a massive gold door, making her way down a flawless marble corridor, and stopping before another set of gold doors.

Two guards stood at attention, their hands on the hilts of their long swords.

"We have brought the woman as requested by King Xerxes," Hegai said with a deep bow.

One of the guards reached for the door and swung it open.

Esther thought she might stop breathing. It was another corridor, this one lavished with plush rugs and intricate wall hangings. Another set of doors mirrored the ones that had just been opened, and another pair of guards stood at attention at the interior doors. Behind her, she heard a sniffling, most likely from Nan. Esther wanted to cry too. She wanted to return to the harem, to its beauty and serenity, to her seven sweet maidens.

Somehow, she took a step and was inside the inner hallway.

Hegai turned to face her, his kind eyes filled with warmth. "We will remain here. You'll go inside those doors and wait for the king to join you. We'll be here as long as the interview lasts." Then he bent forward and kissed her on the cheek. "You look stunning, Esther."

Her eyes burned, and tears forced their way out of her eyes.

"Don't ruin the kohl," Hegai said.

Sarah produced a linen kerchief and dabbed at Esther's cheeks, which made Esther want to cry more.

Nan put an arm around her. "We won't stop praying until we see you again."

Esther closed her eyes and exhaled. The sincerity of Nan's words touched her. When she opened her eyes again, she was determined to be ready. A week, a month, or another year would not change the outcome of the king's decision, so it might as well be today.

"Thank you for everything," she whispered to Hegai then turned her gaze to Sarah and Nan. She simply nodded. If she spoke, she wouldn't be able to hold back further tears.

Hegai told the guards Esther was ready, and they opened the doors.

Esther blinked in amazement, trying to take in the sight before her. She'd thought her quarters in the harem opulent, but they were nothing compared to the vibrant room she was stepping into.

The ceiling extended overhead higher than she could have ever imagined, with windows all around. Esther had never before set foot in a turret. The sunlight glowed into the room and made the gold furniture gleam. She'd never seen so much gold—each piece of furniture, from tables to chairs to the divan, was gold, exquisitely shaped, and covered with cushions of purple and indigo.

She walked slowly to the center of the room along the plush rug and stopped, not knowing what to look at first. A massive lion skin spread in front of the cold hearth, and a trickling fountain made of silver and marble in the corner of the room made her feel as if she were in an outside garden.

On each gold table sat a painted vase of the most perfectly shaped roses she'd ever seen, and they were all white, making the room even more brilliant and ethereal. The rug was a mixture of deep indigo- and gold-colored threads so soft that Esther imagined a person could easily sleep on it. Without thinking, she stepped out of her embroidered slippers and wriggled her toes into the deep plush.

But her feet upon the soft rug wasn't enough. She bent down and ran her fingers along it. It was certainly as soft as silk and as comfortable as a cushion.

"Did you lose something?" a man's voice said.

Esther froze. The voice could belong only to one man—the king. She rose and turned around.

It was no doubt Ahasuerus—*King Xerxes*, she reminded herself. She hadn't thought of his first name for months. His hair was longer than she remembered, but perhaps she was just used to the close-shaved heads of the eunuchs. He wore a thin gold crown—something he definitely wasn't wearing that night at the well, and his indigo robe was belted with a sash of purple over a white tunic.

If she had doubted her memory of the intensity of his brown eyes, she didn't have to doubt any longer. It was as if she could see for leagues into them and never reach their depths. And there was that scar, the one above his left eyebrow, which left her extremely curious. Everything about him was more perfect and more handsome than she remembered. Whatever did he say to Anne to make her so furious? And what did Anne say to the king that caused such a swift dismissal?

Esther's face flamed hot at her own thoughts, not to mention that the king was staring at her.

"Well?" his deep voice seemed to reach out and touch her.

She opened her mouth, not sure what he meant, then by some miracle remembered his question.

"The rug—it's beautiful," she said, her voice barely above a whisper, as if she'd lost her ability to speak.

The king simply stared at her. No smile. No frown. No response.

"And I couldn't resist touching it. It's like silk." Then she remembered her training. Mortified, she dropped into a prostrate position.

It seemed as if she was on the ground forever, yet she didn't mind because of the luxurious rug. But as she held her prostration, she remembered her slippers and realized with new horror that she was barefoot before the king.

She wanted to curl up and disappear or maybe run out those massive gold doors and not stop until she reached Egypt.

"Please rise," the king's voice sounded somewhere above her.

I've already annoyed him. Perhaps I'll break Anne's record.

Esther rose, moving her foot over and sliding the slippers closer, but there was no time to put them on. She hoped to do it without drawing attention to the fact that she was currently barefoot. *He* was not barefoot.

She kept her gaze lowered, not daring to meet the king's eyes. She was not to speak unless he asked her a question. There was no telling what she might say next. Her mind began to race. Perhaps this was all just a test by the Lord, and she was not meant to become queen or to represent the Jews in the kingdom. The Lord meant for her to learn humility and proper reverence. Not to mention patience and servitude. Finally, she relaxed slightly but soon found that she'd reached her conclusions too hastily, for the king stood in front of her.

"The first thing I noticed when we met was how tall you were for a woman," the king said.

Not extraordinarily tall, Esther thought but quickly bit back that reply. *Why is he standing so close to me? Should I be looking at him?*

Hegai had told her the king would ask her to sit on a chair or a divan, then he'd probably sit himself or stay standing. But they were both standing, and he was so close that she could smell fresh pine coming from his robes. Had he just been outside? Then she realized he was reaching for her, and before she could decide what to do, he lifted her veil and took it off.

"There you are." His voice was soft, like a caress.

If Esther had been blushing before, now her face was on fire. She looked up at him against her will. His eyes were on her, searching her own as if looking for some sort of answer.

"You're taller than I remember as well," Esther said.

His lips curved into a smile, and she couldn't help but smile back.

What am I doing? Flirting with the king? He didn't even ask me a question.

"I trust you were treated well in the harem and your room met your satisfaction?"

Esther clasped her hands together, and tears gathered in her eyes. Thinking of the emotional good-bye of Hegai, Sarah, and Nan tugged at her heart.

The king's smile faded. "No? Tell me what happened."

"Oh," Esther rushed to say, her words tumbling out. "The harem was wonderful—as far as harems go—not that I know any others. Everyone was so kind, except for . . . I mean, the harem workers and, of course, Hegai was always there with his advice about every little detail."

"Then why are you crying?" His fingers brushed against her cheek.

"I—I will miss them all," she choked out, embarrassed that she was crying over servants. The king would see her as a blubbering fool and send her home immediately.

The king moved closer and placed his other hand on her other cheek. "You have been a blessing to each of them, Esther."

The way he spoke her name melted into her. "They are too good," she whispered.

He chuckled and lowered his hands. "I think they would say the same thing about you, which is why I've asked you to come for the interview this afternoon." He gazed at her for a moment then turned and walked toward one of the low tables.

When he stopped, he said, "Would you like some refreshment?"

She nodded, astonishment making her legs feel shaky. He wasn't dismissing her yet.

"Come sit with me. I couldn't eat much during the midday meal, yet I find myself quite famished now."

The way he was looking at her made Esther blush again. She wished she could put her veil on, but it seemed the king had kept it with him. Perhaps it was in the pocket of his robe? She slipped on her shoes, still hoping he wouldn't notice, but she caught him watching her.

He said nothing, merely smiled, then clapped his hands.

A servant appeared almost immediately, coming in through a door on the far side of the room—the one the king must have used. The servant prostrated himself, then the king said, "Wine and fruit, please."

Esther smiled at the young man. "Thank you." His ears turned bright red. When he left, she said, "Should I be wearing my veil?"

"No," the king said. "He's not used to being thanked by beautiful women."

She frowned, hardly believing the servant was unused to beautiful women. "Surely he's seen plenty if he serves you."

The king's face tinted, and Esther wished she would have kept her mouth shut. Hegai's counsel of only answering questions was very wise indeed.

"I didn't mean to imply—" she started.

"Come sit down, Esther," he said, his tone sounding amused.

She obeyed immediately, sitting on the edge of the divan as far away from the king as she could possibly be without falling to the rug.

He kept his gaze on her. "I'm pleased that your propensity to please everyone hasn't changed after nearly a year of having seven maidens to yourself."

Esther stared at the king. Mordecai had told her the king was apprised of everything, but this as well? "I *am* here to serve," she said, almost adding *my people*.

"And I find that completely charming." He held out his hand, and Esther stared at it.

"Come closer; you're going to fall off the divan," he said with a chuckle. "I won't ravish you here and now."

She thought her heart would stop with humiliation. "I would never accuse you of—"

His hand covered hers and gently guided her closer until they sat nearly shoulder to shoulder. The king didn't seemed daunted one bit. He leaned back and smiled as if he had no worries or cares, but that wasn't what was making Esther's heart hammer. He hadn't let go of her hand.

Even when the red-eared servant returned and set out the wine with the platter of nuts and olives and honeyed dates, the king kept his fingers around hers.

What does this mean? What are you doing? Esther wanted to ask. Instead, she said, "I must apologize for inspecting your rug so closely and for removing my slippers. I am sure Hegai warned me not to inspect rugs or remove my slippers in his lengthy and thorough instruction."

"Are you sure?" the king asked. "Perhaps it was such a preposterous notion that Hegai didn't think he'd have to mention it."

She swallowed back a laugh. "Very true." She realized she enjoyed the teasing from the king. Surely he wasn't like this at court or in battle. This was not anything like how she had imagined the interview would go.

He leaned forward and unstrapped his sandals. "You're right. The rug is quite nice."

Esther laughed aloud this time, then gasped as he reached for her feet and removed her slippers. If Hegai had any idea what was happening on the other side of those golden doors, he'd probably faint.

The king leaned back again, studying her as if they had plenty of time.

She dug her toes into the rug, reveling in the softness but not relaxing her posture. That would be too forward. Then she realized what she'd forgotten.

"Oh, the wine! I should pour it for you." Esther glanced at the king to see him smiling again.

"I promise, the instruction I received was very thorough, and Hegai missed nothing," she said. "It's my fault that I have been so negligent. We've spent hours pouring wine just so. It's just that you are—" She closed her mouth into a firm line and set about pouring wine into the two gold goblets on the table, marveling that her hands were quite steady.

Then she picked up one of the goblets and handed it to the king. He took it but didn't drink yet. "I am just so . . . *what?*" he asked.

Esther was afraid she'd really crossed the line this time. "Kingly?" She exhaled. "I mean, I wasn't expecting you to be . . ." She looked at him, truly looked at him. If there was a chance she'd ever marry this man, then she wanted him to know what she thought of him. "So *real*. You're a king, yet you're a man too."

His eyebrows lifted.

"But a beautiful man with *everything*, so I thought it would be hard to talk to you. I thought you'd take one look at me and dismiss me. Instead, you took off your sandals."

He stared at her, and Esther finally had to look away. She had no idea what he was thinking.

"When we met at the well, what did you think?" he asked.

Esther peeked up at him. "I didn't think. And when I could think later, I decided I imagined everything."

His mouth twitched. "When the edict came, what did you think then?"

"That you were mistaken. That a king couldn't possibly be interested in inviting me to his palace to prepare me to be . . ." Esther's words faltered. At that moment, she knew that even if the Lord hadn't prompted her to take this path, she wanted to know this man. She wanted to know what he loved, what he hated. What he dreamed about.

"A queen?" he said in a soft voice.

She could only nod. This was all surreal. She wondered if the king would think it strange if she pinched herself. *What is he thinking?*

A silence filled the room, broken only by the king lifting the wine goblet to his mouth. Esther took the opportunity to do the same. Perhaps the wine would help harness her tongue. She took a small sip then another. The flavor was rich, yet light and fruity. She didn't want to appear too eager, so she took one more swallow and set the goblet back on the table.

"You called me Ahasuerus when we first met," the king said, turning the goblet in his hand as if he was inspecting the workmanship, which was exceedingly fine. "And you called me again by my given name when I visited you in the harem when you were ill. Why was that the first name you thought of?"

Esther's cheeks heated. "I truly don't know. Perhaps you looked more like an *Ahasuerus* than a *Xerxes*. I apologize for my imprudence."

"You apologize far too much," he said.

"I—" She stopped, realizing that she was about to apologize again.

The king laughed and set his goblet back on the table. He turned toward her and rested his left arm on the back of the divan. He was practically touching her, and Esther had to calm her breathing.

Her gaze strayed to his scar, and she had the sudden desire to touch it, to ask him what caused such a deep mark. When her eyes met his, her heart thumped at the intensity of his gaze. She wanted to ask him what he was thinking but dared not. Almost as if by a will not her own, her hand lifted. Ahasuerus didn't move, not even when she brushed the scar over his eye with her finger.

Chapter 14

"SWORD FIGHT?" ESTHER SAID, HER finger touching the scar just above his brow.

Ahasuerus was surprised at her touch, but he had no trouble welcoming it. This woman was different from the others he had interviewed. She was less formal, more natural around him and didn't hesitate to laugh. Yet, there was a pureness and innocence about her as well. He knew she was different when he had first laid eyes on her laughing, veil-free face. She was absolutely and completely different from Vashti in every way.

"An arrow too swift to avoid," he said.

His scar was incurred a few years ago during one of his more aggressive hunting excursions. He still remembered the expression on Prince Carshena's face when the arrow misfired and shot straight for his head.

Esther lowered her hand, but Ahasuerus wasn't ready to let her go. He captured her hand in his, threading their fingers together.

The first time he'd held her hand was to help her from the ground at the well. He'd noticed their roughness and strength. "Your hands are soft now," he whispered. The room felt unusually warm, and he could only attribute it to the fact that a beautiful woman sat next to him, one who was beautiful on the inside as well as the outside.

Looking into her eyes, he felt as if he'd arrived home—there was comfort, peace, and tenderness there.

Esther looked down at their intertwined hands. "Sarah and Nan made sure of that."

More harem workers she has no doubt endeared herself to, he thought.

She let out a breath as if she'd been holding it. "I am not used to such idleness."

Of course she wasn't, and that's what made her even more appealing. She didn't expect to be waited on. She cared about servants and had learned

all of their names. Ahasuerus had full reports from chamberlain Biztha—
and he only allowed himself to smile over them after Biztha had left the room.

Her eyes widened as if she'd realized what she'd said. "I didn't mean
that everyone here is idle—"

"I know you didn't." He drew her hand to his lips and kissed the back
of it.

She blushed, and Ahasuerus thought he might be blushing as well.
He couldn't help thinking about Vashti and how they'd never had such a
comfortable, private moment. Everything in their relationship had been
driven by plotting parents.

Esther withdrew her hand and clasped them together.

"Should I apologize for being forward?" he asked.

"You did promise not to ravish me," she said in a small voice. "Kissing
my hand is certainly not ravishing, is it?"

Ahasuerus smiled, although what he really wanted to do was kiss her
properly on her lips, which he'd been watching for the past several moments.
"Tell me the first thing you'd do as queen of Persia."

Her brows lifted, and she looked at him with surprise. Then her mouth
softened into a smile. A moment passed, then two. Ahasuerus was enjoying
the fact that she was truly thinking about it.

"I—" she began in a quiet voice. "I think the very first thing I'd do is . . ."
Suddenly, she was blushing again. "How about I tell you the second thing
I'd do?"

Ahasuerus laughed then grabbed her hands in his, locking them in his
grasp. "I insist on knowing the first thing and nothing else. And don't change
what you were going to say. I'll be able to tell by your expression."

Her cheeks reddened, and she glanced at the wine goblets as if she were
seeking for courage, or simply stalling for more time. "It's rather embarrassing
and probably not entirely appropriate to say to Your Highness."

"Then it wouldn't be true to your heart."

She nodded and lowered her eyes. "The *very* first thing I'd do as queen
is . . . kiss the king."

Ahasuerus grinned, especially when he saw her brilliant blush. Everything
in his body propelled him to lean forward and kiss her, but something held
him back. She was somehow too pure, and he refrained from following his
physical instincts. He'd been married before, and he had concubines who
had born his children, yet . . . Esther was special. He didn't want things to
be the same with her as with other women.

He kept the well-mannered distance between them, restraining himself as never before. "Esther, I want to make today the first day that I stop regretting what happened with Vashti."

Her eyes rounded at the mention of the former queen's name.

Ahasuerus continued, in too deep now to backtrack. "Since Vashti . . . departed . . . I've regretted my actions that led to the dissolution of our marriage. Even though the fault was primarily mine, I had to uphold the image and propriety of the kingdom and laws between a husband and wife." He exhaled. He'd never told anyone this much about his disappointment in himself. "When I saw you in the streets and then when I was notified of your arrival in the harem, some of the guilt slipped away. It was as if the Creator had sanctioned the events surrounding Vashti."

Esther let out a sigh of her own and looked down at their interlocked hands.

The warm smoothness of her skin seemed to travel the length of his arm all the way to his heart. Ahasuerus marveled at how comfortable and natural it all felt. It wasn't an act of seducing but an act that showed she cared about what he felt. Then he saw that tears had filled her eyes.

"Ahasuerus," she whispered. "I can't imagine the pain you have been through, and despite it all, you've had to lead the kingdom. You should have a queen who can rule beside you and share your burdens. I have come from a modest home and was brought up to tend children and clean cooking rooms. You don't need to feel guilty by sending me back home. You need a wife who is trained to live the royal life and can be your companion in all things." She wiped at the tears dripping down her face. "I don't know if I am that woman, no matter the connection we may have felt when we met at the well." Her sad smile was heartbreaking. "I am a simple woman and will be happy in a simple life—"

"Esther," Ahasuerus cut in. "Your gentleness and thoughtfulness is what's lacking in my palace. It's what the people need—a queen who is one of them, who understands them, who has lived as they do." He used the edge of his sleeve to soak up her tears. "To send you home today would be a regret I'd never be able to reconcile."

She brought her hands to her cheeks as she stared at him.

He gently pulled one hand from her flushed cheek and bent forward and kissed it. "Esther, I want you to be my wife. Are you willing to serve as queen of Persia?"

* * *

"Yes, Ahasuerus," Esther whispered. Her voice was gone.

The king didn't flinch at her use of his true name; in fact, he was smiling at her. And she ached to throw her arms around his neck and kiss him. She had to settle for a wildly beating heart. How had this happened? How had King Xerxes just proposed to *her*, an orphaned Jewish woman?

The Lord's Spirit had prompted her to tell the king she would be happy in a simple life, that his days of feeling guilty were over. Yet, he'd still asked her to marry him.

She looked down at the hand he held. "Is this a dream?"

"If it is, it's the most pleasant dream I've ever had," he said with a chuckle.

Joy surged through Esther, joy that she never imagined she'd feel with this outcome. She'd been so fearful, so unsure of marrying a man who had other women before her and children with his concubines, but somehow, those worries didn't pain her now. As she looked into Ahasuerus's eyes, she marveled at the tenderness she saw there.

He stood and tugged on her hand, pulling her up next to him. There was such an intensity in his gaze that her breath caught. "I must leave you now, my betrothed, or I will be in grave danger of breaking my oath of not ravishing you."

She smiled but felt breathless inside. Her thoughts turned to what it might be like to be this man's wife in every way. A blush warmed her cheeks, and she lowered her eyes.

"And don't think I won't forget about the first thing you promised to do when you are queen."

Kiss the king. She snapped her head up to look at him, her face flaming.

He took a step back and bowed. Then he held out her veil that he'd procured from somewhere in the folds of his robe. She reached for the veil.

"I will see you on our wedding day." He turned and strode out of the room.

Esther stared at the door he'd gone through then looked down at the veil in her hands. Her heart felt like it would burst. It had happened—really happened. What would Hegai and Sarah and Nan think? What about the other women, still waiting for their interviews? There would be no interviews for them now.

And Mordecai—and Leah. Johanna.

It was impossible, yet it had happened. A miracle that could only be from the Lord.

O Lord, my God, Esther whispered. *Give me the strength to become what Thou desirest. Guide me, protect me, and bless my people.*

Chapter 15

IT HAD BEEN SEVERAL MONTHS since Haman had seen Rebekah, but today that would change. He could hardly focus on what his wife was telling him about the misdeeds of one of their sons, Ham. Her narrow face was red with anger as she recounted something about how Ham had lost silver in a betting game. It involved another boy and a horse race.

It was too early in the morning to listen to a woman's ranting. He couldn't believe it had been so long since he'd gazed upon Rebekah's beautiful face. His spy, Thar, had brought back a report each week. The man was small enough to fit in with the Jews and not raise any suspicion; all he had to do was dress like one. Thar said Rebekah had the full color of health again. She had made friends among the women of her community. Yes, her husband was still herding goats, but their new hut wasn't as dilapidated as the one they'd had in Shushan. Apparently, the goat-man's cousin was wealthy, and they lived in a couple of rooms at the back of the cousin's home.

Zeresh's voice pierced his mind, and he refocused on what she was saying.

"I don't have time to deal with Ham until I return from Media," he said.

"Must you be gone for so long?" Zeresh asked.

He let out an exasperated sigh. "It's on the king's orders; therefore, it's unavoidable." Since he'd gone on a few hunting trips with the king, he felt he could make a special request and visit some of the smaller courts in individual provinces as a presiding judge. He'd done it as a lesser judge before but not as a chief judge.

Zeresh was saying something else about their son. Haman was tired of listening to her sharp voice. It seemed every moment he was at home, his wife had to give him a full report of his children's misdeeds.

"Tell Ham that he'll be earning back the coins he lost in betting," he finally said.

Zeresh harrumphed and placed her hands on her hips. "That's very well for you to say, but I'll be the one living with him as he mopes about for the next week."

Haman had no answer for his wife because his mind was back on Rebekah. He turned away from her and strode out of the home. Her voice trailed after him, *complaining, complaining, complaining,* but it quickly grew fainter. By the time he'd mounted his horse, he couldn't hear her at all.

He rode hard for Media, intent on reaching it by afternoon. His spy would be meeting him just outside the town. Their plans would begin from there.

Haman was nearly to the crossroads when he saw another rider approach him from the opposite direction. The man wore plain, simple robes, yet he rode a fine horse. It could only be Thar.

As Thar drew near, he said, "Everything is arranged for you, sir. I have a small house and clothing. You can look as Jewish as you want."

Haman chuckled. "Perfect. When can I see her today?"

"It's too late now. Her husband is due for supper at any moment. It's best you wait until midday tomorrow."

Haman nodded, considering Thar's advice. "I will see her tonight from afar. Do they have plans outside the home?"

Thar hesitated. "No, there are no obligations tonight since it's Sabbath. Although on other nights, they frequently receive visitors of their cousin's. They visit in the courtyard as the evening air brings coolness."

"Excellent," Haman said, a smile tugging at his lips. "Lead me to our quarters." He'd be seeing Rebekah soon. Very soon. And tomorrow he'd be speaking to her face-to-face and holding her in his arms. He could almost feel the softness of her skin next to his and smell the scent of her hair.

He couldn't wait to see the surprise on her face then the pleasure. Enough time had passed that she would miss him with a fierceness equal to his and be eager for him. He had been growing his beard longer for a couple of months, in the style of most Jewish men, and with a plain dark robe, he'd blend in. He also planned to hunch over a little so he wouldn't seem so tall.

The small house was private and clean—much to Haman's appreciation. The bed was only a mat on the floor, but he hadn't come to indulge in luxuries.

By the time the sun was setting, he was ready, but when he strode out of his bedchamber, Thar gaped at him. "Her husband will be there tonight."

"I merely want a glimpse." He smiled broadly. "Coming?"

Thar scrambled into action, donning his own robe. "It is nearly Sabbath, so we must be off the roads before dark. And we'll have to be careful when we come back so no one sees us."

"If all the Jews keep to their homes like they should on their Sabbath, we won't have any trouble," Haman said with a smirk.

Thar smiled. "Let's make haste."

The two men walked along the roads, and Haman noted that the homes were decent places with neat courtyards and trimmed bushes. When Thar moved off the road, he said, "We'll approach from the back of the home. There are quite a few trees that will conceal us."

Haman nodded and followed. They wove their way through several stands of trees until Thar drew Haman to a stop. "We'll have to be completely silent from here since the courtyard is not too far."

Lights twinkled through the trees, and at first, Haman wondered if there was a cooking fire going, but he knew the Jews didn't cook on their Sabbath. As they reached a waist-high stone wall, Haman realized the light was coming from hanging lamps edging a large yard.

Thar pointed to a stone in the wall and pulled it out. Haman crouched to look through the gap. Several people were seated on cushions surrounding a long table, including men and women and children as well. It took only a moment to find Rebekah.

She was facing him, and for a fleeting instant, Haman worried that she could see him from his hiding place. Although her face was turned in his direction, she didn't seem to notice anything.

Haman exhaled slowly. She'd changed. Or maybe she hadn't, and he'd just forgotten how beautiful she was. She wore a slight smile. Did that mean she was happy? Her husband must be sitting across from her, if Haman could guess the goat-man's physique. What must have been the cousins filled up the rest of the space, a man who looked like an older version of goat-man, a stout woman, and three smallish children. Did these people never grow?

Then again, Rebekah's petite form suited Haman just fine. And he was sure she appreciated his height. He smiled—no, grinned. She was radiant. It must have been the oil lamps glowing against the evening sky, but whatever it was, she had never looked so beautiful and healthy.

He'd been praying to Ahura-Mazda for her full recovery, and it looked like she was completely healed. The cousin stood, and everyone bowed their heads in prayer, repeating words in whispers.

Haman watched Rebekah's lips move. Even though he couldn't care less about the religious words she was repeating, he wished he could hear her voice. But it was impossible to hear it from this distance. When the prayer concluded, the women stood, reaching for the platters of food on the table. They proceeded to serve the men then the children.

Rebekah moved slowly, pausing to smile at each person, and as she rounded the table, she turned to the side, and Haman saw her profile. Something inside him froze. Even with her wearing a robe over her simple tunic, he knew every curve of her body. Her face, her shoulders, her . . . He pulled back from the wall and squeezed his eyes shut.

Thar tapped his shoulder, but Haman ignored him in an attempt to get Thar to leave him alone.

Haman exhaled then moved forward again, willing his eyes to see a different image now. A different Rebekah. But there was no doubt—not to a man with ten sons of his own.

Rebekah was with child.

Which meant the child belonged to her husband. Haman stared at her for as long as he could stand it. His eyes burned with disbelief, then anger. He blinked and realized she not only looked lovely, but she also looked happy.

But how could she be happy without him? He had been her love, and the only thing that had stood between them was her religion and his wife. He couldn't very well give up his wife—he wasn't king and couldn't live through that sort of scandal and keep his position as chief judge. And he wasn't willing to become Jewish.

In fact, it wasn't until this moment that he realized he truly hated the Jewish people. It wasn't just that Rebekah willingly lived within the confines of the religion; more than that, Judaism had taken away the one thing that was most dear to him: the woman he loved.

Haman reeled back, pulsing with disgust. He'd come all this way, only to . . . His eye caught Thar, who was looking at him with confusion. Haman scooted away from the wall and stood up then plunged back through the trees in the direction they'd come. He wasn't quiet, but he wasn't concerned about that now.

Just before they reached the road, Haman stopped and gripped both of Thar's arms. "She's with child!" he spat.

"What? I—no!"

"Yes, I could see it for myself. Any man who's ever had a wife knows the signs."

"But she doesn't look—"

Haman's fingers dug into Thar's skin. "I know what I saw, and I want you to find out everything you can. When is the child to be born? Who will be the healer to attend her? Or will it be the female cousin? I want every detail possible."

Even though it was dark, Haman could feel the fear pulsing through Thar.

"How will I discover all of this woman's business?"

"You'll dress like a woman and go where they talk to each other." Haman relaxed his grip. "When she delivers, I will finally be able to bargain."

Thar's eyes widened. "What are you planning on, sir?"

"You'll only know what is necessary. From this moment, you are a beggar woman who will find out everything I need to know."

Chapter 16

A DOZEN TRUMPETS SOUNDED AS Esther lifted the hem of her robes and climbed up the broad marble steps. The announcement of her arrival was powerful, reverberating down to her slippered feet. Her back was to the sunrise, the sky just brightening with the new day. The marriage was to take place as the sun rose. Then the wedded couple would retire as the sun set.

The robes she wore were white silk, sewn with pearls and emeralds, and a flower garland lay draped around her shoulders. Her clothing felt heavier than a satchel of rocks, yet Esther had to walk as if nothing weighed her down. She wished Hegai and the harem workers could be in attendance at the marriage, but only royal dignitaries would be there, which also excluded treasury workers such as Mordecai. Esther had never thought she'd marry without even one of her relatives in attendance.

It had been a moon's time since Esther had last seen Ahasuerus, on the day of the interview. There had been no word or instruction from him. She had been schooled by the harem workers about what happened in a Persian wedding ceremony. Sarah had even pulled her aside to instruct her on what would happen in the bedchamber as a married woman and loyal subject to her husband.

Esther's face flushed as she thought of it, and she was grateful for her veil. She quickly turned her focus to the steps in front of her. Since there had been no communication with the king, she only had to trust that all of the details of the wedding had been taken care of. Her only duty was to be fitted for her marriage clothes. Then she'd undergo the final purification process.

But Esther had stayed much busier than just preparing physically. She'd been weaving fabric to make a robe for the king as a marriage gift, spending early mornings and late nights with her seven maidens, first in weaving then in stitching and embroidery. The completed robe wasn't nearly as fine as what the royal clothiers designed, but the thread had come from Egypt—fine and lustrous—and the gift had a personal touch a purchased robe would have lacked.

Three days before the marriage, Sarah and Nan had used what Esther soon learned was called *band andazi* to remove her facial and leg hair, as well as the hair from her stomach and back and under her arms. With special threads, the harem workers pulled the hair from the roots. That pain lasted throughout most of the day. Two days before the wedding, Esther underwent a series of baths and oil massages on both her skin and hair.

There was not one more thing they could do to her to prepare her for this marriage, unless they had a way to calm her speeding heart. As she reached the top of the stairs, she thought of little cousin Ben and how she'd pretended to be his queen on that day more than a year ago. They'd reenacted the Jewish marriage rite. Today, her real wedding would be conducted according to Persian custom.

The doors that led to the throne room stood open. The walls were lined with courtiers, women on one side, men on the other, and all eyes were on her. Esther had never been so grateful for her veil. Her body flushed with heat as the attention of hundreds of people focused exclusively on her. She had never seen the throne room but now knew it exceeded any room in the palace in magnificence. Huge marble pillars seemed to extend to the heavens, and the marble floor alternated tiles of red, black, and white. The dais upon which the throne sat was of pure gold.

Her eyes lifted to find Ahasuerus seated on his throne. She could not read his gaze from this distance, but she noticed he was dressed in all white too. A flower garland hung across his shoulders. His hair was pulled back, and he wore the crown she'd seen on the day of her interview.

The court guests prostrated themselves as she passed them, and it felt as if all of her breath had left her body. She was to be the queen. Truly, the queen of Persia. And the bride of Ahasuerus. She forced herself to take steady, even steps, her heart tapping faster than her feet. As she neared the king, she could see his smile.

Her heart beat even faster, and she wanted to smile back, but she had to focus all of her effort on remaining upright and not fainting dead to the marble floor. She tore her gaze from the king's, but it was back on him in an instant. Was he looking forward to marrying her? To taking her as his?

Esther wasn't naïve, expecting to be the king's only love. Her marriage would be far from the traditional monogamy of her Jewish people. The man she'd be marrying in a few moments would never be hers alone. He already had women and children.

She swallowed against the dryness in her throat and wished she could take a sip of wine or perhaps drink down a whole jug. Anything to help her grasp the moment upon her.

As instructed by the harem workers, Esther knelt before the king. He took her hands in his and kissed each one. Her body shuddered, and she wondered what it would feel like to have his lips on hers. She flushed at her own thoughts. Ahasuerus guided her to her feet then to the seat on the left side of his throne.

The king sat next to her. "Esther."

Not a question, nor an answer. He just spoke her name.

And he smiled at her.

Esther wished they were in a room alone, without hundreds of pairs of eyes on then. Maybe then she'd dare speak to him.

A Magus wearing red robes stood before them, a loaf of bread in his hands. He held each end delicately.

The king stood with a sword in hand and lifted it. Esther flinched as he brought it down into the center of the bread, slicing it open. He took the two pieces of bread from the Magus and handed one to Esther.

She took a bite of the bread, and the king sat down again and took a bite of his piece of bread. Another Magus stepped forward and took the bread then offered the king a goblet of wine. He took a sip and handed it to Esther. When their hands touched with the transfer of the goblet, Esther blushed madly. She brought the goblet beneath her veil and took a sip of the sweetness. She didn't think she'd ever get used to the rich fruitiness of royal wine, so different from what she had always known.

As Esther handed the goblet back to the Magus, the musicians in the corner started playing a low beat on their drums. More Magi stepped forward until there were a dozen in a semicircle in front of the king. The head Magus began speaking in a low voice, reciting a prayer to Ahura-Mazda. The king bowed his head as he listened. So too did Esther.

When the Magus finished, he began again, this time the king repeating the words. Esther joined in on the third recitation as she'd been instructed to do in the harem. When the third and final recitation concluded, the Magus said, "O King, do you enter into this union by your free will?"

"Yes," Ahasuerus said.

The Magus turned his gaze on Esther. "Esther, do you enter into this union by your free will?"

As instructed, Esther remained silent. The Magus repeated the question a second time and then a third. Esther had been told that asking the question multiple times signified that it was the groom who sought after his wife and was anxious to marry her, not the other way around. On the third time, Esther answered, "Yes, I do."

The king reached for her hand and brought it to his lips. Then he stood and drew her to her feet. She knew what to do next, but it was still surreal as she knelt and King Xerxes placed a crown on her head.

The first thing she felt was the heaviness of the gold circlet, and the second was the heaviness upon her soul. She was now queen, and the responsibility seemed enormous. The band of musicians' drums, tambourines, and flutes swelled into the room as voices rose in praise of the king *and queen*. Esther blinked back tears and rose on her trembling legs. Standing next to Ahasuerus, hand in hand, she looked out over the gathered throng.

The next hours blurred as the feasting and entertainment began. Esther had never seen such lavishness. From the platters of steaming meats, fruits, cheeses, vegetables, and goblets overfilled with wine to acrobats, dancers, and magicians.

All the while, Esther was acutely aware of the king next to her and that she was now his wife. Court members approached the dais, prostrating themselves and bringing gifts of spices, silks, furs, jewelry, and pictorial vases—so many gifts that Esther was amazed. One prince even brought a pair of tamed monkeys. They were adorable, but she wondered what would become of them.

Esther couldn't help clapping in delight. Next to her, the king laughed. With such a large array of food, she didn't have trouble partaking only what was allowed by the law of Moses. If anyone noticed her picky habits, she planned to say that her stomach was sensitive.

The gifts kept coming until Esther's mouth was tired from smiling and her eyes blurry from so much opulence.

As the sun disappeared below the horizon, the orange and pink hues slowly faded, replaced by torchlight. Dozens of torches shone in the sconces on the walls so the throne room was nearly as bright as midday.

The king stood, and the courtiers prostrated themselves. Esther moved into her own prostrate position, and Ahasuerus extended his hand toward her. As he helped her up, she was reminded of that day at the well. He'd helped her to her feet then, he dressed in a plain cloak and she in Leah's rose-colored tunic. Now, Esther and the king stood in the position of the highest honor in all the land, wearing their finest wedding white. That day had led her inexorably to this one.

The king stepped off the dais, leading Esther with him, and they walked through the parting crowd. Esther's maidens fell into step behind her, and the king's menservants followed him.

Their entourage left the throne room, and they turned toward the private rooms of the royal family. Esther remembered the day of her interview and how she'd met the king in one of his greeting chambers.

King Xerxes paused at the first set of double doors. He dismissed all of his servants save for one. Esther turned to her seven maidens. Their faces were aglow with excitement and pride. "I will call for you in the morning," she said in a quiet voice.

They looked surprised to be dismissed so completely, but Esther had been taking care of herself much longer than she'd been pampered in the harem. Tonight she did not want any help. Whether or not the king approved or disapproved, he didn't say.

The guards opened the doors, and she followed the king down the corridor to the left to a smaller set of doors. The doors were a blond wood, expertly smoothed, with flowers carved right into the wood.

"The queen's rooms," Ahasuerus said. His mouth twitched, almost into a smile. "I'll be with you shortly."

Esther nodded, and a nearby guard opened the door. She stepped inside to a large room. As the door shut silently behind her, she stared at the surroundings. On every surface in the room was a vase of white roses.

They were unexpected, breathtaking; she knew they were from Ahasuerus.

Esther walked from vase to vase, lifting her veil and smelling each collection of flowers. She was exhausted, but as she moved among the roses, wonder filled her. Had it really happened? Or would she wake up and discover she'd been dreaming? She took off her veil and laid it on a divan.

Then she removed one long-stemmed rose from a vase and walked to the far end of the room, where doors led out onto a marble balcony. She opened the doors and stepped outside; twilight had deepened the color of the sky to violet. As she inhaled the sweet scent of the flower, the moment seemed perfect. She leaned against the balcony railing and looked over the city. She could see firelight from family cooking fires and torches against the gathering darkness.

Amazement coursed through her at the beauty and peace of it all from her viewpoint on the balcony. From here, everything looked serene and calm. And she loved it. She loved her land, her people, and her family. She loved the harem workers; Sarah and Nan; and Hegai, the keeper of women; and she hoped to see them often. Inhaling the fragrance of the rose again, she hoped most that her marriage would be happy.

Her thoughts turned to Ahasuerus and the way he'd kissed her hand while surrounded by the entire court. They were married now, yet she felt she hardly knew him. She closed her eyes, thinking about the past twelve months and all of the preparation she'd gone through in order to have this honor. Was she truly ready?

Mordecai depended on her to be a successful queen—one who would protect the Jews. Would her relationship with King Xerxes facilitate that? "O Lord," she whispered, "bless me with wisdom and strength. Thou hast brought me to this place, and I have married the king of Persia. Bless me with the knowledge and intuition to carry out my duties according to Thy will."

When Esther finished the prayer and opened her eyes, her gaze found the stars that dotted the sky. She recognized the Persian goddess Ashi constellation. Esther had seen the same constellation from her home with Mordecai and Leah. To think they all lived under the same sky made her breath catch with homesickness.

Becoming queen was overwhelming enough, but this being her wedding night made her heart hammer as she thought of the words Sarah had whispered to her about the intimacies between husband and wife.

Her breath nearly stopped as she heard a door shut. Without turning, she knew Ahasuerus had come into the room that he'd had filled with flowers. She looked down at the white rose in her hand. He had given her flowers, but what did he think of her? Yes, he'd chosen her as queen, but was there more depth to his feelings than the apparent fascination that he seemed to have?

His footsteps were soft as he crossed the balcony and stood by her.

She didn't know if she needed to drop into the prostrate, but something held her upright, and her eyes focused on the rose in her hand.

Ahasuerus rested his palms on the balcony rail. "What do you think of all of this?"

"It's beautiful," Esther said. Out of the side of her vision, she saw that he'd changed from the wedding robes and now wore a belted tunic. "I can't believe how close the maps of stars seem up here."

The king turned his face toward her, and Esther could feel the heat of his gaze. "Do you know the constellations, then?"

"I'm still learning, but I can pick out the seven marks."

"And how did you learn these seven marks?" he asked, his tone amused.

"Mostly from my clay tablets, but—"

"You can read?"

Esther shook her head. "No, I've just asked other people what the words say." She cast a glance at his profile. "But I'd like very much to learn to read."

The king was staring at her. "Perhaps you shall."

Encouraged, Esther took a deep breath. "It seems on a night like this, the possibilities are endless. There is so much to learn about all the beauty out there, and reading will open the way." She met his gaze, feeling heat spread through her body. "And all of the flowers are beautiful too."

One side of his mouth lifted into a smile. "I wanted to fill the entire room with roses, but I could only get enough for about a dozen vases."

"Ahasuerus," Esther said, placing her hand on his arm. He didn't move back or seem cross about her touching him or calling him by his real name, so she continued. "A dozen vases of roses are more than enough for any woman. You could have given me a single rose, and I would have loved it."

His smile grew. "I still remember your promise."

"My promise?"

"What you said about the first thing you'd do as queen?"

Kiss the king. Esther's breath stuttered. Had he really thought of what she'd told him all of this time? "Well, then, I guess I'd better keep that promise."

Even though her heart beat wildly, she stepped toward him as he turned to face her. Still holding the rose in one hand, she lifted her hands to his shoulders. They were warm and solid beneath her touch. He didn't move as she rose up on her toes and pressed her lips against his.

His hands stole around her waist as he drew her against him. Esther had never been this close to a man before. His lips moved against hers, kissing her back, his mouth urgent yet tender.

It was quite plain to Esther that the king knew how to kiss a woman. She felt as if she might start to float right off the balcony and soar into the sky like a dove. Despite knowing that he'd kissed many women and had already fathered children, she wanted him to herself.

She pulled away to breathe. "I have a gift for you."

The king didn't release her. His hands moved up and cradled her face as he kissed her again, more slowly this time. Esther closed her eyes as tremors ran all the way to her toes. She'd never thought that a kiss could make her forget all of her concerns. Perhaps the gift could wait.

"Esther," he whispered when he released her. "You are my gift."

Instead of floating, Esther now thought she might melt. One part of her questioned his sweet words, while the other part of her decided to believe them with all of her heart—at least for tonight. She reached a hand up to his face and touched his cheek. Then she touched the scar above his eye and moved her fingers through his hair. Was he really hers?

Tonight, he is.

Ahasuerus smiled and grasped her hand. "Come inside." He led her around the inner room, extinguishing the oil lamps until the room was in near darkness. The moonlight coming in from the balcony cast a pale glow, making the white roses look ethereal.

Still holding her hand, the king led her to a single door and opened it. On the other side was the bedchamber. A few oil lamps had been lit. Esther hadn't explored this far, but it was definitely a bed fit for royalty. The massive cushion stood on a platform, with silk drapes hanging from the ceiling to shroud the bed.

At least a dozen more vases were scattered about the room, but instead of white roses, these were red. "More roses?" Esther said, feeling suddenly out of breath.

Ahasuerus grinned. "I told you we ran out of white."

"What will the people think when they discover the king's gardens have been stripped of all the roses?"

The king wrapped his hands about her waist, pulling her close. Esther's heart purred at his nearness, especially in a room with the queen's bed— *her* bed.

"We didn't pick the pink or yellow ones."

Esther laughed then found herself kissing her new husband again. His arms tightened around her, and in a sudden move, he lifted her up and carried her to the bed.

She lay back against the silk bedding and pulled Ahasuerus to her. The wedding gift could definitely wait.

Chapter 17

DAWN HAD NOT YET ARRIVED when Esther awoke in her new bedchamber. The oil lamps had burned out and everything was quiet, except for breathing next to her. The events from the day and night before flooded through her mind, and she marveled that she was now, completely and truly, queen and wife to King Xerxes.

She turned on her side and realized she was even more amazed that a man had slept in her bed. Ahasuerus was lying on his stomach, a mere hand span away from her, his torso bare. The feel of his lips on hers and his tenderness in all things made her heart swell. She understood now the bond created between a man and a woman when they became husband and wife.

Her hand strayed, almost involuntarily, and rested on her husband's back. His shoulders were broad and bronzed by the sun. She moved her hand along the breadth of his back, smiling as she remembered the discussion about all of the roses last night. Her fingers stopped at a long scar on his lower back. She lightly traced the raised skin, wondering what had happened. Wasn't royalty supposed to be protected from harm?

"Sword training with my cousin," Ahasuerus said.

Esther jumped at the sound of his voice. She hadn't realized his eyes were open and he was gazing at her. He smiled when her eyes met his.

"What happened to the cousin?" she asked.

"He was sent to Greece as a spy. My father thought he'd been a bit too aggressive with the heir to the throne." Ahasuerus's half-lidded gaze took in her undressed state.

Esther felt a blush rising, and she tugged the coverlet up higher.

The king turned on his side, now facing her. "How are you feeling?"

Her cheeks were certainly red now. "I'm . . . perfect." She smiled even though her heartbeat thundered in her ears.

"You *are* perfect, and you're beautiful in the morning," he said in a quiet voice.

"So are you," she said with a laugh.

He smiled then reached over and lifted one of her locks of hair. "I'm glad your promise wasn't limited to just one kiss." He rose up on an elbow and leaned over her then kissed her neck.

Tingles ran through Esther's body. "Do you think the kingdom can run itself?"

"For a few hours, maybe a day." He kissed her jawline. "Two at the most."

She moved her hands up his chest and then behind his neck. "What happens if we refuse to open the door?"

The king moved his lips to her ear and whispered, "You'll hear a lot of banging and shouting."

She giggled.

"Then someone will break down the door and rush in with a sword in hand, ready to defend me in any way required."

"Defend you? Against *me*?"

Ahasuerus chuckled. "Especially against you. Did you not know that a woman can tempt a man into almost anything? Cause him to lose his mind?"

Esther laughed with him, but deep inside, she wondered if that would be the case with her and if it had been the case with his first wife. She tightened her hold around him and realized that once he left her bedchamber, he'd be the world's once again. Only in here, and only for a few precious moments, was he hers alone.

* * *

Ahasuerus knew all chance of sleeping any more had completely fled, even though he'd slept little the night before. His new wife, Esther, had fallen back asleep, despite the sun's rays pouring into the room. The corners of the chamber had brightened, turning the roses he'd ordered for her to brilliant scarlet.

He pulled on his robe then leaned over Esther to kiss her forehead. Would that he could spend all day with her alone, or even two. She was beautiful, yes, and kind, but there was a depth to her that he wished to know better. She was intriguing yet humble and knowledgeable. And her sweet accepting of him last night had touched him.

The fact that Esther could tease him and not be afraid to call him by his real name made being around her feel like she really enjoyed just him. Just Ahasuerus. And that she wasn't thinking about him as the king of Persia.

He'd always wondered what it might be like to live like a normal man, working from sunup to sundown in a field then coming home to supper with a wife and children around a rough-hewn table. Perhaps sharing a few cups of wine with friends in the evening as they discussed the politics in the land. Then he'd return to his small house and warm bed, where his one loving wife awaited him.

Gazing down at Esther for a moment, he could imagine her in such a setting. Despite her beauty and grace, it was as if she could exist in both worlds equally well. The reports from the harem had confirmed that she had a generous heart, as well as many skills, such as weaving and using herbs that would bless any husband and children.

He turned away from Esther and left her room, entering the main chamber, where the scent of white roses filled the air. Near the balcony doors was something wrapped in linen. The wedding gift she'd brought him. He could well guess what it was. The director of the treasury had reported that Esther had put in an order for thread to work on a weaving project.

The king hadn't any problem approving the expenditure, as little as it was, because he knew that in the villages, women liked to make things for their grooms. He'd wait to inspect the gift later in the evening when he saw Esther again.

There would be another feast tonight, but the day would be devoted to a council with the princes who had come for the wedding. The call for sending an army to invade Greece had grown to a new fervor. His armies had been home for only a few weeks, and already the commanders were crying for another invasion. The council would replace his usual day of hearing petitions by the public.

After bathing and changing in his private rooms, he stepped into the corridor. The guards nodded in acknowledgment—they were the only ones exempt from prostrating themselves so they could always be on the alert. Biztha, who was apparently waiting for any sign of the king, rushed forward.

"There was a scene last night," he said in an urgent whisper. "All is well now, but I wanted to let you know before you went to the council."

Ahasuerus looked down at the chamberlain. "Why wasn't I informed?"

"I didn't want to disturb you and Queen Esther," Biztha said. "I hoped to quickly quell it, but there might be some hard feelings this morning."

The side of the king's mouth lifted as he thought about the uninterrupted time with Esther, but he hoped that not being apprised of the "situation" was a wise move.

Biztha leaned forward. "Tarsena seduced one of Meres's wives last night."

It took a moment for the king to comprehend. "What do you mean by *seduce?*"

Tarsena was an old man, a fat man, and Ahasuerus couldn't imagine any of Meres's wives dallying with the prime minister when she had Meres as a husband.

Biztha's face drained of color. "That is what the dispute is about."

Ahasuerus felt sick. This was a serious charge indeed. "Follow me into my chambers."

Once the doors were closed, the king turned on the chamberlain. "Do you mean to say that Tarsena forced himself onto the wife of the prince of Media?"

"That's what the woman told the prince."

"Bring her to me. Not Meres, not Tarsena, just the woman."

Biztha's eyes widened.

"Here. In my chambers. Now!"

The chamberlain turned and scurried out so fast that he forgot to shut the door. Ahasuerus took care of it with a slam. If Tarsena had done what the king suspected, there was no way Ahasuerus could cover the man's deed. Although the king had wished that the prime minister would retire, this blunder was not what he needed for the kingdom at this time. Especially when it had happened on his wedding day, when he was about to marry Esther, a woman who was a commoner.

The king had yet to discover how the general population felt about his marriage to Esther. Gifts had been aplenty yesterday, but those had been expected since they were from the invited guests. How would the rest of the people feel about a queen who had no royal blood in her?

Disgust swept through him about Tarsena—the man never seemed to have control over his actions. Surely he'd been a more reasonable man in Darius's era. Ahasuerus couldn't even imagine how furious Meres must be.

Ahasuerus strode to the windows that overlooked the vast palace gardens. As he gazed down upon the bushes and plants, he remembered Esther's comment about all the roses disappearing—what would the people think?

These thoughts were circling throughout his mind when a knock sounded at the door and it cracked open.

"Enter," the king said.

Biztha walked in with a veiled woman following. He and the woman prostrated then rose. Biztha's face looked pale. "Meres is in the corridor. He wants to speak to you."

"Meres can wait," Ahasuerus snapped. "I'll speak to his wife alone."

Biztha backed out of the room, and Ahasuerus waited to speak until the door closed.

"What is your name?" he asked, trying to keep his voice even.

She practically cowered before him, visibly trembling. "Ava."

"Please remove your veil, Ava. I'll hear your story while I see your eyes."

The woman raised her slim hands and lifted her veil. Two dark eyes peered at the king. Her face was puffy from crying, and her eyes were rimmed in red. But most noticeable was the red welt on the left side of her face, as if she'd been struck.

Ahasuerus clenched his hands, wanting to deliver a blow to Tarsena's ample jowl. He took a deep breath. "You're the wife of Prince Meres?"

She nodded.

"Tell me what happened last night."

Her gaze faltered, and she looked down at her clasped hands. "After Your Highness left, there was more entertainment, but I was very tired. Meres excused me to return to our chamber." She lifted her eyes briefly, tears in them. "I was only there a short time when the door opened. I hadn't even thought to bolt it."

Ahasuerus sank down in the nearest chair, listening.

Her voice broke. "I thought it was my husband, but when I saw the . . . prime minister . . . I thought he'd come to meet my husband." She brought a trembling hand to her mouth and looked away.

"I need to know what happened. Everything."

Her intake of breath was shaky. "He is a large man, and he . . . he overpowered me. I called out, but he struck me and said he'd kill me if I screamed. When he was . . . having his way, my husband came in." Tears budded in her eyes, and she continued to tremble. She met the king's gaze, fear and shame in her eyes.

He stood and walked toward her. Pausing in front of the crying woman, he said, "Your words will be heard in court today as Tarsena stands trial. I'll send a scribe in, and you will tell him exactly what you told me."

"I will," she whispered. "Thank you, Your Majesty."

The king passed her then paused, his gaze resting on the welt on the poor woman's face. "You will be avenged very shortly. Guests at my palace will not be treated this way, no matter who the man is."

She bowed her head in acknowledgment then prostrated herself.

Ahasuerus crossed to the door and flung it open. Biztha waited just outside. Another man stood behind him—Prince Meres. His face flushed with fury, and his eyes brewed like the darkest storm clouds.

"My friend," Ahasuerus said to Meres before the man could speak. "Your wife has been gravely mistreated under my palace roof. The man who did this will stand trial for his crime." He turned to Biztha. "Clear Judge Haman's schedule. The prime minister will appear at court at noon, and Haman will preside."

Biztha nodded, and the king looked over at the guards outside his door. "Bring me the captain of the guard. He has an arrest to make. After the arrest is made, send the scribe Dan into the chamber with Meres's wife to record her story."

Biztha hurried away, and one of the guards bowed and left the corridor.

When Ahasuerus and Meres were alone, the king grasped the prince's arm. "I cannot express my sorrow enough for what has happened to your wife. Her words will be read as a witness against the prime minister."

Meres gave a curt nod, his eyes full of fire. "If that fool is not sentenced to hang, then I'll have him killed before the sun sets. The only reason he still lives is that my shock was too great and I didn't catch him before he fled."

"Judge Haman's sentences are swift and sure," the king said. "You have my word that Tarsena will not live to see another day."

The fire in Meres's eyes dulled to a smolder. Ahasuerus had no doubt the prince would carry through with his threat if the court did not do it for him.

The captain of the guard arrived.

"Gad, we have grave business to attend to," the king said. "Arrest the prime minister without delay. Come with me now."

The captain didn't look surprised, which meant the man sent to fetch him had filled him in. Soon the news would be all over the palace. The king had to act very swiftly.

Two chamberlains and three guards accompanied Gad. The king recognized the chamberlains as Bigthana and Teresh, who oversaw the royal stables, but he didn't have time to question why they were part of Gad's entourage today.

Ahasuerus made his way to the throne room with Gad and his group. Inside, the other princes had already gathered for the council. He paused at the entrance, looking at the assembly. All of the princes from Persia and Media were there, except for Meres: Carshena, Shethar, Admatha, Tarshish, Marsena, and Memucan. They were cousins and half brothers but none in the direct line for heir to the throne.

If Ahasuerus died, the battle for kingship would be fierce. He scanned the faces then found who he was looking for. The prime minister sat in a corner, his arms folded.

Tarsena rose to his feet and prostrated himself as soon as Ahasuerus's gaze landed on him. Then he scrambled to his feet and rushed forward, his wide girth making it look more like a stumble. Ahasuerus's hand clenched into a fist as the man started to explain the night before.

"Your Highness, you have been fed a poisonous tale." His eyes were wild beneath his thick eyebrows. "That woman of Meres's is a seductress."

"Enough!" the king shouted. The room went absolutely silent. "Your trial begins at noon. Captain Gad, arrest this man."

Tarsena fell to his knees as the guards came forward and grabbed each arm.

"Please!" he cried out. "I served King Darius, and now I serve you faithfully. Don't let a harlot come before me. Remember the years I've devoted to the kingdom of Persia. Hail King Xerxes! Hail Queen Esther!"

"Pretty words," Ahasuerus spat out. "Save them for your trial."

Tarsena's panicked complaints echoed in the throne room as he was practically dragged out. When his voice faded, the king looked upon the remaining assembly. Meres entered the room, his face much calmer than the last time the king had seen him. The prince silently took his seat.

"In my kingdom, a female guest will not be mistreated in such a manner. The guilty man will pay a heavy price." Ahasuerus looked right at Meres. "I regret my actions that drove Queen Vashti away. With my new marriage and my new queen, I am raising us to a higher standard."

He took a deep breath, his body feeling like it was on fire with conviction. "I will no longer tolerate all-night feasting and drinking. And I will not tolerate the mistreatment of guests in my palace, especially another man's wife."

Chapter 18

A SOFT CLINK WOKE ESTHER, and she heard a small giggle when she opened her eyes. The first thing she realized was that she was in her new bed, and the second thing was that her husband was gone. She pulled the covers around her and sat up.

Karan, one of Esther's maidens, stood on the other side of the room. She brought a tray of food and set it on a low table surrounded by cushions. The maiden gave Esther a shy smile then prostrated herself.

Will I ever grow used to this? The prostrating? And never being alone? Not even to sleep in on the morning after my marriage?

"Thank you," Esther said to Karan. "Will the king be joining me?" She felt embarrassed to ask the question, but as of now, she felt that she knew very little about the procedures in the palace. Sarah and Nan hadn't been privy to the little personal details of daily life and customs between the king and queen.

"Oh," Karan said, her eyes rounding. "I do not think so. No." She looked toward the windows. "It is past noon already."

Esther drew her brows together. "Is he in council, then? Or perhaps . . . hunting?" What would the king do the day after his marriage if not spend it with his wife?

"You have not heard, then?"

"Heard what?" Esther felt the press of irritation inside. She hoped for a more direct reply and not so much questioning. Esther climbed out of bed, pulling the cover tight about her. She kept her tone polite, but inside, she was quite impatient. "Tell me, please."

The maid set down the jug of steaming tea. "The prime minister is to be executed at sundown." When Karan was met with shocked silence, she continued. "He was found guilty of assaulting Prince Meres's wife last night. King Xerxes's punishment came without delay."

"Prime Minister Tarsena?"

"Yes," Karan said.

Esther had just met him at the marriage festivities. He was an older man, one who'd probably been in his prime during King Darius's reign. Her mind reeled at the thought of the awful act that led to such dire consequences and how fast the man's life had been changed.

"And how is Prince Meres's wife?" Esther tried to remember meeting Prince Meres, but there had been several princes to whom she'd been introduced yesterday.

The maid's sunny disposition seemed to cloud over for a moment. "She will be avenged, and that will have to be enough." She clasped her hands together. "But there has been a great deal of talk in the palace today. The king has forbidden late-night feasting and drinking. And any crime against a woman who is a guest in his palace will be immediately addressed."

Her words struck Esther to the core. Ahasuerus had spoken of his regret regarding Vashti. Was forbidding late-night drinking another step in order to alleviate his regret? Whatever the case was, Esther knew the king must be having a difficult day. To lose his prime minister would certainly change the political landscape.

She wished she could discuss this with Mordecai. He had not thought highly of the current prime minister. Would a new prime minister make a difference in her influence at the palace?

"Chamberlain Hatach awaits in your receiving room," Karan said. "The king has assigned him to oversee your schedule."

"Hatach is waiting right now?" Esther asked.

Karan nodded.

Feeling flustered at the thought of a man waiting for her on the other side of her bedchamber—the one she'd just shared with her husband—she dressed quickly with Karan's help and went out to meet him.

A man stood in the middle of the room, apparently waiting for her. How long had he been standing there, Esther wondered. "Chamberlain Hatach?"

The man prostrated himself then stood. His dark gray hair was smoothed back from his face, his jawline square and rugged, his neck thick as if he'd been a fine warrior in years past. Despite his robust exterior, the smile lines around his eyes and mouth made Esther realize he was normally a pleasant man.

Sure enough, he offered her a broad smile. "It's a pleasure to serve you, Queen Esther."

She inhaled at the title. She'd been called that plenty the day before, but she was far from used to it. Esther wondered if it would be untoward to ask Hatach about the prime minister. Instead, she invited him to sit on the divan and tell her what to expect in the palace.

Despite Hatach's patient explanations, Esther's stomach was in a knot the rest of the day. She knew she wouldn't see the king until the evening feast, and she wished she could speak to him and comfort him if needed about the crimes of his prime minister. What had he thought when he left her side this morning? What did he think about last night? About their very new marriage? Would she be a burden to him? Or could she help him in serious matters such as this?

Her seven maidens surrounded her as they prepared her for the feast. Karan came back with the news soon after sunset. "The prime minister has been executed. Hanged at the gallows."

Although Esther expected the news, her heart clenched. She hadn't known the man personally, and by all accounts, he'd been a vile person, but a life taken jarred her to the core. One of the maidens continued to comb Esther's hair then arranged it into a low twist in which she inserted tiny blossoms.

All of the maidens seemed to be waiting for her response—her response as queen. It was then Esther realized that although her first instinct was to sorrow over the events, both in the crime against the prince's wife and the betrayal the king had felt, she realized the punishment had been fair and just.

And she must focus on that. Weak tears were not fit for a queen. She kept her eyes dry and her head erect as the maidens continued their work. Soon their light chatter returned. Once the henna on her nails was dry, she slipped into a violet tunic. The silk felt luxurious against her skin.

The robe Karan brought forward was a deep purple—the color of royalty. It seemed there was no end to the resplendent clothing Esther might enjoy. Tonight she'd be in the presence of the king, as his queen. Her maidens finished the last touches of putting on her veil, followed by the crown.

The weight of it reminded Esther of when it was placed upon her head the night before. When she turned toward the bronze reflector, she was stunned at who she saw. A year before, she'd spent her days cleaning and caring for her cousins. Today, she was looking at a queen.

Karan touched Esther's elbow. "We must hurry straightaway. The king is expecting his queen before the guests arrive."

Warmth spread through Esther as she thought about the king's anticipation and her anticipation as well. Even though this would be a formal event, she'd sit next to him as the guests—their guests—arrived. When she exited her chambers, Hatach was there to escort her to the banquet. With her seven maidens following, Esther walked to the throne room.

The chamber blazed with torchlights, although the evening was still young. The white silk drapery of the wedding decorations had been cleared away, replaced by colorful and intricately woven hangings depicting scenes of battle and hunting.

Esther scanned the hangings, then her eyes moved to where the king was speaking to a tall man near the throne. They looked to be in serious discussion, but as Esther approached, both men turned to her with a smile.

The tall man's eyes were small and set close together, yet he was a relatively handsome man. He was perhaps in his midforties and had a regal air about him. His hair was about as long as the king's, although peppered with white among the black, as was his short, well-kept beard. Though his robes didn't belie that he was a prince, Esther assumed he was closely connected to her husband.

"Esther," Ahasuerus said, his tone mellow.

She could see by the darkness around the king's eyes that he'd had a long day. She wondered how many days he'd had like that. Esther prostrated herself, and when she stood, Ahasuerus took her hand and kissed it.

"You look beautiful," he said.

She wanted to reply in kind but not with another person standing near. It was a bit disconcerting not to see her husband all day, especially after their night together, and then the next time they were together was in public. She wondered what he was thinking about her. And should she offer her condolences about the former prime minister?

"Esther, I'd like you to meet our chief judge, Haman."

Haman reached for her fingers and bent over them, delivering a soft kiss. "I am enchanted to meet you."

Esther realized she'd just been kissed by a man who Mordecai said hated the Jews. She suppressed a shiver. "Thank you, Chief Judge." She tried to recall what Mordecai had told her about this man.

The king grasped her hand again, and she clung to his. She could never tell him about her dislike for the man he had in a trusted position. Besides, Haman was the one who'd just ordered the prime minister's execution at the king's command.

The next moments were a blur as Haman and the king continued to speak in low tones and Esther tried to keep herself calm. There was no exterior reason to fear the chief judge, yet Esther felt extremely uncomfortable in his presence. Just knowing that Mordecai feared him made her wary.

The guests began to arrive—the princes, their wives, and other royal court members. Esther was grateful that she recognized several of them. She marveled that they could be so jovial soon after a morbid execution, but it seemed the feast would not go to waste.

Esther was seated across the room from the king, with men gathered on one side and the women on the other. Wives of the visiting princes surrounded her, all asking about her beautiful robe and the gifts she'd received the day before. Esther was as friendly as possible, yet she couldn't help glancing at Haman from time to time.

When the gossip turned to Meres and his wife, Esther didn't quite know what to say. She nodded a few times but kept silent in her opinion. Her instinct told her that her words might be repeated in a less favorable light, and anything she said would be held against the king.

Platters of steaming meats were brought in, followed by warm bread and soft cheeses. Esther reached for her wine goblet first and relished the soothing taste. It helped her relax and helped keep her gaze from Haman. She was just starting to enjoy the chatter around her when Karan tapped her on her shoulder.

Esther was surprised to see the maiden at the banquet table. "What is it?"

"A man named Mordecai wants to talk to you, and he's waiting outside the palace gates," she whispered. "He says it's urgent."

What was Mordecai doing? She couldn't leave the feast without drawing attention to herself. How could she explain to the king?

Nearby, Hatach had overheard. "It is not possible for just anyone to have an audience with the queen. Tomorrow, we'll see if he is cleared by the guards and if his message is truly urgent."

Karan looked from Hatach to the queen. "Very well," she said then left the table.

Even though Esther knew it was right to delay a meeting with Mordecai and follow the palace protocol, she didn't enjoy anything about the next rounds of food, nor did she enjoy the entertainment meant to honor her marriage.

What could be so urgent that Mordecai could influence a guard to contact her maiden? Then her heart dropped. Was it one of the children? Leah? Or perhaps Johanna?

At the first sign that the festivities were waning, Esther rose and excused herself. Hatach immediately questioned her, but she put a hand up to silence his questions. There was less disturbance at her departure than she expected, although she heard some tittering as she left—speculation on the reason for her early retirement. Esther's blush was well hidden beneath her veil.

Once outside the banquet, Esther said to Hatach, "I have a feeling that the man named Mordecai has information that cannot wait until tomorrow."

"Then I will be present when you meet with him."

"Very well," Esther said, because she didn't really know what else she could do.

Karan waited for her outside the throne room. The maid's gaze went furtively to Hatach then back to Esther. "Will you come to see the man now?"

Esther stopped and looked over at the guards who stood at the throne room entrance. She lowered her voice. "The man still waits? What is this about?"

"He wouldn't tell me anything. He says when you heard his name, you would come and that he does not want to come too far into the palace."

Her hesitation wasn't long, and with a glance at Hatach, she said, "So I shall meet him now. Show me the way."

Karan, Esther, and Hatach hurried down the wide set of stairs that Esther had climbed the morning before when she walked to her wedding. At the bottom of the stairs, they crossed a torch-lit courtyard. Then Esther followed Karan, with Hatach close behind, through a series of winding passages until they reached a small gate where two guards were posted.

"Allow the man, Mordecai, to enter," Esther said.

One of the guards opened the gate, and Mordecai stepped through almost immediately.

He stopped when he saw her, and his eyes widened. Then he dropped into the prostrate position. When he rose, Esther led him along the passageway, out of Karan's and the guards' hearing. Hatach followed but stayed several paces away. "What urgent news do you bring?" She hoped her voice sounded steady even though she feared what Mordecai might say.

"I have overheard a plot against the king's life."

Esther's mind spun. She knew there was danger surrounding the king and the palace and that guards were needed for protection. But to hear that there was an actual plot was disturbing.

Mordecai gripped his hands in front of him, and from the look in his eyes, Esther knew he was equally disturbed.

"It's among his own chamberlains," Mordecai said, looking past Esther to Chamberlain Hatach.

Esther stared at her cousin in the moonlight. "Who is it?"

"Chamberlains Bigthana and Teresh. They supervise the king's stables."

Esther was relieved it wasn't Hatach. She wanted to run back to the throne room to question the men. She knew both of them were sitting at the king's table right now. Her heart twisted as she thought of something happening to Ahasuerus. "What do I do? How do I stop this?" She drew closer to Mordecai. "Tell me everything you heard. Quickly!"

"I left the palace later than usual tonight, and I twisted my foot as I hurried out of the gate. I stopped inside the closest alcove to rest before hobbling home, and I heard voices above me." He paused as if remembering the conversation. "It sounded something like, 'The king will never know until it's too late.' Then another voice said, 'Many will rejoice in his death.'"

Mordecai looked down at his hands. "I am not a strong man and could not have confronted either man, but I decided I needed to see who had spoken. I reentered the gate with an excuse then hurried along the outer corridor until I found the proximity of the room.

"Just as I reached the area of the alcove on the opposite side of the wall, a door opened and two chamberlains exited. I knew who they were—from their requests at the treasury." He took a breath, lowering his voice. "Their faces paled when they saw me, like they were guilty of something serious. I smiled and hurried past as if I were on some sort of errand, but I've never been so scared in my life."

Esther put her hand on Mordecai's arm. "If they were plotting the king's death, then you are a very brave man."

He exhaled. "Maybe I misunderstood."

"Regardless, thank you for telling me. I will inform the king right away." She had no idea how she was going to pull him away from a banquet without violating some law of decorum. But the fear in Mordecai's eyes was real, and the pounding in her heart told her the danger was true.

She wanted to give Mordecai a kiss on the cheek in farewell but dared not. She didn't want Hatach to see.

"May the Lord speed your errand," Mordecai said then prostrated himself.

Tears pricked Esther's eyes as she watched her cousin hurry away, out into the night. Moments later, Karan was back at her side. Her eyes were bright with curiosity. Hatach's gaze was wary, but Esther didn't know if she could trust him with the information. Was Hatach in league with those who conspired to murder her husband and king?

As they ascended the stairs together, going toward the throne room, Esther turned to Hatach. "How might I go about gaining a private audience with the king when he is hosting a feast?"

He slowed on the step. "The king?" He lowered his voice. "This has to do with the king?"

At Esther's nod, Hatach said, "You can send a messenger, but to pull him out of a banquet—everyone will know."

"I was afraid of that." Esther turned to Karan and put a hand on her arm. "Can you do something for me? It's of the utmost importance. Tell the guards that the queen requests the presence of the captain of the guard."

She didn't know who else to trust, and she could only pray that Captain Gad was not involved in the plot against the king's life. She had met him at the wedding feast, and Ahasuerus told her that he trusted Gad with his life more than any person in the kingdom. So Esther had to put her faith in that. She didn't reenter the throne room but sent Karan on her errand. Two of her other maidens were waiting near the guards by the throne room. Their faces showed relief as Esther crossed to them.

"We'll return to my rooms now." She looked over at Hatach. "I'll call for you if you are needed."

The man bowed and stepped aside.

The maidens bobbed and hurried after Esther. She had much to do and little time to waste. How might two chamberlains carry out their evil plans? In a mock skirmish? In the dead of the night? During a sword training or perhaps while on a hunting excursion? Esther's mind turned over with possibilities, one after the other.

By the time they'd reached her private rooms, she was exhausted and heartsick.

She took off her veil and opened the balcony doors. The memories from the night before—standing on the balcony with her husband, discussing roses and the constellations—flooded back. He had to be warned immediately.

Where was Karan? Where was the captain of the guard?

Her maidens must have sensed her consternation because they sat together quietly, watching her pace the room.

Finally, the door opened, and Karan hurried in, followed by a large man—who looked every bit a warrior. Esther's head felt faint, but she remained in her stance. The man prostrated himself before her.

When he rose, Esther said, "Karan, take the women into the next room. I'll speak to Captain Gad alone."

Karan looked taken aback, and Esther knew it was a highly unusual request. But she was too unsure of whom to trust and could only hope she'd be forgiven of this untoward step. When the door shut behind the women,

Esther turned back to Gad. "Thank you for your haste. I did not plan to meet you for the first time in such a circumstance, but I need your oath tonight."

If there was any curiosity or perhaps even astonishment on Gad's part, he never showed it. His expression was calm, and Esther's heart rate slowed a notch. She knew, or hoped, this man was true to King Xerxes.

"You are to report to the throne room and let the king know that you have been commanded by me to escort him back to my room when his feast has concluded. I've been made aware of a threat to the king's life."

At this, one of Gad's brows lifted.

"He is not to leave the throne room with any prince, any chamberlain, any servant. Only you and your most trusted guards have permission to bring him here."

Gad gave a slight nod. "Very well, Your Highness."

Her voice caught, and she felt dangerously close to shedding tears in front of this man. "Do not delay another moment."

The captain's lips pressed together, and he turned and strode out of the room. The door silently swung shut behind him. Esther sank to her knees and bowed her head. "O Lord, my God, preserve the king of Persia this night."

Chapter 19

AHASUERUS STRODE DOWN THE CORRIDOR until he reached the queen's rooms. He didn't wait for the guards to open the doors for him. He flung the door open to see Esther kneeling on the ground, her head in her hands.

For a moment, he feared something had made her ill. But then she lifted her head, and he saw that she'd been weeping. Was this a tantrum from his new wife? Although Ahasuerus took full blame for asking his wife to remove her veil in public, he couldn't forget her vanity, her perfection, and her insistence of having certain things to her specifications.

Was Esther too inexperienced and innocent of palace life to be a queen after all? Gad had come in right behind him, and Ahasuerus wondered if he should excuse the captain.

Esther rose, her gaze on the man behind him. "Shut the doors, Gad." Her voice was direct and in control, which belied the redness of her eyes.

Ahasuerus collected his temper. Perhaps this was not the female tantrum he feared. "What has happened, Esther?" he asked, controlling his emotions with great effort. When Gad had come into the feast with several guards, Ahasuerus had felt a jolt of panic go through him. Had Tarsena's wife done something awful, like burn herself in her house? It had been done before in acts of defiance against royalty.

But when Gad had whispered that he was there on the queen's orders and that only the captain was allowed to escort the king back to his private rooms, Ahasuerus didn't waste a moment.

The people in court could talk all they wanted. He was sure that gossip would go far and wide about something wrong between the king and his new wife. As much as Ahasuerus cared for Esther, he could not accept another wife who disobeyed or threw tantrums. He'd discover what was behind her bold actions and confront her immediately.

But the woman standing a few paces from him was not throwing a tantrum. Her head was raised high as she met his questioning gaze.

"There has been a plot against your life, Your Highness. Two of your most trusted chamberlains seek to destroy you." Her pause was brief. "The man Mordecai, who works in your treasury, overheard them plotting."

Ahasuerus looked from Esther to Gad then back to Esther. "What did Mordecai overhear?" As Esther told him, he sank onto the nearest divan. It was unbelievable. Both chamberlains had been in his service since early in his reign.

Understanding dawned as he realized that Prime Minister Tarsena had been the one to recommend them both. The king searched his memories—thinking there might even be a family relationship between Tarsena and one of the chamberlains.

His head dropped into his hands as Esther finished her report.

"Do you find any fault in Mordecai's story?" Ahasuerus asked.

"No, Your Highness, I do not," she said in a quiet voice.

Ahasuerus looked up to see Esther's gaze on Gad, as if she were trying to determine the loyalty of the captain. Rising to his feet, he said, "Captain, bring the chamberlains immediately to my private rooms. I'll question them there, and if necessary, they will be tried at court in the morning."

When Gad exited the room, Ahasuerus turned to Esther. Her face was pale. "Is this why you left the feast early?"

"Yes," she whispered. With Gad out of the room, she looked less like a queen and more like a frightened woman.

"Come here," he said. She took a tentative step forward, and he pulled her into his arms.

She wrapped her arms about his waist and laid her head against his chest. "I didn't know what to do. I didn't want to raise an alarm in case it allowed the chamberlains to escape." She looked up at him, her eyes filling with tears. "I'm so afraid, Ahasuerus."

The way she said his name tugged at his heart. The fear and concern in her voice were real. He brushed away a tear on her cheek and leaned down to kiss her forehead. "How did the man Mordecai know to contact you?"

"He's the one who brought me to the harem." She seemed to hesitate. "He hoped if he could get me the message that the matter would be dealt with before . . . before anything could happen."

Ahasuerus touched the lock of hair that had fallen to her shoulder. "Mordecai is a wise man. He works in the treasury, right?"

Esther nodded then leaned against him.

"You are tired, and it will be a long night," he said. "You should retire to bed."

Her arms tightened about his waist. Then she released him and looked up. "Wake me when you have news." She touched his face. "Be safe, my husband."

He took her hand and kissed it. "I will."

Esther was nothing like Vashti, who would have never dared to meet with someone from the outside. He realized that Esther was more faithful to him than he could have hoped.

By the time he reached his own chamber, three guards were waiting for him. One of the guards stepped forward. "Bigthana has poisoned himself, and Teresh ran. The captain will have him soon though."

They are both guilty, then, the king realized. "Have the healer purge Bigthana's stomach," he ordered the guard. "Then bring him along with Teresh."

Ahasuerus strode into his chamber. All was quiet and peaceful within, opposite of the emotions going through his heart. How much more damage would occur as a result of the prime minister's actions? It was unbelievable that the chamberlains were more loyal to the prime minister than to their own king. He owed Mordecai his utmost gratitude, as well as Esther. But first, justice had to be completed.

A knock sounded at the door, and the king was not surprised to see Biztha come inside. "You've heard the news?"

The man nodded, his hands twisting nervously together.

"Their actions reveal their guilt. We'll have court tonight. Clear the throne room of all women, and inform Chief Judge Haman that the hearing will begin as soon as those traitors are delivered."

"Yes, Your Highness."

"We'll find a way to reward the man, Mordecai, later. He is the one who brought it to our attention."

"He's that Jew who works in the treasury."

Ahasuerus nodded. "A Jew who is more loyal than my own chamberlains. Do not let me forget his kindness."

Biztha bowed and left.

For a moment, Ahasuerus stared at the closed door. Then he took a deep breath and exited the chamber to see two more men of his court condemned to die.

* * *

Esther did not think she'd ever fall asleep, but when her bed moved slightly, she realized that's exactly what she'd done. And now the king had come to her room. He lay on his back, his hands interlaced behind his head as he stared upward.

Esther didn't know if he was upset or if he was just thinking. Her maidens had left her room before there was any news about the chamberlains' fate. She cringed to think about what might have happened if Mordecai hadn't overheard them talking.

She scooted over to Ahasuerus and laid her head on his shoulder. He turned and pulled her into his arms, and she nestled against him. Relief washed over her. He was accepting her comfort.

"Have they been sentenced?" she whispered against his neck.

"The chief judge has ordered that they be hanged at dawn." His tone was emotionless.

"Oh, Ahasuerus. This has been a terrible day for you."

He said nothing but exhaled, his warm breath touching her face.

Tears welled in her eyes. She'd only been married one day, but the thought of losing her new husband had caused real fear. Now he was safe, and he was with her, above all others whom he could be with. She wanted to kiss him but did not know how he'd respond in this time of heartbreak. Instead, she stroked the side of his face then moved her fingers through his hair.

His body relaxed, and when he fell asleep, only then did Esther close her eyes again.

Before dawn could brighten the sky, she awoke to find Ahasuerus sitting on the edge of the bed. His head was bowed, and he was whispering something. His torso was bare and his silhouette dark against the gray of the sky that could be seen from the windows. He must have parted the window hangings to allow the morning light in.

Esther watched him for a moment, and when he finished whispering, she sat up.

He turned toward her, and she saw a small gold statue of Ahura-Mazda in his hand. For a moment, she wished she could tell him about the true God, the one God who looked over everything and everyone.

"I need to surround myself with people who are trustworthy and loyal," he said in a quiet voice.

Esther reached for his hand, and he grasped it. "Surely there are many who are trustworthy."

He looked at her, but she couldn't quite read the expression in his gaze. Could he guess that she hadn't been totally honest with him? What would he think if he knew she was a Jew?

"I'm not as confident as you, Esther, to believe that there are many loyal people in the land."

She squeezed his hand, wishing she knew the politics and the people better and that she didn't have to hide her religion from him. "Is there anything I can do to help you?"

"You already have," he said, his eyes on her. "You married me, and then you saved my life."

"That was Mordecai," Esther said.

Ahasuerus pulled her toward him. "But if Mordecai hadn't felt he could alert you, his message might have been too late." He rested his forehead against hers. "Thank you, Esther."

She smiled, although her heart still ached for him, ached that she was betraying him as well. He drew her closer and kissed her. Esther decided to forget what the future might bring and relaxed into his kiss, grateful he was with her at this moment and that he could talk to her about his concerns in the kingdom. When she'd married him, she wasn't sure what her role would be as his wife. She hadn't even expected him to spend a second night in a row in her room since he had other women who would expect him as well.

The more he kissed her, the more she didn't want him to leave. She'd have to spend another day away from him, and when the all-male religious festivals approached, she'd spend days and weeks away from him. She knew he had to leave soon—dawn was quickly approaching—but she allowed herself a bit of indulgence.

"I will pray that you'll find a new prime minister soon," she whispered. "One who will do right in the eyes of the Creator." She'd mentioned his god, although she would be praying to her own. Her heart thumped as he cradled her face and deepened his kiss in response.

Chapter 20

THE DAY PASSED SWIFTLY AS Esther took a full tour of the palace. The traitors had been hanged before her morning meal was served, and Esther knew her husband would not join her until evening, at the final wedding feast.

Esther requested the tour with the intention of learning how everything was run and meeting more people. Also, she hoped to visit her friends in the harem. She wore a robe the color of a ripe orange, a pale-yellow veil, and her crown. Walking along the corridors with Hatach and her maidens, she was humbled as the court members and servants prostrated themselves as soon as they saw her.

Along the way, she stopped and asked several people their names. She and her maidens toured the courtyards, all heavy with foliage, and walked through beautiful archways designed with intricate mosaic tiles. When she arrived at the cooking rooms, she marveled at the high ceilings and row of fire pits along one side.

In one corner, dried herbs hung, and in another corner, a couple of women were grinding herbs against a stone slab.

A large woman with rough, red hands hurried forward and prostrated herself. "Your Highness, is there something you need?"

"Who is in charge of the cooking?" Esther asked.

The woman dipped her head. "I'm the head cook and oversee all preparations."

Esther clasped the woman's hand. "Thank you for your good service. What's your name?"

The woman's face went as red as her hands. "Channah."

"Channah, do you have an herb garden?" Esther asked.

"Oh, yes, Your Highness."

"May I see it?"

"If you insist, Your Highness. But watch your step; there is only dirt for a floor."

Esther smiled and followed the woman through a low door and down three steps. The herb garden was walled in, with large trees in each corner. The ground might be dirt, but the rows of herbs were laid out in a precise and straight manner. It was plain that great care had been taken in cultivating the herbs.

Smells of spice and flora tickled Esther's senses, and she sneezed.

The head cook chuckled. "It's quite fragrant out here," she said.

"This garden is beautiful," Esther said with a smile. She almost said that her cousin Leah would love it as well, but she stopped herself in time. Moving past the head cook, she walked along the rows, stopping every once in a while to bend down to touch a leaf or a bud. She snapped off a lavender stem and brought it to her nose to inhale its fragrance.

Channah beamed. "You may visit the garden anytime, Your Highness. Of course, we have additional spices brought in from Egypt."

"Thank you for letting me see the garden," Esther said. "It's lovely here." She crossed to the steps to reenter the cooking room, casting another glance at the neat rows of plants. There was no splendor or lavishness here, just simple rows of herbs growing out of the earth. They needed only water and sunshine to thrive. So simple and so opposite of palace life.

Voices hushed as she entered the cooking room. "Thank you," she said, nodding to the servants who stood gaping at her. By the time Hatach led her and her maidens to the harem, Esther was quite amazed. The palace employed hundreds of people, all working in their own little dominion. And Esther was determined to get to know each area, no matter how small or lowly. These were the people who were invaluable to the palace running and supporting the royal lifestyle.

A guard opened the door into the harem, and Esther immediately felt the onset of nostalgia, which was ironic to consider. Hatach waited by the entrance as Esther walked into the courtyard. It didn't take long for Hegai to spot her, and he came rushing over. She grasped his hands then kissed both of his cheeks. His face reddened with the attention.

"You look splendid, Your Highness."

"It is wonderful to see you," Esther said.

A screech followed by running footsteps caught her attention. Nan ran through the courtyard then halted suddenly and went into a prostrate position. When she stood, there was a big smile on her face and tears in her eyes. "I know it's only been two days, but I've missed you so much."

Esther laughed and pulled the woman into her arms. Sarah came next and received an equally enthusiastic greeting from Esther.

Hegai folded his arms, his brow wrinkled. "We heard of the executions."

"Yes," Esther said. "The king has had much to deal with—and so soon after our wedding."

Nan looked at her with eager eyes. "How was the wedding?"

The wedding was a vivid blur of color and music in Esther's mind. "It was beautiful. The king wore all white, and you would not believe the piles of gifts we received."

"And the wedding night, how did you fare?" Nan said in a conspiratorial voice.

"Nan!" Sarah reprimanded. "You're addressing the queen of Persia!"

Nan's face reddened. "Forgive me, Your Highness."

Esther put her arm around Nan with a smile. "I know you only ask because you care for my well-being." She looked at Hegai, whose mouth was set in a disapproving line. "My wedding night was wonderful."

Nan clapped her hands together, and even Sarah smiled.

Hegai cleared his throat. "Would you like to sit for a drink and rest for a moment?"

Taking up his offer, Esther sat with them in the garden, describing the wedding festivities and the many people she'd met so far. "It's amazing what it takes to run the palace. Did you know there is an entire herb garden just for spicing the foods? As well as spices brought in regularly from Egypt?"

"Yes," Nan burst out. "A camel caravan arrives every fortnight with goods for the king. That's where most of your silk comes from."

Esther smoothed her robe over her knees. She'd almost forgotten what it would be to wear a coarse linen tunic. She wished she could share some of her wealth with her cousin's family and Johanna.

She looked into her friends' eyes. "Is there anything you need that I can help you with?"

Hegai shook his head. "You have done so much already for us. We feel proud that we were able to assist in your preparations."

Nan and Sarah nodded their agreement. These people were so different from the ones who frequented the court. They were humble, hardworking, and kind. She wished the king could get to know them.

She sipped the wine that Hegai had brought.

"The harem feels rather quiet now after all those years of preparing women to interview with the king," Hegai said.

"Have all the women settled back in their homes now?" Esther asked.

"We have not heard," Sarah said. "We can only assume their dowries were generous enough to secure a husband."

"And the women who remained?"

"They are in reserve for . . . the guests of the king." Sarah clasped her hands together on her lap, an uncomfortable smile on her face.

Esther nodded. She had assumed that marriage for the king wouldn't change his or his guests' habits. Although Sarah hadn't exactly said the king would still visit the harem, Esther could assume it would be the case as well.

At least he hadn't been here the past two nights.

There was one area in the palace Esther wouldn't visit today, or any other day, and that was the concubines' rooms. They were women who must hold a place in the king's heart for him to select them and father their children.

Sitting in the garden reminded Esther of all the months of waiting and wondering she'd done before her interview with Ahasuerus. After he'd chosen her, the time had sped by as she had prepared his marriage gift, something she had yet to give him.

"You will have to see the stables," Sarah said. "The king has magnificent horses."

"And the weapons room," Hegai said, his eyes shining. "He is said to have weapons spoilage in there from the Greek war."

"The war in which King Darius was defeated?" Esther asked.

"Yes, and many in the kingdom are in support of avenging that loss," Hegai said. "But we should not speak of such things. Some are saying the prime minister's swift execution happened because he was a supporter of going back into battle."

"And the king is not a supporter?" Esther asked.

Hegai lowered his voice. "If he were, our army would already be there, siding with the Spartans against the Athenian empire." He shook his head. "It's too dangerous to speak of such things, even in the harem courtyard."

"Thank you for telling me," Esther said. "I know very little of battle strategy." She could ask Mordecai, but she couldn't very well call him in for a council without bringing attention to the fact that she was meeting with a Jew.

When Esther left the harem, she was ready to return to her rooms but decided to visit the weaponry room first. Her maidens and Hatach followed her obediently, probably thinking how strange she was.

Karan took a couple of wrong turns before they reached the right set of doors. The posted guards looked surprised to see the queen and her entourage.

They stood quickly from where they sat playing the board game of twenty squares.

Esther greeted them. "May we tour the weapons room?"

The guard on the right leapt to his feet and stuttered, "I-If it be your desire." He reached for the door and opened it. "I'll l-lead you around so no harm will come to you."

Esther smiled to herself. She wasn't planning on picking up any weapons. The doors opened into a low-ceiling room with small windows that sat near the roof. The first thing she noticed was the thick dust. It made her throat tickle.

As she stepped forward, following the guard, her feet brushed against the layer of sand that coated the stone floor. Weapons were stacked on shelves that ran the length of all four walls. Some were piled on the floor. Javelins and spears were propped against the walls, and one shelf entirely held bows. Swords and arrows mixed together in haphazard stacks. Large baskets filled with knives looked to be the only organized part of the room. Esther wondered why the weapons had been allowed to fall into disrepair.

Esther slowed as they passed by helmets and breastplates. The metal had started to deteriorate and rust. She reached out and ran her fingers along the top ridge of a helmet. The rust stain was rough and scaly.

"Are these the weapons the king would use if there were an attack on the city?"

"Every soldier and guard has his weapon with him at all times," the guard said. "These weapons would only be needed if we had to prepare more soldiers. The king has his own room of personal weapons. These are all surplus."

"So only if there was an emergency?"

"Correct," the guard said.

"Perhaps the weapons should be kept in better condition and organized so they will be useful should an emergency arise."

The guard gave a nod. "King Darius kept this place immaculate. King Xerxes doesn't place the same emphasis on weapons of war."

"Some of this armor looks as if it might fall apart, and that wouldn't be very effective in a battle." She scanned the other piles of weapons. Although she couldn't tell if anything was actually broken, she'd never seen such neglect. "There is an oil made from almonds that will get some of these weapons back to usefulness." It was what Johanna had told Esther she used for her husband's farming tools. She assumed it would work with weapons as well.

"Very well, Your Highness," the guard said.

She completed the circuit of the room then stopped at the entrance. "All of this dirt and sand should be swept out as well. It will keep down the dust when the wind blows in from the windows."

The guard nodded. "Right away."

"Thank you." As Esther left with the maidens, she hoped the guard didn't resent her orders. She wondered how long it had been since Ahasuerus had seen the state of his weapons room. Maybe he wasn't concerned about it. But while he was busy with many other things, Esther felt she could help out in small ways.

While walking back to her rooms, she passed a set of elaborately carved dark-wood doors. "What's this room?"

"The chamber of writings," Karan answered.

There were no guards at these doors, and Esther wondered how that was so. Perhaps the writings were of lesser value than rusted metal?

"Let's go inside," Esther said.

Karan smiled and opened the doors. The chamber was dim. Dark red silk hangings covered the windows, and thick rugs ran along the floor. There were tables piled with metal and clay tablets, some of them looking cracked. Large cushions dotted the floor, along with several divans. She caught the smell of old oil, as if the oil lamps had long since been extinguished.

No one was inside. It looked like a forgotten room. She wondered how it had looked in Darius's day.

Esther walked in and crossed to the far wall. "Let's part these drapes so we can see better."

As the maidens scurried around opening drapes, the room came to life. Light spilled across tables and into the corners of the room. It revealed the rugs to be a deep scarlet flecked with gold thread. The cushions and divans were covered in tufted wool of many colors—faded greens and blues blending together into one hue.

Esther had heard of the libraries of Athens and Nineveh. In her mind, they'd teem with intellectuals discussing religion, art, and architecture. Servants would move in and out with jugs of refreshing tea.

But here, in this vast room of tablets, there was nothing but disarray, as if the purpose of the room had been forgotten for other pursuits.

"Does the king ever spend time in this room?" Esther asked mostly to herself.

Karan was nearby. "I don't think anyone comes in here. Perhaps in King Darius's day they did. Our king is very fastidious in keeping records of the kingdom's daily events, but what's in here is from bygone days and other countries. It seems there is not much interest in them."

Esther walked to one of the tables and trailed her finger through the dust. She blew on her finger, watching the dust particles shimmer in the sunlight. Picking up one of the clay tablets, she turned it toward the rays of sun. The writing was beautiful. She wished she knew what all the symbols meant.

Her gaze moved to a swatch of linen. On closer inspection, she realized it wasn't linen at all but a much stiffer fabric. The surface was rough, with lines running through it as if it had been woven. Tiny figures were painted on it. "What's this?" Esther said.

Karan joined her at the table. "I've never seen it before."

Esther examined the figures, marveling at the intricate use of color dyes. There were rows of dark-skinned people wearing little clothing and animals with skinny faces. "I think it's telling a story."

"The people look like Egyptians," Karan said. "At least, they look like the ones I've seen arriving by caravan."

The story panel was fascinating. It was like catching a glimpse into another land.

"We must find out what these are saying," Esther said, setting down the panel and picking up another one. The second one was full of strange symbols.

Hatach crossed over to the women and peered at the panel pieces. "It's the writing from Egypt."

"Beautiful," Esther murmured, studying the symbols. Her second day as queen was proving to be quite fascinating.

Chapter 21

"BINITI HAS DELIVERED A HEALTHY son," Shaashgaz said, prostrated on the marble floor of the throne room.

King Xerxes bade the keeper of the concubines to rise.

The portly eunuch nearly jumped to his feet. Perspiration bathed his face as if he'd run the whole way to the throne room. And perhaps he had. Shaashgaz was certainly out of breath.

"How does Biniti fair?" the king asked. This was her second child.

"She's strong and giving suck to the child."

The king let a smile escape. A healthy child and a safe birth were good omens indeed. He'd wondered if Ahriman, the god of destruction, had cast his evil eye over Persia the past couple of days. Since his marriage to Esther, treachery had abounded within the palace walls. Had it been Ahriman who had overpowered his twin brother, Ahura-Mazda, and voiced his displeasure?

Now, with the arrival of a healthy child, it seemed Ahriman was satisfied and Ahura-Mazda was dominant again. Today, the king would offer sacrifices to both gods, as well as the Creator, Zurvan Akarana. He didn't want any gods to feel neglected.

Shaashgaz's gaze was expectant.

"Do you have anything else to report?" the king asked.

"Biniti has requested the queen's blessing on the child," the eunuch said, twisting his hands together nervously.

The king considered the eunuch's request. None of the other concubines had had their children blessed by a queen. Vashti had refused to do it. She wouldn't go near any of the concubines, but Esther might consent. "You have permission to beseech the queen," he told Shaashgaz.

The eunuch's gratitude spilled out in a stutter. "Th-thank you, Your Highness." The man prostrated himself, still mumbling words of gratitude.

As he tottered out of the room, the king leaned over to chamberlain Biztha. "Bring me a report on how the queen receives the request."

Biztha smiled and exited the room as well.

By the time the king saw Esther, it was well after midnight and she was sound asleep. He'd never spent three nights in a row in the queen's chamber, not even in the early weeks of his marriage to Vashti. But the reports of Esther's doings throughout the day had reached him, one after another, each one bringing greater surprise than the one before.

He sat on the bed and listened to her even breathing in the moonlight. She looked guileless and unassuming—like a babe in her sleep. But she had caused a stir in the palace today. While he was in council interviewing royal cousins and princes for the position of prime minister, she'd walked through the herb garden with the head cook.

A smile tugged at the king's mouth. Biztha's report had been detailed in telling him that Esther had spent more than an hour in the harem—the courtyard to be sure—but the queen visiting the harem? It was unprecedented. And then she'd upturned the weapons room.

The king reached over and pulled the heavy fabric up higher, covering his wife's shoulders. "What were you thinking?" he whispered. The report from Biztha was that Esther ordered the weapons cleaned and oiled and everything from the helmets to the arrows to be organized.

Esther's next target was the chamber of writings. She'd ordered for it to be cleaned and for shelves to be built to organize the tablets and papyrus. And then the request from Shaashgaz had been granted. Esther had promised to give Biniti's child the queen's blessing.

Ahasuerus lifted the covers and scooted in next to Esther. He kissed her forehead and lay close enough that he could feel her breath on his face but without touching her. Esther's eyes fluttered open for a moment, and she blinked up at him. "Ahasuerus, you're here," she whispered then closed her eyes again. Asleep.

* * *

Esther woke to an empty room. Her husband was gone, but she knew he'd come in the night. She remembered his kiss on her brow and his whispered words—although she didn't know what he'd said.

Dawn was still new in the sky, so he must have risen early and already begun the day. Three nights. He had come to her three nights now. But her stomach knotted at the thought of what she must do today.

She had been quite exhausted when she had granted audience to the keeper of the concubines the evening before. The man had acted very nervous in her presence, which endeared him to her immediately. When he'd told her his name was Shaashgaz, Esther saw him relax a little bit, and although she was tempted to ask him dozens of questions about the king's concubines, she held back.

Now that it was morning, her maidens came into her room, and she dressed carefully. She didn't want to dress too elaborately, but she also wanted to make sure she looked the part of the queen. The women she'd meet were concubines of her husband and mothers to his children, although she was the one with the title.

If only Hegai were here to counsel her now. She didn't want her maidens to see how nervous she was. It would be her turn, instead of Shaashgaz's, to be breathless. She had never thought she'd be visiting the concubines' rooms.

Once she was dressed in her lavender robes of silk, she decided not to wear her crown but instead a band of amethyst gems around her head on top of her veil.

Karan led the way to the concubines' quarters. They were on the east side of the harem, a large garden separating the two sections, each with its own set of gates and guards. The first thing Esther heard as she stepped through the bronze-plated doors into a massive courtyard was the laughter of children.

Her heart stuttered for her cousins, little Abigail, Ben, and Samuel.

Several children played at the edge of a pond in the center of the courtyard. They looked up when she entered with her maidens. The oldest, a girl perhaps five or six years old, stood, her eyes wide. "The queen! It's the queen!"

Esther kept her smile to herself as the little children scrambled to stand next to the first girl. They all dropped into various forms of prostrations. Within a moment, Shaashgaz came into view. He rushed forward then stopped suddenly, prostrated himself, and rose again.

"Your Highness, welcome!" His face flushed as he spoke.

"These children are charming," Esther said. Her stomach was so tight it was hard to breathe. These were Ahasuerus's children. Ones he knew and most likely loved. Her heart tugged as she saw the resemblance in their features. The wavy dark hair, the deep brown eyes, the broad smiles.

All of the children stared up at her expectantly. How had Vashti endured this place full of children shared by her husband? The children were innocent; they played no part in the relationship between their mothers and the king.

It was as if they lived just on the edge of something they could never grasp. They could see all of the riches, but they'd never inherit or hold an office.

Shaashgaz was speaking again. "Biniti's room is this way. She is with the child."

Esther took a deep breath. She was about to meet one of the king's concubines. The room that Shaashgaz led her into was smaller than expected, but it was richly decorated.

A woman with a gently lined face looked up. She abandoned the embroidery in her lap and prostrated herself. Because of all the beautiful women Esther had met in the palace and those she'd trained with in the harem, she hadn't expected Biniti to be a plain woman.

"Biniti?" Esther said.

"Your Highness, I am honored," the woman said in a throaty voice. It was not soft and soothing as the harem workers had trained Esther and the other virgins to use but had an edge to it.

When the woman rose, her eyes were hard.

Esther felt she'd been jabbed. Biniti's words had been humble enough, but her sharp gaze said much, much more.

Esther was the intruder into the life of a concubine who had been living free of a queen's influence. Yet the woman had asked for the queen's blessing. Why? A soft cry sounded from a large basket in the corner of the room.

"The *boy* is awake," Biniti said, her emphasis on *boy*.

Following the woman to the basket, Esther peered down on the tiny infant. Another innocent child of the king. Biniti picked the child up and thrust him at Esther.

She nearly grappled to hold on to the child; he was so light in her arms. Even Samuel hadn't seemed as small as an infant. Esther looked down into the babe's murky gray eyes. She didn't exactly know what she was supposed to say or do, but perhaps Biniti didn't either. "What's his name?"

"Ramin," Biniti said in a proud voice. "It means *warrior*."

Biniti's tone stung. "I know what the name means," Esther said. Cradling the child in her arms, she closed her eyes. She didn't know if the woman was watching her or closing her eyes as well, but she decided to say a prayer in silence and pray for his health.

She could not bring herself to pray to Ahura-Mazda, either silently or out loud. She wondered what Biniti would think if she knew that the queen was praying to the Jewish god. When she finished, she opened her eyes.

Biniti was watching her.

"He's a beautiful child," Esther said, handing back the baby.

Biniti said nothing, just stared at her with that hard look.

Esther moved out of the room and into the bright courtyard again. More children had gathered together, standing next to women who must have been their mothers. Esther slowed and nodded at them with a smile. She didn't know if she should stop and speak to them.

There were four women. Biniti made five, and she was the only plain one. The others were beautiful, and one looked as if she could be royalty herself. Two of them whispered together then giggled. But it was clear to Esther that they stood as a united front—against her. They thought of her the same way Biniti did.

Not even in the harem had Esther felt like such an outsider. These were women who lived in the palace as well, but it was plain they did not welcome her as the others at court appeared to. Or had the others at court truly accepted her? It seemed only terrible things had happened since the marriage. And some might see it as a curse from their gods. She knew it was a miracle that she had been chosen queen in the first place, but had everyone acted politely because they were in the presence of the king?

She decided to step forward and greet the women and children. Then she asked each of them their names. Even after giving their names, the women still eyed her suspiciously, but Esther couldn't let that bother her. At least that they could see. When she exited the courtyard, her eyes burned as she took slow breaths.

Her calm persevered as she and her maidens returned to her rooms. Once inside her chambers, she asked to be alone. And as the door shut, she crossed to the windows and closed the draperies, casting the room into gray.

She walked to the bed and exhaled. Ahasuerus had spent three nights with her here, but she knew it wouldn't last forever. The look in his concubines' eyes had told her she wasn't the only woman for the king; they were his women too, and they had borne his children—many of them.

Esther pressed her hands against her stomach. Could she already be with child? The darkness of the room seemed to gather around her. She was alone in this palace. Her friends in the harem were restricted to the harem. Karan and the maidens were sweet girls but not women who could guide her like a mother. The only woman who was close to a mother for Esther could never visit the palace—as a Jewish woman, Leah's connection would become too clear. Would she see Johanna again? Would their children ever meet?

I am lonely even in my faith, she thought. Other Jews worked at the palace in various positions, but none came in contact with her.

Esther sank to her knees and rested her arms on the bed. *O Lord, my God, is it my lot to live as a lonely woman?* Tears touched her cheeks, but she made no effort to wipe them away. *My children will be raised to worship Ahura-Mazda. They will not be taught the law of Moses. They won't observe the Sabbath as a holy day.*

Her head sank into her hands, and her shoulders shook with sobs, but all the while she was still chastising herself. She had known what it would be like when she'd agreed to marry the king. She'd known what it would be when she'd accepted Mordecai's counsel. This was the way of Persia. On one hand, it was noble what she was doing, but on the other hand, it hurt so much. So deeply.

O Lord, Thou art the only One I can confess my heart to. The only One who knows my sorrows. Please guide me to become the woman Thou wouldst have me be.

And if that meant sleeping in her grand bed alone as her husband spent the night in other women's beds, that would be the requirement in order for her to serve the Lord.

She must have fallen asleep on her knees because the next thing she knew, someone was lifting her. She opened her eyes to find Ahasuerus smiling down at her.

He'd set her on the divan. "You're here?" She couldn't help but smile back. Then she looked toward the windows. Daylight peeked around the edges of the draperies. "Have I missed something that I was supposed to attend?"

"No," Ahasuerus said, his eyes scanning her face. "You must be very tired to fall asleep on the floor."

"I . . ." *I was praying. And crying.*

"Biztha told me of your reprimand to my guards at the weapons room."

Her cheeks flamed hot. "I only meant—"

Ahasuerus laughed, then sat beside her and took her hands in his. "I think it's wonderful."

She stared at him, hardly daring to believe his enthusiasm. Her tearful prayers seemed to be something like a past dream as she looked into his lively eyes, and her heart fluttered.

He brought her hand to his mouth and kissed her fingers. "And I agree that the chamber of writings should be put to good use again. I'd much rather hunt than read. But my wife may read all the hours of the day if it pleases her."

"I don't know how to read."

He laughed again and touched her cheek. "That's why I've come to speak to you—while my guests drink my wine in the banquet room. You will have a tutor. He will teach you all the letters you want to know. You may learn as many languages as you want."

Esther's mouth fell open. "Then that means I'll learn to read my tablets. Oh—" She threw her arms around his neck, and he pulled her close, chuckling.

She pushed aside her tearful prayers of pleading with the Lord to help her endure and serve. This was a good man. She kissed his cheek. "I still need to give you the wedding gift." She rose and hurried to the corner of the room, where she'd stashed the wrapped article.

Ahasuerus smiled as she sat next to him on the divan and handed it over. "I didn't get you a gift," he said.

She laughed and waved a hand. "All of this is a gift." She was about to reference her previous home, but she stopped herself in time.

The king removed the cloth wrapping and held up the robe. It was lightweight silk with several colors blended together.

"Since I had less than a month, I enlisted the help of my maidens with the weaving. It's meant for nightwear, not really for public viewing. I don't think my stitching would hold up to anyone's scrutiny."

"You haven't been spending years on this like most Persian women?"

"I—" Her face reddened. "I didn't think you'd want the one I'd started at home. It wasn't really fit for . . . you."

"I love it." He leaned forward and kissed her cheek. He drew back and looked deep into her eyes. "I heard you gave the queen's blessing to Biniti's child today."

"Yes." She breathed, waiting for her heart to twist at the mention of his concubine and child. Ahasuerus's arms rested on her waist, and instead of her heart twisting, it expanded. "The child is beautiful."

He moved his fingers along her cheek, her jaw, her neck.

"How many concubines do you have?" she asked.

His fingers stopped moving. "There are five women."

"And how many children?" she whispered. She could have numbered them herself, but she hadn't the courage to.

"Only yours will count, Esther." His fingers moved behind her neck.

His words were sweet, which made her long for children, to have healthy sons who would make him proud, to have beautiful daughters whom he could marry to princes.

"The women did not seem to care for my presence in their courtyard," Esther said.

"Vashti never spent time there," he said, pulling back and gazing at her. "Your cheeks are growing red." His mouth moved into a smile. "Are you envious of those women?"

She turned her face so she wouldn't have to see his laughing eyes.

"Ah, my sweet Esther," he whispered. "You are queen of all of Persia, yet you're envious of a few concubines." He turned her face toward him. "My father had dozens of concubines, as well as hundreds of illegitimate children from other women, running around and all claiming a piece of the kingdom. I don't intend to have so many. I value my peace."

He lowered his face to hers and kissed her softly.

A tremor spread through Esther, warming her body, and she melted against him. As his kisses turned fervent, she forgot her worries and became lost in a world that was all him.

Chapter 22

THE DAYS PASSED SWIFTLY AS Esther found much to do around the palace. Despite her maidens telling her she didn't need to do so much, Esther pushed ahead.

The weapons room would have made any king proud by the time the cleaning and organizing was finished. Young scholars were invited to the palace to use the chamber of writings. And most importantly, Esther started working with the tutor. Master Shan was a small man with a large nose. He talked in a quiet voice, and Esther wondered if it was because he'd spent so much time reading and writing on tablets—things that made no noise.

On the night of the first day of tutoring, her husband didn't come to her chamber. She stayed awake waiting for him, eager to tell him she'd learned several words already, but he never showed up. And when she awoke in the morning, his side of the bed was cold and not slept in. She rose from her bed with a heavy heart.

It had happened. Her husband had stayed with one of his concubines. Her mind flashed over the women she'd seen in the courtyard and the curious eyes of the children. They'd claimed his attention long before she'd even met him. What did she expect?

Tears threatened as she crossed to the windows and drew open the drapery. The sun was already warming the land, and the sky was a bright blue. The king would be in council by now. She'd not see him for an entire day—and possibly another night. Who knew when she might see him again?

The morning passed slowly, and by the time the tutor showed up, she forced herself to break out of her melancholy and focus on the learning Ahasuerus had provided her. He'd given her a great chance. She couldn't waste it no matter how much her heart hurt.

That evening as she prepared for bed, having received no word of a feast nor any summons from the king to attend such an event, she took courage and asked Karan, "Any word of the king's activities today?"

"I have not heard anything, Your Highness," Karan said, avoiding Esther's gaze. The maiden continued to comb Esther's hair in silence.

Esther put her hand on the woman's arm, stopping her movements. "Please. You may tell me. Where did he spend the night? Surely there has been talk." Whispers were constant in all corners of the palace.

Karan glanced over at the other maidens. One by one, they slipped out of the chamber. Then she looked toward Esther, her eyes still not quite meeting the queen's. "He was not in the harem, nor with the concubines, if that's what you're wondering."

Relief shot through Esther, but it didn't last long. "Then . . . where did he spend the night?" It was strange to be asking this young woman about the king—if anyone should know where he'd slept, it should be her, the queen.

"I heard he was visiting Prince Admatha's estate. I can only assume he spent the night there."

"When did he return?"

"I am not certain of that either. He was in council this afternoon but left again for another feast given by Prince Admatha."

Esther swallowed back her disappointment and forced her expression to remain neutral. "Thank you for telling me. I want to be a good queen, and the more I know about my husband, the more I can serve."

Karan nodded and continued brushing Esther's hair.

The strokes were soothing and reminded Esther of the times in the harem when Nan would brush her hair. She closed her eyes for a few moments as Karan worked. Finally, Esther said, "I'll retire to bed now. Thank you for your help."

"Do you need me to stay in your room tonight?"

"No," Esther said, although she was touched by the offer. What if the king returned after the feast? Karan extinguished the oil lamps before she left the room, and Esther was left alone in the darkness.

She slipped out of bed and knelt on the floor to pray. Her prayer was short, her heart too tender to voice her concerns. When she finished, Esther rose and climbed beneath the silk coverings, the luxury of the fabric soft around her.

She had more than any other woman in the kingdom, yet she was alone in so many ways. Why had her husband spent the night at the prince's home? What could have been so important that they needed to talk late into the night? Or to feast or to drink? Had there been women there?

She didn't know how long she'd slept before she felt a warm body nestle against hers.

"Esther," he whispered, and just like that, she was fully awake. "I have found a new prime minister."

The happiness in his voice, as well as his presence, made her smile. "Who is it?" she asked.

"Chief Judge Haman."

The warmth faded from Esther, and even where Ahasuerus's body met hers, she felt a distinctive chill. Haman was the man Mordecai feared the most.

"He was the most natural choice; I should have seen it all along," he said.

Do I have the power to change my husband's mind about his choice of prime minister? O Lord, what should I say? There was nothing she could say, she realized, without telling the king that she was a Jew and that Haman hated her people. Now this man would have immense power in the kingdom.

"Has he accepted?" Esther whispered, too worried that if she tried to speak aloud her voice would tremble.

"He has graciously accepted," Ahasuerus said, his breath warm against her neck. "I will miss having him as a judge—typically a lifetime assignment—but I cannot overlook his usefulness to me."

Esther lay still as her husband touted the virtues of Haman. If it hadn't been for Mordecai's worries about the man, Esther might have been convinced by what the king said. Could someone who hated a group of people really be so fair in judging and really have the best interest of the kingdom in mind?

"Is that why you've been gone from the palace? You were in council with Prince Admatha about whom to select?"

There was a pause, then he chuckled. "Not exactly. Admatha's first son was born, and I went to the celebration." He moved his fingers through her hair, brushing it away from her neck and shoulders.

Esther was quiet for a moment. "Are women not invited to such events?"

The king's hand stilled. "Women were there . . . so I suppose I could have brought you." He pressed his mouth against her jaw. "It's been a long time since I've had a wife."

Esther wondered what other things he was in the habit of doing without a wife at his side. She hoped her husband would take her along to the next celebratory event. And she hoped that Haman's new assignment as prime minister would not be such a concern for Mordecai or her people. These thoughts made her stomach harden with worry, but then Ahasuerus started kissing her and sufficiently distracted her thoughts.

* * *

Esther had mentally prepared herself for the king's hunting. Their marriage was only a few weeks new, but she didn't want to be known as a complaining wife. At least he wouldn't be with his concubines. In fact, Karan had told her he hadn't visited the concubines' quarters since the wedding, except for short visits to the children.

But Esther hadn't realized how her husband's absence would feel. Typically, she didn't see him all day but knew he was in the palace or close by. Now, he was truly gone. Everything in her chamber seemed a bit forlorn, the colors dimmer, the bed harder, and the sunlight weaker.

She tried to stay busy to keep her mind occupied. It was only a couple of weeks, and then he'd return to the palace. She made rapid progress in her reading and visited the harem workers every few days, since she couldn't very well insist they come see her in her quarters. Hegai could move about the palace quite freely, yet Sarah and Nan could do so only with special permission. Only her maidservants or royal guests were allowed in her quarters.

So it was with surprise when she rounded the final corner to the harem gate and met Haman. She'd only met him once before, but she recognized him immediately. She came to a stop, and her maidens halted as well and bowed before the prime minister.

He was probably the tallest man at court, and his close-set eyes reminded her of a ferret. He prostrated himself immediately with quite a flourish, as if he found amusement in meeting her.

"Queen Esther, you look divine." When he rose, he grasped her hand and kissed it, his trimmed beard tickling her fingers. His robe was not that of the judiciary anymore but was a deep purple and looked significantly royal. He was the decision maker in the king's absence. "Visiting the harem again?"

Esther felt uncomfortable responding. Her maidens, as well as the guards at the harem gate, would hear everything. Now she was regretting that she'd told Hatach he didn't need to come along, for she wasn't sure how to answer Haman. Finally, she said, "The harem workers were very good to me while I lived there."

Haman flashed a smile, and Esther noticed he had exceedingly white teeth. "It must be like home to you. And I am sure the harlots love to receive visits from the queen."

Esther looked away from him, toward the nearby gate. His tone had sounded belittling. "As I said, Hegai has been very good to me." She met his amused gaze.

His mouth twisted into a half smile. "You do know he's a eunuch."

Esther's face heated. It was as if Haman was implying something inappropriate. "Of course he is, as are all of the men who deal closely with the harem and the king's concubines." Saying the last made her feel more bold and courageous, as if she had no qualms over her husband's relationships with other women.

He bowed deeply. "As you wish. I'll not interfere with the queen's private matters." He grasped her hand again and kissed it.

Esther had to compose herself in order to not tug her hand away from his touch. She turned toward the gate, embarrassment coursing through her, but Haman's voice stopped her.

"Queen Vashti had her means of entertainment brought to her. There's no need for the queen to go traipsing about the palace to find enjoyment." He chuckled low and deep. "I can certainly arrange for your satisfaction."

She slowly turned her head to look at him. His lips were curved, and his close-set eyes bore into her. She felt cold all over and struggled with an answer. Finally, she shook her head. "I ask you to refrain from such suggestions," she said, but it came out as a whisper.

His smile broadened. "Very well. If you change your mind, I'm at your service, Your Highness."

Esther couldn't move, couldn't speak, and stayed rooted in place as he bowed and continued past her down the corridor. She listened until his footsteps had completely faded before she allowed herself to breathe. He was an awful man, vile, and he'd insulted her. Hot anger pulsed through her, but she pushed it down as she walked toward the harem gate.

The guards were watching her, and her maidens had seen and heard everything. There was no privacy now. There could be no tears. She didn't know what manner of man Haman was, but for him to say those things to her—when he didn't even know she was a Jew—seemed beyond her imagination. How did he treat Jewish women?

She walked slowly through the gate after the guards opened it. What if others in the palace had the same suppositions as Haman? When she saw Hegai rushing across the courtyard to greet her, tears pricked her eyes.

Hegai was a dear man, caught up in a life he hadn't requested, much like many in the palace. He was a eunuch and would never enjoy the full opportunities manhood presented. And he had been nothing but kind to her. She wondered how much she could trust him or how much the rumors about her visits might hurt him. After Hegai prostrated himself, she greeted him then moved to one of the courtyard benches.

"Nan and Sarah will be sorry they missed you today," he began. "They've gone to the market."

Esther had been inside these palace walls for more than a year, so the idea of walking to the market and buying anything now seemed foreign to her. She was in a completely different world now.

She took a breath and leaned quietly toward Hegai. "Do you think you could arrange for Mordecai to meet with me in private? I'd like to thank him for his help in revealing the plot against the king." She looked around. No one else was in the courtyard but Karan, but still she felt that anyone could be watching.

"I'll arrange for him to meet you in the queen's receiving room."

Esther smiled. It would be a place far from Haman and whoever spied for him.

Less than an hour later, Esther waited inside the receiving room. She had to tell Mordecai about Haman and ask him for advice. Someone rapped on the door, and Karan went to pull it open.

Esther's heart leapt when she saw her dear cousin enter the room. His expression was subdued, but she noticed the liveliness of his eyes.

Karan hovered near the door, seeming to wonder if she should stay in the room.

"Karan, you may wait outside," Esther said. Once the door shut behind the maiden, Esther turned to Mordecai and kissed both of his cheeks.

"My dear, Leah and the children send their love," he said.

Unexpectedly, Esther's eyes filled with tears. "Tell me about the children. What are they doing? What do they look like?"

Mordecai smiled and talked of how Samuel had started walking and Ben had declared his infinite distaste in all girls who couldn't climb a tree with him and Abigail had begun embroidering.

Esther memorized every word he said and tucked it away in her mind to savor later. But when Mordecai finished his account, she grew sober. "You have undoubtedly heard the news about Haman's assignment as the new prime minister."

Mordecai looked toward the door as if he suspected someone was listening. "Yes," he said in a low voice. "And he is already abusing his power. As a judge . . . he was fair in most things inside the court, although he took many liberties outside the court. Today, he was wearing the royal purple colors."

"Yes. I saw him a short time ago when I was going to visit Hegai."

"Did he speak to you?" Mordecai asked.

Esther nodded and told him all that Haman had said to her—all that he'd implied. Mordecai's face was red by the time she finished.

"His words are insulting," Mordecai said, gripping his hands together. "But I don't think it's something you can complain about to the king. Haman's opinion might be shared by others who think the queen shouldn't be so involved in palace activities."

"What should I be involved in?" she asked. "The king has complimented me on my resourcefulness. He's even given me a tutor to teach me to read."

Mordecai smiled and touched Esther's arm. "The king is remarkable in many ways. But because of men like Haman and what their cutting remarks might lead to, you'll need to stop visits to the harem. It probably makes all the royal men nervous, including Haman."

Esther thought about what her cousin had said. Could that be the answer behind Haman's comments? He thought she was spying or keeping track of who went to the harem?

"Do you know anything about Vashti and if what Haman says is true?"

Mordecai blew out a breath. "Many things in the palace and among the Persian people are not what we teach in our religion." His eyes looked sad. "I don't know if Haman spoke the truth, but you might find yourself having to stand up for your values."

"All right," Esther said.

"Haman is a clever man, and you would do well to take care," Mordecai said, watching her.

"What do you mean?" Esther asked. "He doesn't know that I am a Jew."

"Men like him have eyes all over the palace and stay informed of everything. If he sees anything amiss, he might start to suspect your true identity."

"What can I do about that?"

"You must stay away from the harem and any place where you might raise questions, which could be anywhere as far as Haman is concerned." Mordecai offered a gentle smile. "When the king is not present at the palace, it's probably best to keep to your own quarters."

Esther understood Mordecai's concern. But she already felt confined in keeping to the palace, and now her cousin was counseling her to not even leave her rooms. Maybe his counsel was sound, but she'd have to think about it. "Perhaps you're right."

Being able to speak with Mordecai already strengthened her faith, but once he left and she was faced with imposing men like Haman, would she be able to keep her religious beliefs hidden? And how long did she have to keep her secret?

"How should we communicate?" she asked. "If Haman is watching everything, it's probably not safe to meet like this."

Mordecai nodded. "You're right. We will have to find a way. Leah and the children ask about you each evening. They will be happy to learn that I was able to meet with you today."

Esther closed her eyes briefly, trying to imagine a time when she might see Leah and the children again—it would happen only if the king knew and accepted who she really was. "How long can I keep my faith a secret?" she said mostly to herself.

"It's not time yet, Esther," Mordecai answered. "Until the Lord lets us know, you will have to trust in Him."

"It's so difficult," she said. "To keep something this important from my husband. I'm also afraid. What if he rejects me once he finds out? I can't stop thinking about Vashti. She was dismissed for less."

Mordecai's hand grasped hers and squeezed. "You will find a way for the people to get to know you and love you. When you tell the king you're Jewish, there will already be a strong foundation."

Esther wanted to believe her cousin, but she wasn't sure. The king had his closest advisor put to death, and he didn't hesitate to be rid of those who'd plotted against him. When they were alone, he was tender and caring. But she'd seen both sides of him and knew there were no second chances with King Xerxes.

Chapter 23

"I WILL GO TO THE market today," Esther announced as Karan combed through her hair. "We'll bring guards, and I will select a gift for the king to give him upon his return."

Karan's hands stilled. "Are you certain, Your Majesty?"

No, Esther thought. *But I will not let Haman keep me cowed.* And if she was going to get the people to know her, she had to meet them. She would need all the help she could get when she told the king the truth, for she was determined to tell him the truth. She'd realized that more than anything in his absence. If she wanted a true marriage with Ahasuerus, he had to know her true self.

"And bring me silver coins," Esther said. The king would go almost straight from the hunting excursion to the month-long protocol in honor of the Creator, Zurvan Akarana, held in the inner court. She would not see him during that month because no one was allowed to approach the king in the inner court unless invited.

The men of the royal court, including the visiting princes, would spend the month with the Magi, listening to the history of the Persian gods and learning about the religion that was the basis for their beliefs. Esther didn't understand why it would take a month, but the king had explained it a little before he left—it was more tradition than anything else. And it was the precursor to making important decisions for the country. Esther knew the king hoped to put to rest the cry for war with Greece once and for all. If the people of Persia knew that pursuing peace was a decision made in council during protocol, they'd consider it a commandment from their god.

The sun indicated it was nearing midday by the time Esther reached the main palace gate. Her entourage had grown, doubling then tripling, as orders were given to secure her venture. More than a dozen guards led the way, and more brought up the rear. Esther had her seven maidens with her, as well as Hatach.

Esther exhaled as the gates opened. At last, she'd be stepping outside the palace. She just hoped her delicate slippers would hold up on the road. She'd worn her lightest robes, but they were still heavy beneath the glaring sunlight.

She was a few steps past the gates when someone called out, "Your Highness!"

Esther recognized Haman's voice, and dread shot through her. Why was he calling her, and what would he say in front of all of these people?

She stopped and waited for the man to catch up. He prostrated first, and when he stood in front of her, she said, "Yes?"

"I heard you are traveling to the market this morning." Haman clasped his hands together, his jeweled rings flashing in the light.

She gave a small nod.

"Then allow me to accompany you." He tilted his head, his smile too bright. "I am sure the king would wish it."

"I am safe, my lord. Certainly the king will wish for you to care for the concerns of the kingdom during his absence," Esther said, inwardly cringing that she had to be firm with him. She didn't want to spend the day with this man. Not after the things he'd said to her and not after knowing he might be spying on her.

His smile remained. "I must say that *you* are the greatest concern of the kingdom in His Majesty's absence. Therefore, you *are* my greatest concern." Haman's gaze trailed from Esther's face down to her slippered feet. "Allow me to suggest you take the litter. A queen does not walk in the dirt to the market."

Esther paused. Haman was probably right. Should she go ahead and continue walking or listen to him? She didn't dare look to Hatach for his recommendation. "It's only a brief journey."

One side of Haman's mouth lifted, and he scanned the length of her body again, causing Esther to shudder inwardly.

"Even so," he said in a smooth voice, "I'll arrange for the litter to be brought right away so there will not be any more delay."

Esther had barely agreed before Haman was throwing out orders. Within a few minutes, a group of guards came back carrying a high-backed chair with a canopy to block the sun. They lowered it to the ground, and Esther entered the litter and sat down.

A horse had been fetched as well at Haman's order, and he mounted, apparently deciding he wouldn't be walking either.

The travel was slow with the litter and all of the accompanying people. Esther tried to remain calm and tell herself this was part of the process. She was no longer a village girl who could run to the market at any time.

The people in the roads stopped to stare at the passing procession, bowing to Haman then bowing to her. Esther waved at the people and received smiles in return. Once the litter reached the market, the gathered crowds surprised Esther. Perhaps word had spread, and everyone now seemed interested in catching a glimpse of the traveling queen.

Haman stayed close and commanded the guards to keep the people clear of her path. It was difficult to choose which booths to look at first because all of the merchants looked so pleased that she had come, and they kept bowing over and over, praising her. For a moment, she wanted to laugh at the absurdity of it all, but she didn't dare. She hadn't been to a Persian market in the heart of the city before. It was certainly more colorful and vibrant than the Jewish one she'd frequented.

After leaving the litter, she walked past the vast displays of nuts and fruits. Gemstones twinkled in the sunlight, and there was one display dedicated to curved daggers with jeweled hilts. Would one of them be fitting for her husband? She moved on, much to the protest of the various merchants. Silk fabric made into scarves and robes caught her attention, but she wasn't here to buy for herself.

Then a table of the largest display of thread drew her notice. The colors were tantalizing: deep greens, brilliant blues, soft yellows, and vibrant reds. She made her way to the display. As she picked up the dyed threads, she sneaked a few glances around. Did she know anyone here among the crowds? Any Jewish families from her neighborhood? No one looked familiar. Her heart sank. There was no way Johanna would shop at this noisy, crowded, very *Persian* place.

She selected several colors, set on stitching a scene about something in the palace. The merchant was so excited that his face turned as red as the scarlet threads. Once Karan had tucked the package of threads under her arm, the other merchants pressed forward, eagerly calling out to the queen.

Haman moved close to her and touched her elbow. "Unless you want to purchase another item, we should probably leave. The crowds are growing and will soon be difficult to manage."

Esther resented his intrusion, but her heart was beating quite fast at all of the commotion and attention surrounding her. So, knowing she was disappointing many hopeful merchants, she climbed back onto the litter.

* * *

Haman paced the gathering room of his home. It was well past midnight, and Thar had yet to arrive and report. Over the past weeks, Thar had gathered a good deal of information about Rebekah and the upcoming birth. The female cousin would be attending, which worked out perfectly for Haman. She would be easy to intimidate.

He'd already commissioned three guards, including Thar, who would abduct the child. Rebekah would be mad with grief to have her child taken. Haman regretted putting her through a period of sorrow, but it was the only way.

It would all work perfectly if her husband pursued the guards, who would then kill him in a skirmish over the stolen child. Rebekah's grief would double, like any good widow's. That was when Haman's role would come into play.

The timing had to be right: after her husband's funeral and when she'd given up hope of recovering her child. That was when Haman would send a messenger to deliver a handful of silver to let her know he'd heard of her misfortune and was offering his services in any way she needed.

He wasn't sure how it would play out from there. Perhaps she'd come to him directly. Perhaps she'd send a message back with the messenger. Perhaps she'd ask for more money or enlist him to find her child. Whatever happened, it would eventually lead to him locating the child, and he'd then let her know the joyous news. In order to be reunited with her child, she'd have to go into hiding, under his protection. And she would finally, and willingly, be his.

Haman smiled to think of it then quickly sobered. What was taking Thar so long?

He darted to the front door as he heard the sound of a horse arriving. He cursed at the man's carelessness. Thar had ridden the horse right into the courtyard, where anyone might hear his arrival.

Haman wouldn't be surprised if his wife came running out to see what was going on. He had a ready story, but he hoped not to use it. He strode through the courtyard, ready to have Thar flogged. But first, he must hear the man's report.

Thar jumped off his horse and raced toward him.

Haman's stomach wrenched. There was something terribly wrong. He'd never seen Thar act like this. As the man drew closer, the perspiration on his face shone in the moonlight.

"What is it, man? What's the haste?" Haman hissed.

"Sir," Thar said, gasping for breath. "She's gone. She and the child are gone."

"Where did they go? Did her husband discover our plot?"

Another gasp for air. "No, she . . ." He made a slight choking sound. "She has died giving birth." He clasped his hands together and brought them to his forehead. "Oh, sir, there was nothing to be done. The family sent for the healer, but Rebekah and the child are both . . ." His voice fell to a whisper. "Dead."

Haman stared at the man before him, the horrible words ringing in his ears. It was impossible. This man was a liar. Haman swung his fist and cracked Thar on the side of his face. The man went down, and Haman fell on top of him, hitting again and again.

Thar curled up and covered his face. "I'm sorry! I'm sorry!"

Haman couldn't think beyond the desire for Thar to take back the words he'd said. For him to have not spoken them. For them to not be true. Haman was breathing hard now, and slowly, he realized what he was doing.

Thar lay in a heap on the courtyard floor, his face and hands bloody. Haman sat back in a daze and moved off the man.

"Is it true? Do you promise on your life that Rebekah is dead?" Haman asked through gritted teeth. Pain had started to swell his throat, his chest, his head. How could this be happening? How could beautiful, sweet Rebekah be dead? Her child was supposed to be the catalyst in the plans, and now, there was nothing.

Haman climbed to his feet and hoisted Thar up as well. He supported the man as they walked out of the courtyard. On the other side of the wall, the two of them sat in the dirt under a low tree. "Tell me everything," Haman said.

He closed his eyes as Thar spoke, recounting what he knew. Haman imagined the worst—the pain, the fear, the last moments of Rebekah's life. Why? He wanted to scream at Thar, at the heavens. Why did this have to happen to his beloved?

He knew the answer. That beast of her husband was responsible. He caused her to be with child, and her body wasn't ready for it. She hadn't fully recovered from losing her first child—*his* child. The anger stoked inside Haman, and spite overpowered his thoughts, growing hotter and fiercer as he thought about the goat-man claiming his husband rights and spending time with Rebekah.

Now she was gone, and it was the Jewish man's fault. In fact, it was the Jewish people's fault that Haman would never hold his beloved again— the Jews and their one god. He'd never again hear her laugh, feel her warm body, or see her beautiful eyes close right before she kissed him.

Someone had to pay for her death. Her husband, certainly, but it was bigger than just one man. If the Jews lived with such false ideals and forced their women to marry their own kind when they were destined to be with someone else, then the Jews didn't belong in Persia.

Thar had finished his recounting, and after several moments of silence, Haman said, "Go get yourself cleaned up. I'll contact you with my next plans." As the man limped away to retrieve his horse, Haman knew he wouldn't be contacting Thar or anyone else.

What Haman had to do was create a plan grander than any in the history of Persia, one on such a large scale that it would involve *all* Jews. Men, women, children. Every last one of them. Haman would find a way to get rid of them all so he'd never have to look on their soulful faces again. He never wanted to be reminded of the cruel death of his loved one. He didn't want to hear any of their prayers or listen to any preaching about their Lord or the self-righteous sermonizing that had taken his Rebekah from him.

King Darius might have given the Jews asylum in Persia, but now it was time for them to go into either permanent exile or death. It didn't matter to Haman, so long as they were gone forever—they and their clannishness, their determination to stick to their own kind.

Haman rose to his feet and fetched an oil lamp then walked to the underground treasury in the back of his house. Using the light from the lamp to see, he descended the stone steps. Not even his wife knew of the wealth he'd kept hidden there.

In all, it was about ten thousand pieces of silver, an amount that would impress even the king. Tomorrow, Haman would make the rounds of the palace and investigate every Jewish person who was employed there. All of their positions would be scrutinized, and then he'd present his findings to the king.

Even if it took all of his silver to pay for the disappearance of the Jews, it would be worth every coin.

* * *

Morning couldn't come early enough even though Haman had hardly slept. He didn't need sleep and doubted he'd sleep well until Rebekah's death was avenged.

Haman's wife still slept as he pulled out a silk scarf hidden beneath his bed. It was one he'd given Rebekah and she'd returned to him before she was married. He'd kept it as a reminder of her. Now, he tied it around his waist, the cool weave soothing to his skin. He wouldn't go to Rebekah's funeral. He didn't want to see anyone associated with her again. He didn't trust himself—who knew what he might do?

This scarf was all he needed to keep her close and alive in his memory. He pulled on his tunic then his elaborate robes that told everyone and anyone that he was the prime minister to the king.

Slipping out of the house as dawn cracked the dusky sky, he walked to the stables to wake the stable boy. Once Haman was mounted on his horse, he set off toward the palace. Grief and hatred weighed heavily on his heart, but he was determined to fill his next days with action.

As he approached the palace, the guards bowed to him then called for a stable hand to take Haman's horse. He entered the palace and found it was a hub of activity, although it was still early in the morning. He went to the cooking rooms first. The head cook bowed as soon as she saw him. "Tell me the names of your Jewish workers," Haman said.

"I have no Jews working in the cooking room." Her eyes narrowed a bit, and her hands went to her hips. "You'll find one in the treasury, and another is scribe. Several others make deliveries, but I do not cook for them. I can't abide their strange eating habits."

"Thank you for your information," Haman said, pressing a silver coin into her hand.

She beamed at him and gave him another bow.

He left the cooking room with a smile on his face. His next stop was the chamber of writings, which Queen Esther had reformed. It seemed the scribes went there when the king didn't require their service.

Sure enough, two scribes sat in the chamber, and both looked up as Haman entered. They scrambled to their feet and bowed. Neither looked Jewish—they were both clean shaven—but Haman wanted to be careful. "Is either of you Jewish?"

They both shook their heads. "Only Dan is. He's not here yet."

"Ah," Haman said. "He's late in his duties, I see." He turned away before either one could reply and strode out of the room. He stopped at the harem and questioned Hegai. The man seemed to stumble over his words but assured Haman that none of the harem workers was Jewish. Haman hadn't imagined so, but he was being thorough.

By midmorning, he'd covered most of the palace, finding out delicious details about the Jews who worked within. He'd have an interesting report for the king. His next stop was at the treasury. As prime minister, he was privy to the king's finances. Opening the door, he had to stoop to get inside. King Darius had purposely built the entrance too small for any cart or for a man to be able to carry out any large amounts of treasure.

Guards were also posted inside the treasury. They immediately bowed to Haman, as did the two treasury workers. He nodded to each one and was about to ask his questions when he noticed one man behind the two treasury workers. He wore the same robe as a treasury worker, but he was a small man with a thick beard and prominent nose.

Definitely Jewish.

Then Haman realized the man hadn't bowed with the others. Haman stared at him, waiting for the man to acquiesce, to bow to him as was befitting of the prime minister's position. Haman folded his arms in the silence of the room. He felt everyone staring at him; he could practically feel their fear by the fact that no one dared to breathe.

Heat started at the back of Haman's head and spread to his neck, then face and chest. This man—this Jewish man, no doubt—was insulting Haman's office as prime minister. He was insulting the king—for the king had appointed Haman to his position. And now, the Jew refused to show reverence for such a post?

Haman's hands slowly closed into fists. "You're in direct violation of the king's orders."

The Jew didn't even blink. In a quiet voice that could barely be heard in the stone room, he said, "I only bow to the Lord God Himself."

Haman pasted on a slick smile, even though fury boiled inside him. "You're excused from this room. I will deal with you later."

The man must have been surprised, but nothing in his expression showed it. He stepped forward then walked around the long table and past Haman. Once the door closed, Haman set about questioning the other two treasury workers. "What is the Jew's name?"

"Mordecai," one of the treasury workers said.

Just the sound of the Jewish man's name caused Haman to shudder because it was so . . . Jewish. He asked the workers all about Mordecai, when he reported to the treasury, when he departed in the evenings, if any of his accounting had been too high or too low.

By the time Haman left, he had trouble keeping a grin off his face.

Chapter 24

AHASUERUS HAD BEEN GONE LONGER than he'd wished, so when he reached the top of the hill that overlooked Shushan and the palace came into sight, he welcomed the view. The extra day and night were due to Prince Meres's spotting a set of lion tracks. *I have certainly taught him well.* The king chuckled to himself. He glanced over at the prince and found that he was nearly asleep astride his horse.

This brought real laughter from the king. They'd worked hard, slept little, and had probably drunk too much. But there hadn't been women on the excursion, so Ahasuerus had let down his defenses a little. Besides, he was surprised at how much he'd missed Esther. The extra day and night of hunting meant he'd have very little time to spend with her before going into the month-long protocol.

Even though they were newly married, he hadn't realized she had such a pull on him. Yes, it was true he hadn't escaped to the harem or visited any of his concubines since his marriage, but that wasn't entirely unusual. At least that's what he told himself.

As he descended the hill, he noticed a procession winding its way through the streets, and the rider on the lead horse carried the royal flag. The king pulled his horse to a stop and stared. The guards and others in his party stopped as well. What was going on? The only ones who traveled with the royal flag were himself and Haman.

Ahasuerus narrowed his eyes as the procession grew closer. It was heading straight for the hill. Was Haman coming to greet him? Did he have urgent news about something? Then the king realized there was also a litter situated in the middle of the procession.

Esther? he thought at the same time as Biztha called out, "It's the queen!"

The king urged his horse forward, wondering if everything was all right. He hadn't given her permission to leave the palace, and now it looked like she had not only left but also brought half of the palace with her.

The procession didn't seem to be in any hurry, and as the gap closed between the two groups, Ahasuerus saw that Haman was with them as well. When they reached each other, both parties stopped, and the servants set the queen's litter on the ground. The drapery around the litter parted, and Esther stepped out.

She was veiled, but the sight of her made Ahasuerus's heart rate increase. He climbed off his horse to meet her. She walked to him and prostrated herself.

He took her hand and drew her close. "What is this?"

"I've come to welcome you home," she said.

Even though he could see only her eyes, he could tell she was smiling. He had the sudden urge to lift her veil and kiss her, but it would have to wait. Too many eyes were watching, and too many tongues would talk.

"I hope nothing is amiss," the king said to Esther.

"Only you have been missing," she said.

Just then, Haman approached. After prostrating, he said, "Your queen has been busy in your absence."

The king thought he detected an edge in the prime minister's voice but decided to look past it. Haman was as loyal as they came, and that included loyalty to Esther.

"Have you rearranged the entire palace, then?" he said, looking at his wife.

"Nothing so great as that," she said, but her fingers tightened around his.

Haman chuckled beside her. "She's been to the market and made purchases. The merchants have fallen in love with her. But don't worry. I've traveled with her on every excursion."

"I owe you my gratitude, then, Haman," the king said. He wanted to question Esther and find out why she'd ventured beyond the palace to the market. But he decided to save that conversation for when there weren't dozens of pairs of ears listening.

Haman bowed. "When she insisted on coming out to meet you, I was compelled to support her."

Again, the edge in Haman's voice. Perhaps Ahasuerus would hold a private audience with the prime minister to find out why he was spending so much time with Esther. Haman didn't have the best reputation with women. Ahasuerus exhaled. He had no reason not to trust Haman, and he trusted Esther implicitly. The king glanced at those who'd arrived with Esther and saw her chamberlain, Hatach, standing not too far off. The man would have been sufficient to accompany the queen.

He turned to her and spoke in a quiet voice. "And why did you insist on coming out to meet me?"

"I thought I'd like a ride on your horse."

The king had to forcefully prevent his mouth from falling open. Everyone's eyes were on him, waiting for his answer to the queen's strange request. He'd never ridden on horseback with a woman before. "Are you sure?" he finally said. "Perhaps I could ride in the litter with you?"

Her eyes smiled. "I'm afraid we'd break some backs if we did that." She looked toward his horse. "It's a beautiful animal."

Ahasuerus exhaled, his mind made up. He led her by the hand to the horse. "You'll climb up after me." Once he was seated, the servants scurried to help Esther mount.

She sat sideways in front of him, and he put one arm around her and used the other to hold the reins of the horse. Her scent was clean and fresh, opposite of what his must be after days of hunting in the wilderness.

"So you caught your lion, did you?" she asked as they rode.

Ahasuerus chuckled. "Yes, but that's not what I want to talk about." She was silent after that, and he just smiled. When they reached the edge of the first housing area, people came out of their homes to watch the procession. They prostrated themselves as they spotted the royal flag. Then seeing that the queen was with the king, they started cheering and tossing flowers.

"Haman was right. The people do love you."

He thought again how he was right in choosing a wife who wasn't already royalty. It seemed that the people had grown fond of the queen in his absence.

Esther turned her head. "They also love their king."

He smiled above her head, thinking of the temperament of the Persians. One day they loved him, the next they were angry with him. "Persia is grateful to have a queen again."

Esther caught a few of the flowers tossed in their direction and held them in her lap. This brought even more excitement from the crowds lining the streets. The closer they grew to the palace, the thicker the crowd became, which the king knew made his guards wary. But it seemed the people were only in a celebratory mood.

Once inside the palace grounds, the king ordered a council to begin in one hour, but first he'd bathe and change his clothing. After he'd changed, he made a detour to Esther's rooms. She sat on the divan by the window, working on a piece of embroidery.

He dismissed the chambermaids then crossed to her. He folded his arms, watching her for a moment as she embroidered with a focused intensity. "What are you stitching?"

She broke her concentration and looked at him.

The king's heart hitched. He could get lost in her luminous eyes.

"The scene outside the window," she said. "They have the most beautiful threads at our local market; some of them are the richest colors." She held up the cloth. "See, I found a color that matched the sky exactly."

He took the cloth from her then looked at the sky. "You must have had the merchants all begging for your attention."

She smiled. "In truth, I just wanted to find a welcome-home gift for my husband. But there were too many things to choose from, so you might have to settle for this embroidery when I finish. It was quite the experience. They seemed to think I was made of pure gold and could change their lives."

Ahasuerus watched her with a smile as the sunlight from the window brightened the silver embroidery stitching on her yellow robe. "Just visiting with them probably did change their lives."

She laughed, and he realized how much he'd missed her laughter. He drew her up from the divan and into his arms. She seemed ready for him and easily wrapped her arms around his neck and turned up her face.

"Whatever did you do to get Haman so disgruntled?" he asked.

"Oh." A shadow crossed her face. "He insisted on accompanying me everywhere I went outside the palace," she said in a slow voice. "I didn't think he'd care to spend the time."

"You know he's been a judge for many years. So if anyone knows the temperament of the Persian people, it's he." He touched her cheek and was rewarded by her soft sigh. "He just wants to protect you."

Again a shadow crossed her face, but before he could question it, she moved her hands into his hair and pressed against him. "I've missed you, Ahasuerus," she whispered.

"You're very good at changing the topic," he whispered back. "The next weeks will be long without you."

She pulled his head toward her and pressed her mouth against his. He decided to let her have her way. The beginning of protocol could wait a little longer.

* * *

Ahasuerus sensed Haman's impatience during protocol in the inner chamber of the Mazda Temple. They hadn't had a conversation since Ahasuerus had returned from hunting. Was Haman's impatience about Esther's activities? When Esther had told the king about her visits to the market, he hadn't seen any harm in them. The queen's presence in the market had done good for the people. They seemed to love her—which made him very happy.

Everyone was waiting for him. "During our hiatus this month, we'll make our final decision on Athens and Sparta. That decision will be made known to the people, and they will support us in our decision." While on the hunting excursion, there was plenty of time to think without the busy schedule of the palace. The king knew he would not take sides between Athens or Sparta. It was just a matter of convincing the others to support his decision fully.

One of the princes grumbled but said nothing further. Ahasuerus wanted to put his father's and his own embarrassing defeats behind him. The kingdom had nothing to prove. Persia was a mighty nation and would continue to prosper. But he didn't want to lose hundreds or thousands of men in a third invasion.

Ahasuerus didn't just want the princes to agree with him to his face but to support him in their hearts as well. He knew there were still some who lusted for war and more power and more land, but marrying Esther had solidified the ideals he was already leaning toward. Persia didn't need to go out and seek war. They'd continue to build their defenses and fortify, yet there were plenty of things to enjoy and find fulfillment in at home. He'd seen that plainly in the last couple of hours alone with Esther in her room.

He couldn't reveal that to the council before him now—that his decision was because of the love and security he felt in Esther's arms. He could almost visualize her now, which made him want to return to her rooms. He knew he wouldn't find her there—she was with the tutor—but when he was around her, he felt different than he'd ever felt around his concubines.

He knew she truly cared for him—there was no explanation except that it seemed to radiate from her. And he knew he cared for her as well, beyond her beauty and her intelligence and calm temperament. *I love her*, he realized.

He didn't know if he dared tell her.

Biztha brought the opening protocol to a close and ordered a servant to bring in supper.

Ahasuerus felt incredibly relaxed. He leaned back in his chair, which was almost as luxurious as his throne in the main court, and watched everything with a tangible detached feeling. The protocol had gone smoother than he'd expected, he and Prince Meres had caught their lion, and he was looking forward to returning to his wife at the end of the month.

When the meal was brought in, the king moved to the head of the long table. The food tasted especially good for some reason. The cooks they brought with them on the hunt did a fine job, but there was nothing like partaking at a royal banquet. He only wished Esther was by his side now. But women were restricted from the protocol.

Haman approached him. "I'd like to request a private meeting with Your Highness. I have matters of the utmost importance to discuss."

"Of course," Ahasuerus said easily. Was this about Esther's activities? He certainly had seen nothing to cause concern. "Let's go now to discuss what you need."

Haman's brows lifted in surprise. A private meeting so soon was unusual, but most of the princes were still eating. No one would need the king for a few moments. They walked into a side chamber of the temple that was surrounded by high columns. Although there was no door, the chamber offered privacy. The king motioned for Haman to sit on a large cushion.

When they were both situated, Haman said, "I have grave news."

The king straightened, alert at once. "From Greece?" Why hadn't Haman said anything at the protocol?

"No, from around our own land." Haman paused. "There is a certain people who live among us and even serve in the palace. Your father welcomed them in their time of exile from Babylon, and they reside in all the provinces of the kingdom."

"Yes, the Jewish people have been here many years," Ahasuerus said.

Haman nodded, and the king wondered what the prime minister's concerns were.

"As I've reported," Haman continued, "I have traveled to various provinces and sat in the local courts to observe that the laws of Persia are being followed."

The king watched Haman carefully. What had the former judge found?

"I've discovered several things that are concerning," Haman said. "The Jewish laws are different from our people's. From *your* laws. And that is how they are ruling—according to their own governing laws. We are the ones who've provided them with a new homeland, yet they do not abide by *our* laws."

Ahasuerus thought this through. He knew they had strict regulations in dress, food, habits, and religious observance. But he hadn't considered how that might carry over to how they governed themselves in each province.

He could see where the conflict would be if one man's crime was treated differently depending on which court he went to.

Haman's low voice continued. "They leave the fields early on their Sabbath so they may be home before the sun sets. This means there is less production, and they are paying less in taxes. The loans King Darius gave them—both in property and silver—have yet to be repaid. At the rate they're working, it will be decades yet."

The king frowned. The treasury oversaw tax collecting. There always seemed to be a shortage in silver even though he didn't live as extravagantly as his father. It was another reason Ahasuerus didn't want to go to war.

"By the time Sabbath ends for them, it's too dark to work again." Haman puffed out a frustrated breath. "They're working less than any other Persian by nearly a half day each week."

"Half a day?" the king asked.

Haman's nod was solemn. "Whereas Persians work until it's well dark."

The king shook his head. He knew a little about the Sabbath day observance by the Jews. Ahura-Mazda demanded his own holy days. But every week? Missing a half day of work?

"Since King Darius's day, we've had other groups of people who have wished to live within Shushan's borders, but we've turned them away." Haman spread his hands. "Their citizenship would have been more productive than that of the Jewish people's."

"The provinces are well populated; there wouldn't be room for more people," the king said.

"Yes." Haman paused. "And we may regret turning down the others. Jewish people won't buy from our Persian markets, and in many cases, they'll only sell to their own people. They continue to separate and ostracize themselves." He shifted on his cushion and leaned slightly forward to drive home his key point. "Worst of all, they use their 'law of Moses' to make decisions in court. They don't heed the laws of the land established by their own king. It's like they don't have a king at all."

Ahasuerus let that sink in. This news was growing graver by the moment. What had his father known about the exiles he'd allowed into his kingdom?

But Haman wasn't finished. "The Jews refuse to join our armies and expect us to protect them. They are bleeding the kingdom dry."

Not all of this was new to Ahasuerus. There had been rumblings in the councils of his father that Ahasuerus had heard as a young prince. Had his father not foreseen these problems?

Haman watched Ahasuerus expectantly. "Even the Jewish people who work in the palace don't work as hard as the rest. The cook refuses to feed them because they've insulted her cooking." His face reddened. "It's like they don't care about our land. They don't care about our traditions or our kings, and they act like they are superior. There are rumors that the more pious Jewish people do not attend royal processions or festivals because they refuse to prostrate themselves before the king or any other royal person."

Ahasuerus stared at Haman. This was certainly treason. Just one of Haman's complaints amounted to a treasonous act, but all of them combined were a horrific disgrace. It made him sorrowful, then his feelings twisted into something harder. The anger started deep within his chest then spread to his limbs.

"In your own palace," Haman said in a hushed voice, "there are Jews who don't work as much as the others. Dan, the scribe, is among them. He is later than the others in the morning and leaves early for Sabbath."

The king knew who Dan was. One of the younger scribes, Dan was quick minded and quiet. But he had not always been in attendance with the other scribes, the king realized now.

"What other positions do Jews hold within the palace?"

"None in the cooking room," Haman assured him. "There are a couple in the stables and another in the treasury. Having a Jew in the treasury brings me great concern." He looked toward the inner court. No one had come to disturb them yet, so he continued. "I have witnessed the rebellion of the Jews myself and within the walls of your own palace. Surely you've heard all of the arguments over the years about allowing exiles into Persia, but there have been enough allowances made. The Jews continue to produce children who share their beliefs. What if . . . what if they outnumber us one day?"

This was something Ahasuerus hadn't considered, but it made him feel cold all over.

"Soon, there will be too many to contend with," Haman said, his eyes wide. "As the prime minister, I've decided to invest my own money and time into solving this situation." He lowered his head for a moment then met the king's gaze. "I will pay ten thousand talents of my own silver to your treasury for a decree from the king demanding that the Jews leave Persia."

The king stared at the prime minister. Ten thousand talents of silver would fill a large void in the treasury. And Haman was right that the Jewish people needed to be dealt with. Ahasuerus had encountered many of the issues Haman had brought up—even at the racetrack, when the Jews had refused to attend the royal race. And that was just a small thing compared to Haman's other complaints. The Jews were a growing problem, and with their defiance toward the throne, they'd made their feelings about Persia clear.

Haman brought his hand to his chest. "You may do as you will with the silver. It is money the Jews should have paid you themselves. They must leave. Then their lands, fields, and homes will be free for other inhabitants who agree to be tax-paying citizens and loyal to the king of Persia."

Ahasuerus stood and paced the columned area. His father might have welcomed the Jews, but he had been desperate in times of war with many of the men gone. The Jews had filled in as workers in the fields and in other places. But now that Persia was prosperous again, the Jews seemed to take more than they gave. Perhaps the decree Haman suggested was the right move.

If Ahasuerus was to convince his council not to go to war with Greece again, he wanted them to understand that his first intent was to protect and preserve Persia. That included cleansing it of anything cankerous.

"And if the Jews don't leave," Haman said in a quiet voice, "their punishment will be death."

The king stopped and looked at Haman.

The prime minister raised his hand, sorrow in his expression. "It would be the last thing we'd desire to do, but we must let the Jews know we are serious. If they do not leave, they forfeit their lives."

"They would be foolish not to leave," the king said. Then he pulled off the ring from his hand that contained the royal seal. "Take this seal and send the decree to every province through our governors."

Haman's gaze lowered, and he rose to take the ring, then he prostrated himself. "Thank you, Your Majesty. This will be a significant day in Persia. Our land will be cleansed of all treachery."

The king watched Haman bow again and walk through the columns, back to the inner court. Ahasuerus had never interacted with the Jewish people on a personal basis, except for briefly, such as with Dan the scribe. But surely that man would be intelligent enough to leave Persia and find another place to dwell. And there were plenty of scribes to replace a Jew. Dan had never done anything to bother him, but the king understood that he couldn't allow slothfulness or rejection of the crown, not in any form.

And not bowing in reverence to royalty could only make things worse. The king let out a heavy sigh then returned to the inner court. There would be some shake up with the decree, but there would also be a chance for the Jewish people to find a new home, far away from Persia, where they could govern themselves and not live off another nation.

Chapter 25

HAMAN RUSHED FROM THE TEMPLE to the palace. It wasn't far, but he didn't want to waste a moment. Even though he had the king's seal with him, it all seemed too good to be real. Not until the decrees were delivered to every province could Haman truly rejoice. Once inside, he made his way to the chamber of writings, sure that he'd find the majority of the scribes there. His heart was bursting with joy. Rebekah's death would be avenged once and for all. Her people—the self-righteous people who had forced the two of them to remain separate and had caused her horrible death—would finally pay.

Whereas before, Haman had thought Ahura-Mazda frowned upon him, he now realized the god had orchestrated all of these events. Yes, it was with great sorrow that Rebekah had been sacrificed in order for Haman to gather the courage to be so bold with the king. But it had worked out better than he had ever thought possible. Something at the back of his mind told him he should be grateful to Queen Esther. The king had softened since his marriage to her, and he had been more willing to laugh, sympathize, and listen to his advisors—such as the prime minister—and Haman was indeed grateful.

He bit back a smile of satisfaction as he entered the chamber. Dan was there. The scribe would be part of writing his own decree of death. Haman wanted to laugh. "I have an important errand from the king that needs to be attended to immediately," he announced. He smirked as the scribes set to work at a furious pace. They removed moist clay from their scribe boxes and pressed it into tablets. As he dictated the words that would be read throughout the entire land before the day was over, he watched Dan from the corner of his eyes.

"Every Jew will be destroyed, both young and old, little children and even women, on the thirteenth day of the twelfth month." He looked at all of the scribes' faces. "Write it down. As you can see, there is little time to be wasted."

Dan's naturally pale face turned alabaster. At one point, his knees buckled and he visibly shook. The other scribes were smart enough not to try to help or console him. If Dan knew what was good for him, he'd make his escape while he could.

"On the thirteenth day of the month of Adar, every Persian will enjoy the spoils that the Jewish people leave behind, either willingly or unwillingly."

The scribes continued to imprint the tablets, and when they finished, Haman said, "See that every governor and every lieutenant receives his own tablet to carry to each province without delay." He pulled off the king's ring, which he had slipped onto his finger earlier. "I will imprint the boxes for the tablets with the royal seal so the people know we're in earnest."

When the scribes had completed the tablets, Haman went on his next errand, his most secret errand. He paid a visit to the captain of the military. With a fresh tablet in hand, he altered the words so it would create a new message that only the captain would see. And with the king's ring stamped into the tablet's box, even the captain would have to obey.

When that was accomplished, Haman returned to the temple. The meal was long over, and the Magi were in the inner court, recounting the ode to Zurvan Akarana, father of Ahura-Mazda. In turn, the Magi recited the story of how Akarana offered a sacrifice to the Creator in order to have a son. The Creator gave him twins.

Haman slipped in without interrupting and silently took his place near the king, who gave him a nod. When the recitation of the Magi was over, and just before everyone fell into meditation, the king turned to Haman. "Have the decrees gone out?"

"Yes," Haman said, trying to keep his voice sober and his expression serious, even though he wanted to shout with elation. Even if the Jews packed up and fled their neighborhoods, they didn't stand a chance. Not with the captain of the military carrying out additional orders. "The decree is on its way at this moment."

* * *

FOUR WEEKS LATER

Having the king gone from the palace should have started feeling normal, Esther thought. But it was different this time. He wasn't in another part of the land, hunting. He was in the temple next to the palace, sequestered for the Akarana devotion. The king had told her it occurred once a year and involved meditating and remembering the story of the Creator. The royal leaders of Persia became sufficiently grounded in the history of their gods so they could continue to make serious decisions during the next year.

She spent the morning on embroidery and ran out of the indigo color, so she sent her maidens to the market for the thread. Although she hadn't relished Haman coming with her when she left the palace in the king's absence, she wasn't ready to face the frenzy that her appearance would create without a royal guard present. Though she was still grateful for Haman's absence now.

Karan and a few of the other maidens were more than eager to go on the errand—they were probably excited to get outside of the palace. She asked the remaining three maidens to walk with her to the chamber of writings for her tutoring session. But once she stepped out of her private rooms, Hatach stopped her.

He prostrated himself. "The royal tutor is not at the palace today. He's on an important errand for the king."

"Oh." Esther hadn't considered that the tutor would be running errands for the king while the king was at the temple. "I will make my usual rounds of the palace, then." It had become a habit with her. She checked on the various palace operations on a daily basis.

Hatach bowed and led her to the main corridor outside the queen's chambers. She stopped with surprise when she saw Karan coming through the doors that separated the royal rooms from the rest of the palace. There couldn't have been enough time for her to make it to and from the market.

Karan quickly prostrated herself then stammered out, "Your Highness. The man Mordecai, who warned you about the plot against the king, is outside the palace walls creating a great diversion."

What could be wrong with Mordecai? "What's he doing?" she asked with growing dread.

Karan's eyes were wide as she spoke. "He's rent his clothing and wears sackcloth and ashes as if he's in mourning." Her voice softened to a whisper. "His cries are terrible to hear. They pierced my very heart."

A jolt passed through Esther. Had something happened to Leah? To their children? She almost didn't dare ask. "Is it his family?"

"His family is safe," Karan said. "I inquired of the guards, but they refused to answer any more of my questions."

Mordecai's family was safe. That was a relief. But then why was he acting so grief stricken? The breath seemed to leave Esther, and she needed to sit down. "Come with me," she told Karan. The maidens followed, as well as Hatach, until they were all seated in the queen's gathering room. Esther wished she could be alone and pray in privacy, but this needed to be attended to immediately. Her prayer was internal, silent, and swift. *O Lord, O God, direct me to make the right decision.*

She looked at her maidens then at Hatach. "Send clothing to the man. Perhaps the king expelled him from his post and he's decrying his poverty. Clothing will let him know he is still a valued citizen."

Karan hurried to carry out Esther's command, and while Esther waited for her return, she closed her eyes, silently praying and thinking. Why wasn't Mordecai in the king's treasury? Why was he without the gates today? It seemed ages before Karan returned.

Her face flushed as she reported. "Mordecai refused the clothing."

Esther blew out a breath, her mind churning and her heart sinking. "Has he calmed at least?"

"No," Karan said, her voice trembling. "His cries are terrible to hear. If I didn't know better, I'd think he'd lost a limb."

New worries pulsed through Esther. Perhaps something *had* happened to him. "Is he injured? Sick?"

Hatach stepped forward and bowed. "I will find out what ails the man, Your Highness."

It wouldn't do for her to rush outside the gates to confront Mordecai. Esther nodded, hoping the chamberlain would be successful. She clasped her trembling hands together. "Very well."

With Hatach gone and the wait continuing, she tried to remain composed, but she wanted to run to the palace gates to find Mordecai herself. He was the leader in the community she grew up in. Everyone looked to him for guidance and answers, and now it appeared that his mind had gone or something so terrible had happened that Esther couldn't even fathom it.

The minutes until Hatach's return seemed to crawl by. Esther could only pace and silently pray to the Lord. If something happened to Mordecai, where would that leave her? She would be completely cut off from her people. It was difficult to find ways to speak to Mordecai, but just knowing he was close was comforting and gave her strength.

Esther barely noticed that her maids were still in the room, quietly whispering their concerns to each other. When Hatach returned, everyone fell silent. Esther studied his face. What sort of news was he about to deliver? He carried a tablet with him, but her stomach twisted at his pallid skin and furrowed brow. "What is it?" she said, her voice just above a whisper.

"It is grave indeed." His voice matched her quietness. He reached for her hand and grasped it.

Esther was startled at the action, but it confirmed that she was not going to like what she was about to hear.

"There has been a new decree signed by the king." He hesitated as if the news was too grave to speak. He looked down at the tablet in his hand. "Mordecai gave this to me to show you. Copies of this have gone out to every province and have been read by every governor and lieutenant."

Staring at the tablet, she knew she couldn't read all of the words, so she asked, "What does the decree say?"

Hatach couldn't meet her eyes for a moment.

Esther clenched her hands together. "Please tell me. I must know why Mordecai grieves as if death is at his door."

Hatach raised his eyes, and Esther's heart plummeted. His coloring had faded. "Perhaps death is at his door, Your Highness. It's most puzzling and most astounding . . . Every Jew has been ordered destroyed if they remain in Persia on the thirteenth day of Adar." Hatach paused. "Even the children and the women."

Esther couldn't move. His words couldn't be true.

"Why? Why would the king . . . ?" she whispered. She reached for the tablet and held the weight of it in her hands. Her eyes blurred as she tried to read the imprinted letters, but they merely jumbled together.

She couldn't comprehend what had moved her husband to send such condemnation against her people. Even if he didn't know his own wife was a Jew, the Jewish people were an integral and thriving part of Persian society. Yes, she knew there were a lot of differences, but they seemed to live side by side in relative harmony.

"Read me the words on the tablet exactly," Esther said as she sank to the divan, holding the tablet toward Hatach. *Please, Lord, let this report be false.* "Every word." Moments ago, she'd been on her way to meet with her tutor. Before that, she'd been stitching. How could her entire world change in such a short time? And what risk was Mordecai undertaking to draw her attention to this crisis?

Hatach took the tablet and spoke quietly. "As I said, many of the Persians are puzzled at this decree." He slowly read the horrible words. When he finished, he lifted his head. "Those who participate in the slayings will be rewarded with silver, and they'll also enjoy the spoils left behind." His voice shook, and he paused as if to collect his emotions. "It appears that the prime minister offered the king ten thousand silver talents to be rewarded to those who do the evil deed, and he convinced the king to approve the decree."

Haman's name suddenly echoed through Esther's mind. She should have known he was involved, but now, hearing that it was his idea and he'd been the one to convince the king, she felt better, yet worse at the same time, if it were possible. A small bit of hope started in her breast. If Haman had come up with the idea, at least that meant it wasn't the original idea of Ahasuerus, and if it wasn't his idea, maybe someone could persuade him to give it up.

Esther had never discussed the Jewish people with her husband, for obvious reasons. But now she wished she had. Then she'd at least know how he felt about her people—without Haman's or any other's influence.

Ahasuerus had been willing to go outside of royalty to find a queen for Persia. Did that mean anything? Perhaps he was more open-minded than his prime minister and others in the kingdom who despised the Jews.

"I do not understand it," Esther said in a faint voice.

"I will not speak against King Xerxes, but you must know, Your Highness, that Mordecai said many people in the kingdom are perplexed at the decree," Hatach said. "And I confirmed it with the guards. The Jews are not the only ones upset."

Hatach's observation brought a bit of comfort. Even though the chamberlain wasn't Jewish, he seemed to be genuine in his distress. Esther looked at the tablet in Hatach's hand, still reeling from what it said.

"Mordecai has a message for you, Your Highness," he said.

Esther perked at the news. Perhaps Mordecai had found a solution. She wasn't nearly as familiar with the politics of Persia as he.

Hatach seemed to hesitate before saying, "Mordecai has requested that you go in unto the king to supplicate on behalf of the Jewish people."

Her body felt hot and cold all at once. Her husband had been sequestered in the inner court now for thirty days, and she had not seen him in all that time. Hatach himself had explained that women were not allowed to attend the protocol, and neither men nor women could approach the inner court without the request of the king. To do so was to risk her life. It was direct disobedience to the laws of protocol.

Esther exhaled. Mordecai must not have known that the king was still in protocol, but how could he not? Mordecai worked at the palace. Did her cousin not understand that it would risk her life?

What if I am the only hope to stop the decree from going forward? She wondered if this was why God had brought her to the palace—to save her people. But surely it wouldn't be at the price of her life. Surely Mordecai and even the Lord God Almighty would not ask that.

"Return this message to Mordecai," she said in a thoughtful voice, "that whosoever approaches the king in the inner court without summons will be put to death. Unless the king holds out the golden scepter and grants life, that person will die." She exhaled in defeat. "And I have not been summoned in all the thirty days that the king has been in protocol."

Hatach didn't look surprised. "I will take Mordecai the message."

Once Hatach had left the room, Esther strode to the balcony doors and opened them. The hot wind blasted into the room, but she needed a change of air. From her balcony, the one on which she'd first kissed her husband, there was no view of the front gates of the palace. She looked over the land, the farms, the homes, the people, and wondered how many Jews were in Persia.

Her stomach tightened into a hard ball. How could this be happening? She braced her hands on the balcony edge, remembering her wedding night and how unsure she'd been as a bride and how innocent she'd been of politics. In the days that followed, she'd realized she truly loved her husband. She'd felt the confirmation from the Lord that she had made the right choice, though she was giving up the open practice of her faith and her children would not be raised to worship the true Lord.

It was much too long before Hatach returned. She went back inside the room to hear his report. "Does Mordecai have a reply for me?"

Hatach looked at his hands. "Mordecai says Haman has ordered all of the Jews killed before they can leave. He has stationed soldiers at all of the borders to prevent anyone from escaping. The king does not know this, and he must be told. If the king does not stop Haman now, all of the Jews will be killed."

Esther's body stiffened. Haman had orchestrated this when the king was in protocol, out of touch with his people and the city. "So the decree that gives the Jews warning is not a warning at all?"

"No, it's a death march. The Jews will have nowhere to go but straight into a soldier's unforgiving sword." Hatach gripped his hands together. "Mordecai's message is this: think not of yourself that *you* will escape the palace more than all the Jews."

Esther inhaled. Mordecai had told Hatach that she was Jewish. She watched his wavering gaze, waiting for the condemnation to show, but all she saw was sorrow and sympathy. Her heart eased a little. She looked over at her maidens. Karan and the other women sat in their various places, their eyes wide at the news.

"Mordecai didn't want me to tell anyone about my religion," Esther said in a quiet voice as everyone's attention was riveted on her. "But it seems the time has come, and now I have Mordecai's blessing." She exhaled, her heart hammering in her throat. "For, you see, Mordecai is my cousin. And I am a Jew."

Karan covered her mouth, and tears fell from her eyes.

"If the king doesn't put a stop to Haman," Esther said, "I'll be included in the destruction."

"No!" Karan cried out. "You must do something."

Esther spread her hands, wishing she knew what to do, wishing she knew how she could change all of this. She looked over at Hatach. "What else did my cousin say?"

"Mordecai said you were chosen for this time and the peace in the kingdom of Persia relies on you now." Hatach's voice trembled. "All of the Jews of Persia will be destroyed unless someone speaks to the king and gets him to change his mind. Mordecai says it must be you. He says that is your purpose."

Esther closed her eyes. So this *was* why the Lord had endorsed her marriage to Ahasuerus—to be the sacrifice that saved her people. She felt her eyes burn but refused to let the tears fall. Was her life more valuable than the lives of thousands of Jews? What if she approached the king and she was condemned to death? Would it be worth it? She would die, and then her people would die.

But what if he listened to her and accepted her as his Jewish wife? Then her people would live. Mordecai, Leah, Abigail, Ben, Samuel . . . Johanna and her husband. All of those who were dear to her. All of those who were innocent—men, women, and children who had meant no harm in Persia but wanted only to find a friendly country in which to raise their families and worship the Lord. And now if they stayed in Persia, or even if they tried to leave it, they would be put to death.

Who am I? What am I?

She opened her eyes and met Hatach's questioning gaze. "Tell Mordecai to ask all the Jews in Shushan to fast for me. They should not eat or drink for three days, night or day. I will fast as well with my maidens." She looked at Karan, who nodded at her. "On the third day, I'll go to the inner court and beseech the king, despite the law that forbids me to enter."

One of the maidens sniffled, tears running down her face.

"If I perish, then I perish for my people." She sank onto the divan, her body trembling, yet she knew beseeching Ahasuerus was the right thing to do. She felt weak, but inside, she was warm, and that could only be because of the Lord.

Hatach left the room, and the maidens crowded around Esther. She couldn't hold back the tears now, but they were not tears of grief; they were tears of resolve. It was as if she clearly saw the path the Lord had set before her. In three days, her earthly fate would be decided, but whether she lived or died, she knew she was doing what the Lord intended for her.

Chapter 26

I HAVE NOT SEEN MY husband for thirty days, Esther thought. *And today might be the last time I lay eyes on him.*

Her hands shook as she smoothed the front of her robe. She was meticulously dressed. Karan and the maidens had clothed her in her richest and most beautiful robes—those of deep violet—in hopes that the king would welcome the sight of her.

She had no idea how things had progressed in the inner court. Would Ahasuerus be pleased? If so, would it quickly turn to anger when he learned her true identity? Was this the last day she'd see a ray of sun or the leaf of a tree? Would the happy moments of her marriage be forgotten? Would she ever see any of her family members again?

"Hegai and the others have arrived," Karan said, bringing Esther's attention back to the present.

Esther wanted a moment with her friends from the harem. She at least owed them a farewell. She wished she could have done the same for Mordecai and Leah. Regardless, she walked into the queen's gathering room and was greeted there by her friends whom she'd sent for.

She was out of breath by the time she embraced them. The days of fasting had left her weaker than she'd ever been, but strangely, she felt peaceful and calm. When she had greeted Hegai, Nan, and Sarah, Esther told them she was a Jew and that she was going to the inner court.

Hegai and Sarah stared at her, and Nan started to cry. Esther didn't have much energy to console them. "If I don't see any of you again, I want to tell you how much you mean to me. You've been so important in my life." She clasped her hands together. "And now I must go to the inner court to plead for my people."

She left a silent room and stepped into the corridor. All of her maidens accompanied her through the palace and out the gates. The guards looked surprised to see the group of women exit, but they did nothing to stop them.

Esther knew if the Lord wasn't holding her up, she'd very well faint in the road. Her head felt light, but her heart felt peaceful, solid. When they reached the temple, the guards hesitated before letting them enter the doors, astonishment plain on their faces as well.

Once inside the cool hallway, Esther stopped. "Wait here for me," she said to Karan and the maidens. "Only I carry this burden."

Karan covered her face and turned away, and a couple of the maidens started to cry softly.

Esther could hear voices down the corridor. She didn't recognize the tones yet, but she started to pray as she walked. She visualized herself prostrated before the king, confessing that she was a Jew. Then Ahasuerus would . . . what? Turn her away? Love her? He'd been betrayed by his prime minister; his chamberlains had plotted his death. Would he see this as a betrayal too?

And then she was within view of the inner court. It was a wide, long room with cushions lining the walls. Low tables that probably contained food during meals were covered with tablets and writing utensils. Ahasuerus sat on a throne toward the back of the room, and he was speaking to a man seated on his right. *Haman.*

She was beyond feeling fear. She was too weak to soak in any sense of anger or revenge. She could only beg and plead for herself and those she loved.

Esther noticed there were no women, no entertainers, no messenger boys in the room. Those present appeared to be either princes or other royal officials. She waited, her eyes on Ahasuerus. She didn't let her gaze waver, although she heard the voices fade and felt the assembly notice her.

The room stilled, and the king turned his head.

Even from a distance, Esther saw the astonishment in her husband's eyes, and that was when her body started to tremble. *O Lord, my God, give me the strength to stand.*

Her eyes locked with the king's for a long moment. She had not forgotten what he looked like even during the long absence, but seeing him again was like seeing him anew. Her heart reached out to him as a wife, but it also reached out to him as a supplicating servant. He held her fate in his hands.

Esther wasn't even sure if she was breathing or if anyone else in the inner court dared to breathe.

Ahasuerus lifted his hand, and Esther realized he held his golden scepter in it. He was welcoming her. Not condemning her. *Not condemning me.*

Her breath went ragged. She almost sank to the ground. Instead, with the last bit of strength, she stepped forward then took another step and another. Soon she was passing in front of the other men and walking into the inner court. She had made it this far, and it took everything inside her not to collapse.

Something held her up, and something kept her feet moving. When she reached the king, she sank to her knees and touched the scepter, still outstretched in his hand. Then she prostrated. It was only with the help of the Lord that she was able to climb back to her feet.

"Esther, what is your request?" the king asked, burning curiosity in his gaze. "If it's within my power to give it, I will give it, for half the kingdom is yours."

I am a Jew, was on her lips, when something else entered her mind. *Not yet.*

How could that be? This was the purpose of her visit. The days were quickly approaching until her people would perish. Her eyes traveled to Haman and met his glittery and very inquisitive gaze. And suddenly, she knew what to say. It was as if the Lord had spoken directly to her.

"If it pleases you, and the prime minister, I would like to invite you both to a banquet this evening." She couldn't look at Haman to see his reaction, but the king smiled. Relief surged through Esther, giving her another bit of strength to remain standing.

Ahasuerus nodded. "We'll be honored to come to your banquet." Next to him, Haman offered a deep bow.

"Thank you," Esther said, trying to keep her voice strong and normal sounding. She turned and started the long walk back through the inner court. All eyes seemed to follow her, and it wasn't until she was safely in the corridor that any sort of conversation resumed.

She wanted to sink to the ground and cry. She'd done it. She'd come this far. The king had welcomed her, and he was coming to her banquet. Now she just had to prepare one before his arrival . . . and then she'd tell him all that he needed to hear.

* * *

Ahasuerus entered the side room next to the main court, where Esther had arranged for a private meal. He and Haman had come through the back way so as not to draw a crowd at the front gates. He wished for a moment that Haman wasn't with him; Ahasuerus would have liked to greet his wife alone.

He hadn't seen her for nearly a moon, and he'd been startled when she'd arrived at the inner court to invite him to a banquet. Although she had been veiled, he could read in her eyes that she had something important to tell him.

So why did it require the presence of the prime minster as well? Ahasuerus searched his mind for a possible answer but came up empty. All he knew was that he'd been away from his beautiful, kind wife too long.

She rose to her feet from a cushion as he entered the room. She wore all white, reminding him of their marriage day. His heart tumbled at the sight of her. She wasn't wearing a veil, apparently having decided the meal with Haman wasn't too public.

And Ahasuerus appreciated it. He appreciated looking at the woman who was his wife. She was still the same woman he'd met more than a year ago at the well, but she was even more queenly now. She'd learned much, and quickly, and she held herself elegantly. She was every inch a queen, both gentle and powerful.

When he reached her side, he lifted her hand and pressed a kiss on it.

"You're here," she said in a faint voice.

That's when he noticed that she looked thinner. He knew she refused to eat many of the rich foods and meats served at the banquets. Perhaps she wasn't getting enough food. "Are you well?" he asked in a quiet voice.

Of course, Haman would have overheard, but he acted as if he weren't listening. The man had been almost infuriatingly happy the past few weeks, ever since the signing of the edict. The king suspected Haman to be disappointed though, since Ahasuerus was sure many of the Jewish families had fled as soon as they heard the condemning words.

"I'm well now that you are here," Esther said, slipping her delicate hand from his.

Ahasuerus wanted to reach for it again and pull her into his arms. He had not indulged in any visits to the harem like some of the princes had during protocol. If he were going to return to the palace for a woman, it would be to Esther.

He surveyed the food laid out on a low table. It was the usual display, albeit on a smaller scale, but he sensed a difference. Perhaps it was because Esther had overseen it just for him. As they ate, Ahasuerus's curiosity increased until he could wait no longer.

He took a final sip of wine then turned to Esther. "What is your petition? Name it, and it will be granted." He waved at the table of leftover food. "This was not necessary if you're seeking a favor."

Her smile was brief. Should he be worried? Was she unhappy?

"I'm grateful for your favor, husband," she said in a soft voice. "If you still want to grant my petition, then please come again tomorrow for another banquet. At that time, I will be ready to make my request."

Ahasuerus nodded, but if Haman hadn't been there, he would have drawn an answer from his wife that instant. Even so, he kissed her cheek in farewell and left for the inner court again. Tomorrow he'd see Esther again, and in a few more days, the protocol would be over.

* * *

Haman smiled to himself as he walked through the palace. Everyone knew about the decree against the Jews, and in the eyes of all he met, he saw the fear blended with respect for his high office. No one dared not to bow to him now. He'd made it clear that it was his idea and it was his ten thousand talents of silver that would be paid out. And the king had gladly given him the power to enact what would prove to be one of the most life-changing acts in all of Persia's history.

Gifts had been arriving at his home, some from the Jewish people themselves—all begging his clemency, which made Haman want to laugh aloud. But now wasn't the time. He'd pay a visit to the harem and see if there were any fresh harlots, and then he'd return home for the afternoon. He wouldn't be expected back to protocol until the evening.

Inside the harem, Hegai hurried forward to greet the prime minister, prostrating himself, his face flushed. Even the keeper of the women understood how powerful the prime minister was now.

"What's your preference today?" Hegai asked.

"Do you have anyone new?" Haman said. He smiled as Hegai hurried off to find the perfect distraction for him.

An hour later, Haman left the palace by the side gate that connected to the harem. He walked around the side of the palace until he reached the road that led to the front gates. He shook his head at the sight that greeted him every day now. Jews were lined up outside the main gates of the palace, sitting on the ground, bobbing and praying their hearts out. In the center of it all was Mordecai, wearing those filthy, tattered rags. Did the man think he'd get an audience with the king dressed that way?

Suddenly, disgust pulsed through him. If these people had understood their places from the beginning, this wouldn't be happening. He strode toward the pathetic man, Mordecai. Those gathered in the road quickly moved out of his way, bowing as if that could ever change his mind now.

He came to a stop in front of the Jew, but Mordecai didn't move or look up. He just continued to sway and mumble some sort of prayer.

"This is all your fault," Haman hissed. "If you had shown respect to your king and to your prime minister, your people would have been spared."

That caught Mordecai's attention, and he looked up. He face was pale and streaked with dirt and grime as if he hadn't bathed in weeks. He smelled foul.

"You're foolish to sit outside the palace and wallow in your misery. The king will never listen to any of you," Haman said.

Mordecai's head lowered, and he continued in his prayers.

Haman smiled to himself. He was glad the man hadn't bowed to him that day in the treasury. Because now there was something greater to be done—and all of the Jews would finally be gone. Rebekah's death would be avenged, and Haman's riches and power would only increase.

Leaving Mordecai and his people to wallow in their self-pity, Haman returned home. He ordered his wife to gather their closest neighbors, their families, his concubines, and all of the children.

When everyone was gathered, with wine goblets in hand, Haman said, "I've brought you here today to celebrate with my wife, Zeresh, and me. I've risen in preference in the king's eyes, and as his prime minister, I've also become his greatest confidant."

He cleared his throat and returned the smiles from his guests and family members. "The king has ordered that all servants, and even the princes, must bow to me. My riches will increase, and my children will secure places of power within the kingdom. Each of you has been loyal to me all along. And for that you will be rewarded."

Several people clapped, and then everyone was clapping and cheering.

Haman held up his wine goblet. "My success is your success. Just today, I was invited to a private meal by the queen. The only ones in attendance with the queen were the king and me. If this doesn't attest to my esteem, nothing will. Tomorrow I have been invited to another private banquet."

More cheers, and Haman took a long, satisfying swallow of the wine. "It's no secret how I feel about the Jews who've invaded our land and live off of us like infants."

Several people chuckled.

"Today I met Mordecai, the Jewish treasury worker who refused to bow to my station. He still refuses. It doesn't matter how many warnings or chances we give these people; they'll never change their ways. The only answer is death."

The crowd cheered, and Haman smiled indulgently.

"Can we not simply hang the defiant Jew?" Zeresh asked.

Murmurs of approval spread throughout the room.

His wife smiled broadly. "Let the gallows be fifty cubits high."

Several nodded, and one man said, "Tell the king that Mordecai should be hanged as a warning to all the Jews. He's been defiant enough, and more might follow his example. If they do, they will also meet an early death."

"Very well," Haman said. "I'll see that it's done in all haste, and then I'll tell the king tonight of our plans."

Chapter 27

THOUGHTS OF ESTHER KEPT AHASUERUS awake. It was late at night, and he'd left the princes in the inner court, drinking wine. As tired as he was, he couldn't get his wife's sudden appearance at protocol out of his mind. Why had she risked death to interrupt protocol, and why was she delaying her petition? And why had she invited the prime minister to the banquet as well?

Ahasuerus knew he'd find out at the next banquet, but that didn't stop the questions from pestering his mind. He thought of what had occurred since his marriage to Esther. Nothing came to mind that would lead to Esther's actions. Perhaps if he went through the chronicles of the daily records in the palace, he'd remember something.

He called for Biztha. "Ask chamberlain Harbonah to find the chronicles of the first weeks of my marriage." Biztha nodded and hurried off. It was a while before Biztha returned with the keeper of the records, Harbonah, each of them carrying several tablets.

"Start reading the day that I was married," the king said and listened to the account of the festivities.

As Biztha read, the events surrounding the first few days of the king's marriage came flooding back. He heard again of the crime of former Prime Minister Tarsena toward Meres's wife. The king shook his head, remembering the turmoil of it all and how Haman, then the chief judge, had sentenced Tarsena to death.

Then an assassination plot was uncovered. "Wait, what is the man's name who delivered the details?" the king asked.

Biztha consulted the record, but Harbonah already knew the answer. "Mordecai. He's a Jewish man who works in the treasury."

The king stared at Harbonah. "He sounds like a devoted man to the kingdom. He must be an exception to Haman's complaints. He should certainly be exempt from the decree."

"Yes, he should," Harbonah said in a quiet voice.

The king considered this news for a moment. Didn't the Jew deserve an honor of some sort? "How did we reward Mordecai's brave service?" The king knew how the plotters were rewarded. Haman had wasted no time in ordering their executions.

Biztha looked through the record, his brows drawn together in confusion. "It's not recorded here that Mordecai was rewarded."

"I believe there was no honor given," Harbonah confirmed.

"He was overlooked?" the king asked. "No honor or dignity was bestowed upon him?"

Biztha's face flushed. "It appears so, Your Highness."

"We must reward the man who saved my life," the king said. Esther had been the one notified by Mordecai, and then she had presented the information to him. Was this what she wanted to petition for? Perhaps to reward Mordecai in a handsome fashion? Or at least exempt him from the banishment decree? "What's your advice?"

Biztha's expression fell. "I am not . . . sure. Let me see if one of the princes is still in the court. Or Haman has been waiting there as well. He said he wanted to speak with you as soon as you had an open appointment."

"Bring Haman here, then. We need to reward Mordecai and not allow ourselves to overlook him again."

"Very well," Biztha said then left the king's chamber.

Moments later, Biztha returned with Haman, who quickly prostrated himself and then met the king's gaze. "I came to speak with you, and when you weren't in the inner court, I thought I'd have to wait until the morning," Haman said.

The king nodded. "I have neglected to honor a man who deserves the greatest honor. What shall I do for him?"

Haman smiled. "If you truly desire to honor a great man," his smile grew, "I recommend that you dress him in a royal robe—perhaps one you used to wear. Let the man feel honored for a day. Give him your best and fastest horse to ride upon, and let him wear the royal crown."

The king nodded for Haman to continue. It would certainly get the attention of everyone in the kingdom if he honored Mordecai in this way. It would bring notice to the loyalty of the man and to the fact that good citizens would be rewarded publicly.

"You might have the robe and the horse delivered by one of your princes, perhaps Meres. The prince could clothe the man in the royal robe and then bring him on horseback through the streets." Haman paused and rubbed his hands together. "Prince Meres can proclaim to the crowds, 'The king delights in honoring this good and loyal man.'"

The king stared at Haman for a moment, then a smile crept to his face. "Let it be done as soon as the sun rises. But instead of Prince Meres doing this errand, you will be the one to carry it out. Take the apparel and the horse, doing everything you suggested, and clothe Mordecai the Jew in my old robe. The Jew has never been rewarded for uncovering the assassination plot against my life. Because of his good deed and his loyalty, Mordecai will be exempt from the decree against the Jews."

Haman's mouth opened in surprise, and Ahasuerus wondered if perhaps Haman thought Prince Meres should do the honor. "Biztha will find the robe." The king nodded to his chamberlain.

When the men left his room, Ahasuerus wondered again how Mordecai had been overlooked earlier, but Haman's plan was sure to delight the man.

* * *

Haman cursed at the stone wall and then punched it again. He'd followed Biztha and taken the robe the chamberlain had produced. And then he had to restrain himself from ripping it into tiny pieces. How could this have happened? How could he have been so foolish to suggest what he had to the king? But even as he rubbed his sore hand, he knew there was no way he could have known.

I thought he was talking about me.

This was some cruel fate.

The royal robe lay at his feet, neglected. It should have been him wearing it, not a filthy Jew who refused to bow or even to bathe. Not Mordecai—the one man who'd stirred Haman's hate of the Jews to fury. Perhaps Haman should have made Mordecai's failings more clear to the king in the beginning, but now it was too late. The king had commanded him to parade Mordecai through the streets as some sort of hero, and that was what Haman must do.

When the sun finally made its presence known, Haman decided to get it all over with as quickly as possible. He recruited a few guards to accompany him. True to form, Mordecai was at the king's gate. Did the pathetic man never go home?

Haman refused to look at the Jew while one of the guards made his pronouncement, covered Mordecai's shoulders with the royal robe, and helped the man mount a horse. Without looking at the Jew, Haman knew that Mordecai probably thought his pleas to heaven had been answered.

Haman would make sure those pleas would be cut short as soon as possible—at the end of a high tower and a short rope.

The next hour was the most painful of his life. Even losing Rebekah to her horrible husband's intrusive child was nothing compared to this. He ordered the guards to lead the way and deliver the message of honor to the people. Haman followed behind, keeping his head covered and his eyes down. He refused to look at Mordecai, but his eyes didn't miss the cheering and the hope in the gazes among the Jewish people. Haman would enjoy dashing those hopes.

As soon as the procession ended back at the palace gate, Haman made his escape. He hurried home, but by the time he reached the outer courtyard, he wanted to stab himself with a dagger. How would he ever get the image of Mordecai's triumph out of his mind?

He yelled for his wife. "Zeresh!" Then he fell to his knees and cried out again, "Zeresh!"

She came running out of the house.

Haman reached for her, grabbing her legs and wrapping his arms around them. "He thinks he is exempt from the decree, but he will not live. I pledge it on my life!"

"Who? Who are you talking about?" she asked, grasping his arms. "What's happened to you?"

"Call for those who are loyal to me," Haman choked out, turning his face upward. "We need to plan what to do with Mordecai the Jew, the man who has betrayed me the most, the man whom the king now honors."

Zeresh gasped and covered her mouth.

"Now, woman! There's no time to waste."

She fled the courtyard, and Haman staggered to his feet and somehow made it inside his house. He sank onto the cushions in the main hall and covered his face with his hands. It was too terrible to comprehend. Even the deaths of thousands of Jews would not make up for this injustice.

Someone arrived at the door, and when Haman lifted his head to see who his servant brought in, he was surprised to see Biztha.

Haman rose to his feet, trying to compose himself. "What is it?"

"The queen's banquet is very soon. You are to be in attendance."

"Yes," Haman said in a faint voice. The queen's banquet. And he was invited.

Yesterday, he'd gloated over the fact. Today . . . how could he bear answering the questions the king was sure to have about the procession for Mordecai?

"The king asks that you make haste," Biztha's voice broke through Haman's thoughts. "He does not want to be delayed."

* * *

Esther's heart thundered in her chest. The king and Haman were late. Would they come at all? There was little time left. She'd already heard of families leaving and being stopped at the borders. And death had followed. Some had escaped and returned to their neighborhoods, but that would only be temporary as well. As the execution date approached, the Persian neighbors would turn upon their Jewish neighbors, carrying out the decree of the king in order to achieve their reward.

Finally, she heard voices, and she held her breath, listening. Her husband's deep voice reached her, and she thought she heard the name of Mordecai spoken. Her pulse quickened, but it was too hard to decipher what had been said. In a moment, they were in the room. Ahasuerus's smile was faint, and Haman looked significantly less pleased today. The king kissed her hand in greeting, and Esther took a deep breath, hoping her news would be well received.

Haman also kissed her hand in greeting, and it was everything she could do to not pull away. Her heart shuddered at his touch.

But what made her tremble was the gaze of her husband: curious, skeptical. How would he react to what she was about to tell him?

When the food was served, Esther could hardly eat a thing. She noticed that Haman ate very little as well. Her husband watched her closely while he took a few bites. She caught him frowning more than once. Then finally, he wiped his fingers on a cloth. "Esther, what is your petition? You have delayed long enough. I have other matters to attend to."

She exhaled and tried to smile, but her stomach twisted furiously, preventing any soft expression. *You must say it now*, she told herself. Everything was in place to tell him. "Your Highness, if I have found favor in your eyes, then let my life be spared."

His eyebrows drew together, and Esther thought she saw a flash of concern in his eyes. "Why would your life need to be spared?" he asked, grabbing her hands.

She took another breath. "I have grave news, and I plead that the lives of my people may be saved as well."

The king stared at her and spoke in a sharp voice, his patience worn. "Speak plainly, Esther."

Her stomach felt as if it might turn inside out. "My people have been betrayed, and we have been ordered to be destroyed." She watched him closely, but he still didn't comprehend. This was harder to say than she'd thought.

His grip tightened on her hands. "What do you mean? Who intends to destroy your people?"

Her hands went cold in his. "I am a Jew, Your Highness. And my people are the Jews of Persia."

Esther heard Haman's gasp, but her gaze was on her husband. Ahasuerus dropped her hands and looked away. No sound came from him.

"The decree that you sent out includes *me*, for I am Jewish too," Esther said. Her husband still remained silent, not looking at her, and she swallowed hard. "The decree that Haman asked you to approve has been revised. There are soldiers stationed at the borders, killing Jews who try to flee."

Ahasuerus stood and crossed the room, keeping his back to her. His hands balled into fists at his side.

What is he thinking? What will he do? Esther knew she could be banished at any moment, executed, or sent back to her people to die with them. But at this moment, she still had the king's ear. "Your Highness, the Jewish people are not perfect citizens. They are stubborn and flawed. They came to this land as outcasts and have made it their home." She moved into a kneeling position. "But they're good people. They love fiercely and only want to protect their families. They work hard so that when the time comes for Sabbath, they can rest assured they've done their best."

Hot tears budded in her eyes. Her husband hadn't turned around, and she didn't know if he was listening. But she had to finish what she came to say. Even if they were the last words she spoke to him. "I am one of them, and they are a part of me. I have hidden my faith from you and from the court, but I can no longer hide from you. If it be your will, I'll return to my people and accept with them the punishment of your decree." The tears came fully, splashing onto her cheeks. She leaned forward, cradling her stomach, silently praying that he would turn around and speak to her. Forgive her.

He didn't move, didn't speak for several moments, but then slowly, he turned. His eyes looked bloodshot, and his expression was hard. "Why did you not tell me you are a Jew?" he ground out, his voice barely controlled.

He's angry. "I should have told you before we married," she choked out. "What you must think of me now I cannot know. But if any part of our marriage has meant anything to you, I plead for you to spare the lives of my people. We will leave Persia and find a new home, but let us live." She held back a sob, sending desperate, silent prayers heavenward.

The king's eyes closed, and he exhaled. "What has happened to my country?" he said, his tone harsh.

Esther didn't know what he meant, but she braced herself for his wrath.

Instead, he opened his eyes, his face flushed as he gazed at her. "How could you marry me and not tell me who you really were?"

"I—" Her heart thudded. There were a dozen reasons. Fear of the consequences. Obedience to Mordecai's request . . . But there was one true reason. "Because I thought you *wouldn't* marry me. And I love you, Ahasuerus. I wanted to become your wife more than anything. I didn't realize it at the time, but I know it now. I wanted to tell you so many weeks ago, but my courage failed me."

Behind her, Haman stood. He left the room, maybe to call for the guards to arrest her. Esther couldn't imagine what was going through the prime minister's head. But she didn't owe him an explanation—that was reserved for the king.

"You thought I'd put you away like Vashti?" the king asked, his eyes widening briefly.

Esther wiped the tears from her cheeks and nodded.

He was silent for a moment then asked, "Who ordered the soldiers to kill the departing Jews?"

"Haman. He ordered the soldiers to kill any Jews who try to leave Persia," Esther whispered. She took a deep breath. "The Jew Mordecai is my cousin. It is he who brought me to the harem, and it is he who uncovered the plot against your life."

The king rubbed his face then looked toward the entrance. "Where did Haman go?"

"I don't know," Esther said.

Then his eyes were back on her. His gaze was intense, looking deep into her soul until she ached. What was he thinking? Did he hate her? Would he send her to a swift execution? Although fear at his next pronouncement lanced through her, she remained kneeling and met his gaze directly. She would accept whatever his command.

In a surprising move, he stepped forward and said in a quiet voice, "Do you truly love me?"

She thought her chest would burst, and tears sprang to her eyes again. Maybe he would believe her. "With all my heart."

His eyes seemed to flash, and he looked toward the door again as if hesitating. Then he strode out of the room without another word.

Chapter 28

AHASUERUS FOUND HAMAN IN THE courtyard. The coward was sitting on a bench, his hood drawn over his face. His head lifted as the king passed the guards and strode toward him.

Ahasuerus's mind reeled, both with the news that he'd married a Jewish woman and with the fact that his most trusted advisor had deceived him.

"What have you done, Haman? Are the words of the queen true?"

Haman's face was a mixture of red and purple. The veins on his neck stood out as he opened his mouth to answer. Then his gaze slid past Ahasuerus to someone behind them.

The king turned. Esther had followed him. She looked as delicate and as beautiful as the day he'd first seen her laughing in the village square. There was no laughter now, but her eyes were the same depth, the same innocence. It was at that moment that he made up his mind. Comparing the vile darkness on Haman's face to the pale sweetness of Esther's—it was plain who had the pure heart. And who sought to gain power at all cost. Haman wanted to destroy, and Esther wanted to save. It was like comparing the sun to the darkest, dankest hole in the ground. How could he have not seen it before?

Anger reared up in the king against Haman, clutching his heart, and he wanted nothing more than to send his wife away from the monster he'd allowed to persuade him to do evil. The king knew well Haman's hatred of the Jews, and Ahasuerus had let himself be played into authorizing the decree. He gazed at Esther and tried to see her as Haman must see her. A Jewish woman, yes—but instead of despising her like his Persian heritage suggested, Ahasuerus knew he loved her. And he always had. Even with her concealment and even in this precarious moment, he cherished her life above all that he knew. And for some reason, he also trusted that she loved him. He'd seen it in her eyes more than once during their short marriage. It had been in her touch, in her whispers, and even in her laughter.

And today he saw nothing in her eyes that told him any different, despite what he'd just learned.

A movement from Haman captured the king's attention, and he turned to see that Haman had fully prostrated himself on the ground. His gaze was on Esther. "I beseech you, O Queen," Haman called out, his voice pitiful and trembling. "Spare my life, and I will be your servant forever."

Disgust rushed through Ahasuerus at the man's expression—dark and twisted. There was no sincerity or remorse from a caught criminal, which was exactly what Haman was. Jewish families had already been slaughtered because of Haman's trickery. They had not been given what the decree had promised. Haman crawled toward Esther, crying out, "O Queen, spare my life!"

Haman's pleas grew louder and more forceful. Desperate. "Please. I will do everything at your command."

Esther moved out of his path, but he continued toward her until he'd grabbed at the hem of her robes. She jerked her robe away, casting a fearful glance at the king, but Haman lunged forward and clasped her ankles, his hands pawing at her legs. "I will be your eternal slave, anything for my queen, but please spare my life."

"Stop!" she called. She twisted away from the prime minister. Haman grappled for her again, but Ahasuerus pushed himself between Haman and Esther, throwing Haman aside.

Haman cowered, his hands lifting in front of his face. "Have mercy!"

Rage shot through Ahasuerus, and he had to take several breaths before he could speak. "Because you've assaulted my wife, your punishment will be swift," he said. He heard Esther's gasp. She must know now that he was on her side. He called out to the guards. "Bind this man!"

The guards hurried forward and wrenched Haman's arms behind him.

Haman cried out, his feet scraping against the stone floor. "Have pity on me! Take what you will! Everything that I own is yours, including the ten thousand silver talents. I only wanted to cleanse Persia of the vermin that have infected it."

"Cover his head with his hood," the king said in an icy voice. "Then bring me the captain of the guard and tell him to deliver the decree given to him by Haman."

With Haman's face covered, at least the king didn't have to look at the man's pitiful expression. But that didn't stop Haman from moaning and bellowing out pleas. The king walked around the man, wanting to kick him like a dog, but he restrained himself and waited for the captain. Gold winked from Haman's hand—it was the ring the king had given him to create the seal on the decree. Ahasuerus bent over and removed the ring from Haman's finger. He was sorry he had ever trusted the man with such power.

Ahasuerus crossed to his wife and took her hands in his. Her hands were cold and trembling. She stared at him with red-rimmed eyes. "You do not condemn me?" she asked in a shaky voice.

He touched her cheek and found it wet with tears. "I do not, nor do I condemn your people." Slowly, he brought her hand to his lips and pressed a kiss on her palm. "The people of Persia love their queen." He gazed into the depth of her eyes. He saw relief, hope, and love there. It was all he needed to see. "And I love my queen as well."

She fell against him, and he held her up, afraid she might collapse. Her arms went around his waist as her shoulders shook. He held her and let her cry until Gad arrived. Only then did he release his wife and turn to face the captain.

Gad had arrived with several guards and chamberlain Harbonah, the keeper of the records. Harbonah carried a tablet, but Gad took it from him as they walked into the courtyard.

Gad strode toward the king and held out the boxed tablet. The king immediately recognized his seal imprinted on the box, making it an official declaration from the king. When he read the words, his stomach fell. He had not doubted Esther, especially after seeing how Haman reacted, but to see the cruel orders with his seal next to them made anger flare up in his chest.

"Notify your guards at once to cease this order," the king said.

Gad's expression didn't change. "Yes, Your Majesty." His gaze flickered to the huddled form of Haman.

As if to answer the captain's question, the king said, "Haman will be punished for his crimes against my wife's people, the Jews, and for his assault on my wife as well."

Gad's eyes flew to Esther. This time his expression showed astonishment. The guards who'd come with Gad, as well as Harbonah, looked equally surprised. But they quickly recovered and all bowed.

Harbonah cleared his throat. "Haman has built a gallows fifty cubits high for the Jewish man Mordecai."

Esther gasped, and the king let the information sink in to all those in the courtyard, recalling how only that morning he had honored Mordecai for his service in saving his life. His gaze went to Haman, who hadn't moved for several minutes. How had this mess all happened?

"Why have you done this, Haman?" the king asked.

Haman was limp in the soldier's hands, but he lifted his covered head to answer. "The Jews have been a plague since your father provided them exile. We must correct your father's wrongs!" His voice rose, hoarse and raw. "Spare my life, and I will show you the error of your ways."

There was only one way to put an end to it. Another look at Esther's tear-stained face confirmed it. "Hang the prime minister on the gallows he's constructed for Mordecai."

Epilogue

ESTHER LOOKED AROUND THE BANQUET held in honor of her first-year wedding anniversary to Ahasuerus, King Xerxes of Persia. The banquet room was a delightful sight. The tables were piled high with meats and fruits and vegetables, arranged beautifully among jars of roses that her husband insisted on reaping from the gardens again. Esther had never seen so many roses.

"For you, my love," a voice said next to her ear. Esther turned to see her husband leaning close, holding out a white rose with all the thorns removed. His brown eyes seemed to envelop her, and she wished they weren't in a room full of people so that she might wrap her arms around his neck.

Staying demure, she smiled and took the flower. "You're too generous. I wonder what the gardens look like now."

"The gardens can never compare to your beauty, so losing a few roses won't matter," Ahasuerus said with a chuckle. "And here's another for the child."

Her hand went to her rounded stomach. She was in her fifth month, and she'd already felt the babe move. She and Ahasuerus had spent many mornings lying in bed, his hand on her stomach, trying to predict each tiny movement—a hand, a foot, an elbow, a knee?

"Your cousins look happy," he said, and Esther turned her attention to Mordecai and Leah, who sat on the other side of the room. Johanna and her husband, Aaron, were there too, and several other Jewish couples, including Dan and his new wife.

She caught Johanna's eye, and her friend smiled. She was with child as well, and the two babes would be born only weeks apart. It was still hard to grasp that not long ago, Esther had confessed her true identity to her husband. And Haman, the prime minister who had brought such fear and grief to her heart, was gone for good.

Shortly after Haman's execution, the king had bestowed Haman's titles on Mordecai. The kingdom was stunned, and it served as the final act to prove that the king had broken free of his father's austere shadow and made the kingdom of Persia truly that of Xerxes. That, and declaring to the people that the queen of Persia who ruled side by side with her husband was a Jewish woman.

The king gave Mordecai his seal, the one taken from Haman, and Mordecai wrote a new decree that gave the Jewish people the right to defend themselves against any enemies who came against them, inside or outside of Persia.

Esther suppressed a small shudder at the memory. In this room filled with celebration and happy people, it was easy to forget the weeks of darkness that had followed Haman's execution. Those loyal to him and his family still came against the Jews in the cloak of secrecy, and the Jews fought valiantly until Haman's ten sons were hanged at the gallows and thousands of other rebels against the king had also been killed.

The wicked seeds Haman had planted in the hearts of many Persians were terrible indeed. It seemed bands of bloodthirsty men who'd been turned down to fight against Greece were ready to battle anywhere. There had been many gloomy days as reports of skirmishes and deaths had come to the palace. But Esther was proud of her people for defending their rights and lands, and she was proud of her husband for letting them do so.

"Do you think we can cancel the entertainment?" Ahasuerus was speaking in her ear again. His warm breath fluttered her veil, and she flushed.

"Everyone is watching us as it is," Esther said. "If we cancel the entertainment and leave early, what do you think they'll be saying?"

Ahasuerus's arm stole around her shoulders, and he lowered his voice. "I don't care what they might say. Let the chamberlains and the entire royal court spend the rest of the night discussing their king who is in love with the queen."

Esther's face was certainly red now. "We must have the entertainment, dear husband. Everyone is looking forward to it."

He chuckled. "Spoken like a queen."

She smiled at him, and although he couldn't see her smile, she knew he could read it in her eyes. Since the rebellions had died down, they'd slowly focused on making some adjustments in the palace. The cooks prepared food that was acceptable according to the law of Moses for those Jews who served in the palace. The Jews weren't penalized for leaving their stations early on the Sabbath eve. And Jewish religious celebrations were accommodated.

And there had been allowances on Esther's part as well. She agreed that their children would be taught both religions, and they would be allowed to choose as they reached adulthood. Esther had come to respect the beliefs of her husband and his deep spirituality, which didn't include the Lord she believed in.

In turn, Ahasuerus pronounced a new holiday. Each year on the anniversary of Haman's death and the day following, the Jewish people would celebrate their deliverance, and would call it the Days of Purim.

The king stood, and everyone fell silent, watching. He held out his goblet of wine. "The queen and I are grateful for each of you who have joined us tonight. We hope the coming months will bring new harmony to our land and we'll prosper together."

He paused, looking down at Esther. "We also celebrate the upcoming arrival of the heir to the throne. Our child couldn't ask for a better mother."

Or a better father, Esther whispered to herself.

The king raised his goblet high, and everyone cheered. It was a beautiful sound and filled Esther with joy as she looked across the room at each table to see those she loved the most.

Ahasuerus took his place next to her again, and his hand slid into hers. His touch warmed her, making her feel more secure and loved than ever. She had not chosen this life of royalty, of sharing her husband with thousands, of spending her days learning how to run a country with a king, but the Lord had given her this blessing . . . to serve her people.

And she would never question it again.

About the Author

HEATHER B. MOORE IS A two-time Best of State and Whitney Award–winning author of the Out of Jerusalem series and the historical novels *Abinadi, Alma, Alma the Younger, Ammon,* and *Daughters of Jared.* She is a coauthor of The Newport Ladies Book Club series, with *Athena* and the upcoming *Ruby* as her titles. Heather is also the author of the nonfiction work *Women of the Book of Mormon: Insights & Inspirations* and coauthor with Angela Eschler of *Christ's Gifts to Women.* Visit Heather's website for information on upcoming projects: www.hbmoore.com.